NEW JERK IN TOWN

AN ENEMIES-TO-LOVERS ROMANTIC COMEDY

SYLVIE STEWART

ROLLING HEARTS PRESS

COPYRIGHT

First Edition: 2020
Copyright © 2020 by Sylvie Stewart
Editing by Duli Noted

The Nerd Next Door (*Carolina Kisses #1*)

The Last Good Liar (*Carolina Kisses #3*) (*Jan 2021*)

The Fix (*Carolina Connections #1*)

The Spark (*Carolina Connections #2*)

The Lucky One (*Carolina Connections #3*)

The Game (*Carolina Connections#4*)

The Way You Are (*Carolina Connections #5*)

The Runaround (*Carolina Connections #6*)

Carolina Connections Box Set

Between a Rock and a Royal (*Kings of Carolina #1*)

Blue Bloods and Backroads (*Kings of Carolina #2*)

Stealing Kisses With a King (*Kings of Carolina #3*)
(*Oct. 2020*)

Kings of Carolina Box Set

Then Again

Happy New You

Game Changer

About That (*FREE for a limited time!*)

Full-On Clinger

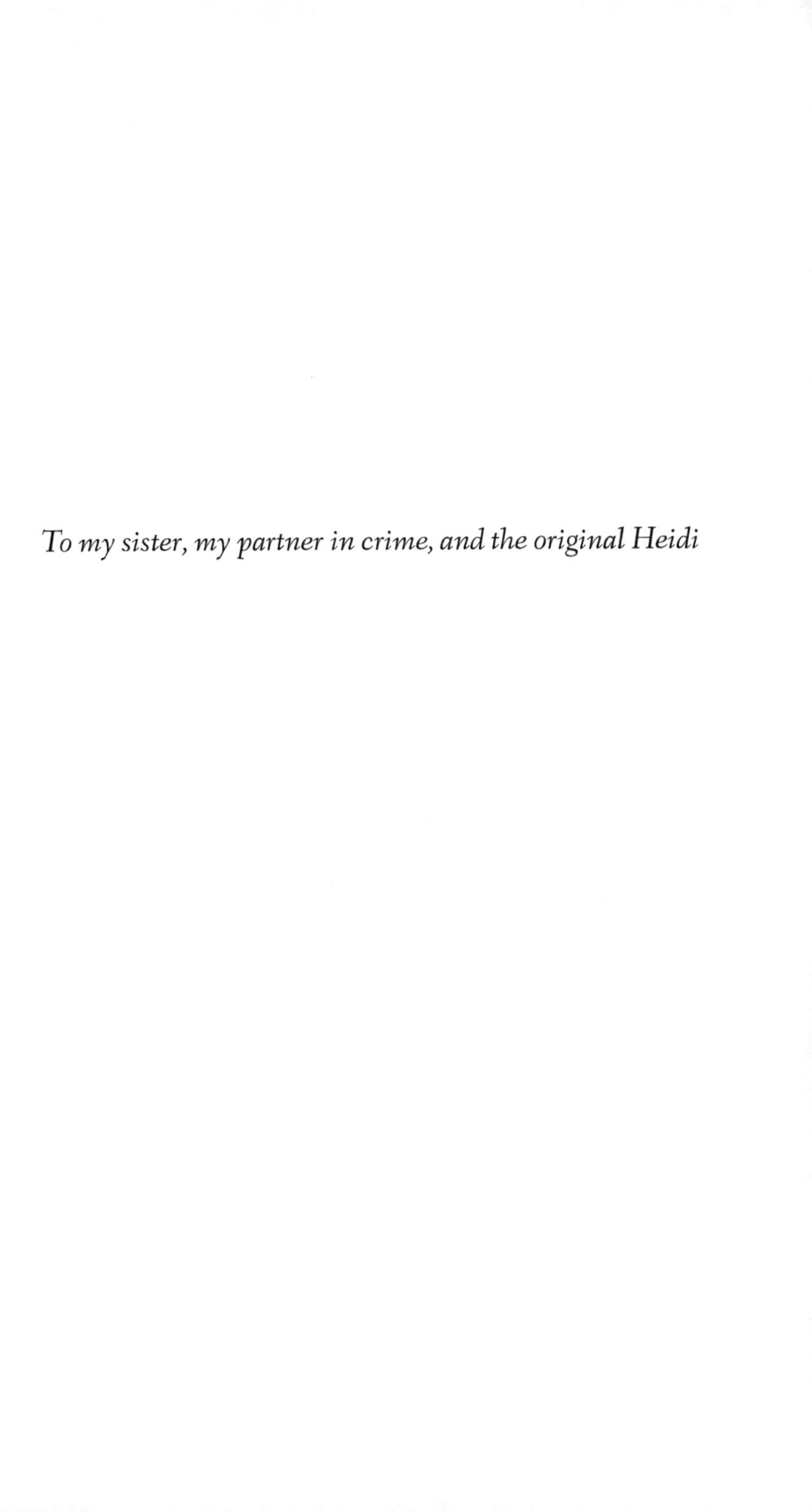

To my sister, my partner in crime, and the original Heidi

MILO

"Because I said so."

Yeah, those are the words that just came out of my mouth. Which wouldn't be all that disturbing if I were, in fact, a parent, but I've been lucky enough to dodge that bullet so far.

Felicity's head falls back, and she laughs hard enough for me to know I'll never live this down, so I do the only thing I can and walk straight out of her room—the one she still insists on calling the guest room. I can't call it anything but hers.

"You can dream all you want, but I'll still win!" Her taunt follows me down the narrow stairs to the main floor of the house, and I feel my stomach growl with hunger.

She has her mother's blood in her veins so, unfortunately, she might be right in the end. That's what genetic hard-headedness will get you, and my sister Sherry—Felicity's mom—could give a jackass a run for its money.

In fact, Sherry's had a lot of practice, given her shit choice in men over the years. Case in point: her latest jackass is the very reason her daughter is now staying with me instead of basking in the toxic swamp that is Sherry's current live-in relationship.

There was a time when I interfered and chased assholes away from my sister, but I eventually realized it was a waste of energy. She was going down her chosen path no matter what. Not even a North Carolina-bound hurricane could stop her from doing exactly as she pleased, which mostly happened to be tangling herself up with one cocksucker after another. Now all I can do is my level best to keep that apple from falling too close to Sherry's fucked-up tree by keeping Felicity on the straight and narrow where guys are concerned.

I pull open the refrigerator and make a point not to inhale as I take in its paltry contents: two bottles of beer, a half-gallon of milk, a few condiments, and some highly dubious takeout containers. I run a frustrated hand through my hair and listen to the shuffling of Felicity's combat boots across the floor over my head. The sound has become just another familiar part of the symphony provided by any good beach house. The creaks and groans of the clapboard construction and the slapping of the loose shutters blend with the rushing wind from across the Atlantic. I swear the house shifts on its foundation hourly. One day, I'll wake up with only rubble surrounding me and the tide rushing in to sweep everything away.

The fridge door falls shut again, and my gaze shifts to the range nearby. I've been meaning to replace the damn thing before its temperamental wiring causes the whole house to go up in flames. Although, come to think of it, the insurance money would come in handy right about now. Any hunger I felt fades at the thought of my bank account and exactly how little money sits in it. Breakfast will have to wait.

"You need to get laid."

I whip around at Felicity's comment. I must have been deep in my personal pity party if I missed her boots clomping down the stairs.

"How did you get to be such a heathen?" My backside hits the edge of the counter, and I give my beard a good scratch.

She just raises a brow at me.

Right. I forgot for a minute she spent the last sixteen years living with Sherry.

"At least mind your own business," I grumble. I'm fully aware that Felicity knows what every other teenager in the world does about sex—which is fuck-all, by the way. But they think they know everything. All *she* needs to know is not to sleep with some asshole and make sure she triples up on protection even if her chosen guy is up for sainthood.

"You *are* my business." My niece has the nerve to grin before she pinches my cheek in a way, I assume, is supposed to tell me I'm adorable. How in the hell did I get here?

Without hesitation, I grab her wrist before swinging it down and twisting her body in one fluid motion. I've got her arm pinned behind her back and her front facing the opposite counter before she knows what hit her.

She tries breaking free, but my hold is firm. "Hey! How many times have I told you to stop doing that to me?"

My words are low and controlled. "I'll keep doing it until you learn how to do it yourself when some asshole tries to touch you without your permission."

"Fine." She stops struggling, and I release my grip. When she turns back to me, her grin has been replaced with a scowl. "You're a real pain sometimes, Milo."

"Thank you."

Felicity rolls her eyes like the pro she is and shuffles over to the cabinet where we keep the cereal, all the while muttering about how she should have gone to live with her friends Ted and Haley because they'd at least have the decency to wait until after breakfast to assault her. I watch as she pours the sugar shit into a bowl and settles at the table, shoving aside unopened mail, dirty plates, and half a dozen comic books.

"Forget something?"

"If you think I'm drinking the milk in that petri dish of a fridge you've got there, you're nuts."

Just to spite the little smartass, I turn back to the refrigerator and pull out the half-gallon of milk before setting it on the table with a clunk. My backside lands in the seat across from her, but her eyes don't budge from her comic book, so I unscrew the lid and bring the container to my lips where I proceed to chug for a good thirty seconds. It's not exactly farm fresh, but it could be worse. I drop the milk back down with an overly exaggerated, "Ahhh." This finally captures her attention, but only results in a slow head shake I interpret as more pity than anything.

"Good luck with that." She shoves a fistful of cereal in her mouth and goes back to the comic as she crunches away.

I slide the carton aside and lean forward on my elbows as I take in the lanky figure before me. Her long t-shirt is frayed at the cuffs, and her hair is pulled back in a disheveled ponytail—quite a departure from the multi-colored cloud of short hair she's sported for the past few years. It's the same dark brown as mine now and just as unkempt. There's nothing artful about the way she's arranged her hair and outfit, and that's her way. But the artfulness lies elsewhere.

"So, are we going to talk about this for real, or are you just going to ignore it?"

Her fingers casually flip a page and she mumbles over her mouthful of cereal, "I'm not ignoring it. I'm just telling you not to worry about it. I've got it covered."

"As clever as you are—and, believe me, I know you are—there's no way you've managed to magically come up with three grand, plus whatever you'll need for supplies."

She swallows and sends a quick glance my way. "Maybe not yet, but I have a plan. Like I said, don't worry."

"And like *I* said, *I'm* paying for it." I check the exasperation in my tone before continuing, "I'm an adult who happens to have credit. You, on the other hand, do not."

"Ah! But I have a job." Her brows shoot up as she gives me her full attention this time. She kindly refrains from mocking me with the unspoken, *"You, on the other hand, do not, asshole."*

I brush past it. "A job which pays you shit and one that you're giving up for art school."

"Yeah, but I have savings. And they're taking me back when I come home from Virginia."

It's no use. My fist hits the table, and I practically growl at her. "You're not spending your savings on school! That's bullshit! Save it for college or a car or, I don't know, one of your stupid comic books!" Her eyes drop to the table, and I hate myself a little. *Breathe, asshole.* "Sorry, Liss." I scrub a hand through my hair and check my voice again. "It's just that a kid shouldn't be expected to pay for their own high school education."

Her voice is so quiet I almost don't hear her response. "Neither should an uncle."

My back settles into the chair, and I watch her again while I rein my temper in. The fact of the matter is Felicity has had kind of a shit time of it, and if anyone deserves a break, it's her. So I'm paying for her to go to this fancy-ass program for a trimester so she can follow her dream of becoming an illustrator. It's a done deal.

"Look." I sigh. "The payment's due in a few days. I know you have pride and you're determined as hell, but this isn't happening unless you let me pay, Liss."

I see the crack in her armor the moment I mention the deadline. We both know she doesn't have this kind of money, just like we both know there's no way her mom would pitch in a penny.

She pretends to read another page of her comic for a minute, and I wait until she shoves it aside and pins me with her brown eyes. The usual determination is tinged with sadness, and I want to punch something. "If I let you—and that's an *if*—it has to be a loan. I'm not letting you pay for it outright."

I nod immediately since this is the closest we've come to a resolution in weeks. We can argue about repayment later. "I can accept that," I lie.

"Then I'll think about it." Felicity pushes back from the table, leaving her half-finished cereal bowl behind. The comic, she takes with her as she heads to the stairs again to finish getting ready for school. But it wouldn't be like her to let me stay one step ahead. "You may want to think about showering and shaving once in a while or you'll never get laid."

I close my eyes and don't even try fighting that battle. I've won one, and there are plenty more ahead.

FELICITY ISN'T WRONG ABOUT THE REFRIGERATOR—something I'm forced to admit after the milk exacts its revenge later that night. So I accept my fate and make a trip to the scratch-and-dent a couple days later on a hunt for both a fridge and a range. This means enlisting my buddy Bran since the place doesn't deliver and all I've got is my Yamaha and the beater I mostly just keep around for Felicity. Bran subscribes to the school of thought that a man is more of a man if he's got a truck, a notion I'm not about to dissuade him from since it's currently benefiting me. Although, once I get a few beers in me, I might slip up and give him a decent helping of shit over it. Bran's what we refer to as an easy target.

"I'm changing your offer of a beer to a case instead." Bran's voice is choked.

I wipe my forehead with the kerchief from my back pocket and glance around the black beast wedged between us. Bran's wheezing like he just finished an Ironman.

"We're not even in the first door, Nancy." I shove the cloth back in my pocket and return my grip to the refrigerator, ignoring the pull in my thigh.

"You said you needed to pick up 'a little something,'" he grunts through clenched teeth as he shoves his end further over the threshold. "Not an entire damn appliance aisle!"

"Hold up!" I kick a rug aside and check for more obstacles. The fridge is so wide, we need to bring it through the front door instead of using the side one that leads straight into the kitchen. "Okay, we're good to go on my count. And we'll compromise with a twelve-pack of Hornet's Nest. One. Two. *Three!*" I pull while Bran lets out a battle cry from the other side and puts his back into it. The refrigerator resists at first and then, with a loud crack and a shower of splintered wood, breaks through the threshold and knocks me back a few steps—where my head connects with the entryway wall.

Bran's red, sweat-beaded face appears around the side. He takes in first the ruined door trim and next my position against the opposite wall, where I'm checking out the growing lump on the back of my head.

"Uh, let's just call it even, yeah?"

An hour later, I slam the passenger door of Bran's black Ram 1500 and meet him on the sidewalk in front of the SWiN, a local restaurant he frequents due almost solely to the fact that he can score free beers there whenever he wants. He's been dragging me with him a couple nights a week ever since he hunted me down upon my return home a few months back.

"Is Rayna working today?" My grumbling belly reminds me I haven't eaten yet today, and it's closing in on four o'clock. This is becoming a worrying trend. It's a wonder the three cups of coffee I inhaled this morning haven't eaten through the walls of my stomach by now.

Bran can't hide his dumb-ass grin. "It's Friday, ain't it?" As if I have his girlfriend's schedule memorized.

I don't respond, instead holding the glass front door open for him so he doesn't get lost in sex fantasies about Rayna and crack his head on the glass. We've both known Rayna since we were all kids spending summers on the beach and sneaking liquor from whoever's parents had a stocked supply. She was way too cool for Bran back then, but Rayna's a smart woman, so she eventually gave the guy a shot a few years back. Since he'd never stopped mooning over her, he made quick work of locking that shit down, and the rest is history. They're set to get married next year sometime.

"Hey, Camille," Bran croons, and I glance over just in time to see the owner of the SWiN check to make sure her hair's in place. Which brings me to the second reason I don't mind tagging along whenever Bran suggests stopping by. Camille Blume has a huge lady boner for my friend—well, as much as a seventy-something, half-insane woman might have one—and it *never* gets old.

"Brandon." She breathes his name with a kind of reverence mostly reserved for pre-teen girls discussing boy bands.

But I've got to hand it to Bran. He doesn't disappoint as he rakes a casual hand through his blond, Ken-doll hair and crosses the room to envelop the woman in a tight hug. "You look stunning, as usual, Camille."

"Oh, stop." She pulls back and bats at his chest, letting her hand linger for a second too long before her eyes land on me and her arm drops to her side like a heavy weight. "Mr. Papatonis." All the warmth she's been showering on Bran turns to ice at the sight of me.

"Mrs. Blume." I don't waste my breath trying to charm her because that ship has sailed—as in, it's likely docked somewhere off mainland China by now. And, besides, charm and flattery have never been in my wheel-house. But I need to maintain some civility, not only because she's a senior citizen, but because she holds the key to some of the best food in Wilmington. And I've tried my entire life not to be stupid, with varying degrees of success.

Bran pulls her attention back. "I apologize for barging in like this, but we wanted to drop in to say hello. You see, we just finished moving some heavy appliances..." he trails off, not even pretending to hide his meaning.

"Not another word." Camille's smile returns, and she shoos Bran toward the bar. "You have a seat, and I'll get Rayna out here to give you a bite and something cold to drink." She turns to the double galley doors of the kitchen without another glance my way.

Bran makes no attempt to hide his shit-eating grin. "And that, young Jedi, is how it's done."

His smug tone has me shaking my head as I grab a seat on the barstool next to him. "You sure do have that elderly population all sewn up, don't you? I guess I'll let you have that while I settle for the nubile young things wandering around town instead." Never mind it's the offseason and the beach is deserted.

"Help yourself, my friend," he replies without hesitation as his stool swivels in the direction of the kitchen. "I'm more than fine."

My gaze follows his to where Rayna stands by the double kitchen doors, smiling and waving goodbye to a dark-haired woman. As the woman moves to the restaurant's front door, Rayna turns to us and approaches. But I'm not looking at her. My eyes are glued to the back of the brunette as her denim-clad ass sways out the door, and the hairs on the back of my neck stand at attention. If I didn't know any better, I'd swear I just saw a ghost.

CHAPTER TWO

JILL

I blame it on TV.

I mean, if it weren't for *Brothers of Moon Bay* choosing this town for filming, I wouldn't be here at all. Instead, I'd be back in Sunview hanging out with my sister, Jenna, and my nieces, shoving my face full of popcorn while binge-watching *Schitt's Creek* and getting drunk on cheap wine. Or maybe I'd be on my way to some glamorous job awaiting me in Charleston while the man of my dreams sits twiddling his thumbs in anticipation of my arrival. But no. Fate or God—or whatever—is enacting some grand plan without my permission.

Okay, fine. I was the one who convinced my parents all those years ago that selecting one's family vacation destination based solely on the filming location of a CW show was perfectly logical. Damn teenage me for being an unrelenting, yet adorable, nagger.

And, yes, I am the one who insisted on this ridiculous

journey to "find myself" as thirty began its looming countdown. But, to be fair, I never expected my stupid subconscious to lead me down memory lane and steer my piece-of-shit car *here*. To the only place where everything made sense and the last place I want to be right now. I mean, surely winter in Charleston or Sunview would be highly preferable to the off-season in a beach town, right?

But after two months of drifting, here I am, still no closer to the meaning of life, yet ever closer to an empty bank account. This thing is turning into more of an *Eat. Pray. Sleep-in-my-Car.* situation with each passing day.

I tip my face up to the ridiculously perfect blue sky with its puffy cotton candy clouds and huff out a breath. It doesn't even have the decency to form a cloud of condensation. Stupid, perfect weather. "Seriously?"

When no reply comes, my eyes drop back down to the "Help Wanted" sign I've been trying to ignore in the restaurant window before me, and I snag my bottom lip with my teeth.

"Don't go in there, Jill," says the reasonable half of my brain before the idiot half butts in. *"What can it hurt? We have to pee anyway, so why not?"*

The urge to cross my legs threatens to overpower me at the suggestion. I'll just ask to use the bathroom and be in and out in two minutes. This is merely a brief stop on my way to my true destination and not God's way of telling me I'm about to be Carolina Beach's newest resident. 'Cuz that ain't happening. I'm choosing to pretend God is not directly to blame for my engine giving out in this town, stranding my broke ass in front of this restaurant and its dumb sign.

Can you blame me for suspecting a conspiracy?

"You think you're so smart," I mumble under my breath as I swing the glass door open and a stale, tinny rendition of a strangely familiar tune plays from somewhere above my head. By opening the door, I also seem to have lifted the lid off an old music box in need of tuning. It takes me a moment to place the song, and then it hits me at the same time my eyes adjust to the indoor lighting. "My Favorite Things" from *The Sound of Music*. Jenna and I used to watch that movie all the time. I'd always insist on playing Maria and make her be Captain von Trapp—and Mother Superior, of course. A swell of nostalgia runs through me, and I have the urge to call her right now and wave the white flag before begging her to come rescue my ass and take me home. But that feeling is overtaken by the oddest sensation of just having trespassed into another realm. One where time suspended in 1938 Austria and vomited kitschy shit everywhere. And I mean *everywhere*. What the actual f—

"We don't open for another hour." A gruff female voice startles me, and I back into the door, pushing it all the way shut and bringing the music to an abrupt halt.

Since she's not looking my way, I can only see the woman's profile as she sits at a table near the back of the dining room rolling silverware. I'm pretty sure there's a horror movie out there that starts like this, but now I really have to pee. So I tempt fate and take a step closer. The woman appears young—maybe mid-twenties—and her blond hair is cut in a short style that feels somehow familiar.

"Sorry. I..." And then it hits me. She's Julie freakin'

Andrews—complete with her Maria-spinning-on-a-mountaintop dress. Of course, it isn't *actually* Julie Andrews, unless Dame Andrews got a facelift and her plastic surgeon is a certified genius. But the blond bowl cut and the Alps get-up are a dead ringer.

I quickly gather myself. "Sorry. I was just hoping to—"

But she cuts me off. "If you know what's good for you, you'll turn right around and escape while you can." She finally looks up at me, her expression bored as she scans me from head to toe. I realize I'm less than impressive in my current outfit of ripped jeans and a faded "Boobytrap backwards is Partyboob" t-shirt that I'm almost completely certain has a salsa stain over my left nipple. *What? You try driving while eating a taco.* But it's not like I'm out to impress Julie—or anyone else, for that matter.

And I'm too distracted trying to quell my urge to ask her for a little "The hills are alive" action to even begin contemplating the ominous nature of her warning. Instead, I attempt a friendly laugh. "No, I'm just here to use the restroom."

The sullen convent dropout tilts her head, sending me another disinterested frown. She's very good at it. "It's your funeral." She rises from her chair and stalks through the double galley doors of what I assume is the kitchen, her dress and petticoat flouncing in her wake.

My eyes skip around the dining room, catching sight of a row of glassy-eyed dolls and a herd of goat marionettes tangled in one another's strings, and my good sense finally catches up with me. Surely, there's a restroom somewhere a bit less creepy. And, besides, everybody knows when the world's best nanny tells you to hightail it, you hightail your ass and be quick about it.

Unfortunately, I'm not quite quick enough to evade the new voice that stops me just as my hand reaches for the door.

"Wonderful! I've been looking for a new Louisa."

I paste a regretful smile on my lips and pivot back to tell this new woman that there's been a misunderstanding. That I just had to pee, but the urge has been freaked right the hell out of me, thank you very much. I'll find a cheap local garage to tow my car and be out of town in two days, tops. Not that I want to blow what money I have left on that piece of crap, but a girl needs a car, right? And, hey, I can enjoy the peace of the off-season beach-town vibe while I wait.

When I think about it, I'm lucky my car chose to die where it did. This wasn't some scheme God cooked up to trick me or teach me a lesson or some such bullshit. Nope. It's a pitstop and an opportunity to relax, that's all.

But as soon as I turn, I know I'm in deep trouble. Because standing outside the kitchen with her hands clasped together in delight is the world's most adorable grandmother—the beloved kind you can never say no to because she thinks you fart rainbows and brags about you to all her friends.

That whole conspiracy thing just regained a hell of a lot of merit. I send a silent touché to God. *"Well played, big guy. Well played."*

"And you're sure I can't be Maria?" I ask Camille (a.k.a. Grandma).

I'm beyond the point of no return, I'm sad to say, and have somehow been coerced into being the newest server at, wait for it... Schnitzel with Noodles—or "the SWiN" as the locals apparently call it.

Believe me, I know.

My back straightens in the booth with a new thought. "Or what about that lady the captain ditched to be with Maria?" My memory is a bit fuzzy, but I seem to remember that chick being hot. And there's no way I'm making good tips while dressed in the outfit Camille just handed me. It covers all the goods and some—which is great for a fourteen-year-old in wartime Salzburg, but not so much for me.

"Baroness Schräder? Don't be ridiculous." Camille points to a sign over the bar behind her that reads "Schräder Haters" in that unmistakable Gothic lettering. "She's not welcome here."

"Right. How silly of me." I muster a smile while I contemplate, not for the first time, exactly what kind of crazy train I've just boarded.

"And I already have a Maria." Camille's smile gleams as she gestures toward the kitchen where the girl who warned me away is presumably sewing clothing out of ugly-ass curtains.

"And you'll need to wear your hair in braids." She nods and pats my hand on the table between us.

Oh, *hell no*. Not only does she want me to dress like a circa-World-War-II home-schooled child, but I have to wear braids too? If Jenna could only see me now, she'd be snort-laughing her ass off.

"Now, dear, I'll give you a copy of the menu to take home with you and study before your first shift on Tuesday." She slides the leather-bound folio toward me. "You can come in this weekend to shadow and get the lay of the land." I flip the folio open reflexively.

And... dayum.

My eyes scan the menu and don't find a single entree under twenty-five bucks on the whole thing. In fact, some run closer to the forty-dollar range. Is everything here made with truffles or something?

I close the menu and smile, this time a genuine one. "Well, at least I'm not Gretl." Camille would probably make me wear a diaper.

"Don't be silly, dear." Camille shakes her head in bewilderment, causing a silver curl to fall over one eye. "She's too young to be a server."

The crazy train has officially left the station, heading for dingbat central. And it appears I have a first-class ticket.

I'm blaming this on TV too.

"Honestly, I'd recommend selling it for parts and getting a whole new vehicle. Transmission replacement is gonna cost you 2500 if you're lucky."

I gape at the guy as he fishes for something in the pocket of his Carhartts, casual as can be—as if he hasn't just upended my world. I can't afford a new car. Hell, I can't even afford the off-season rate at a cheap motel while I wait for my first paycheck. Damn my conscience for making me wire my entire emergency fund to my ex.

I inhale, willing calmness to settle over me. I'll just have to hope the restaurant does brisk business and its patrons prefer to tip in cash. Although, from the mouth-watering scents emanating from the numerous pots and pans I spied in the kitchen, brisk may prove to be an understatement. Fingers crossed.

After the strangest interview of my waitressing career, I hurried my ass so fast to the ladies' room that I hardly had time to notice the nun crossing her legs designating the correct door. Then Camille took me to the kitchen to meet Rayna, her chef, where I also introduced myself to the grumpy convent misfit. However, instead of telling me her name, she instructed me to call her Maria and left without shaking my extended hand. Rayna was downright delightful in comparison, and she didn't even break a sweat as she juggled cooking three different dishes and chatting with me. She inspired more confidence than Camille and Maria, that was for sure. But it would still be at least two weeks before I got a paycheck.

"And you're sure it needs replacement? Not just a little adjustment here or there?" I conjure up a flirty smile as a last-ditch effort, hoping it might buy me a miracle. The guy is kind of cute in a bad-boy, always-has-a-spare-cigarette sort of way. But it's no use. Zeb—if his name badge is to be trusted—returns my smile with an expression laced with too much pity for my liking.

"Sorry, sweetheart, but she's given up the ghost." And

out comes the pack of cigarettes. At least he has the good manners to offer me one before lighting up.

"No thanks." I wave him off, racking my brain for what in the hell to do next. *Come on, Jill, think.* "Um, you don't happen to know of any cheap places to stay around here, do you? I mean, ones that aren't…" I was going to say, "sketchy as hell," but realize maybe I shouldn't go there. I shrug instead.

Running a hand over his slicked-back hair, he eyes me up and down. Oddly, it doesn't come off as rude or lascivious, despite my salsa boob, tight jeans, and previous attempt at flirting. "I'm assuming you're looking short-term?"

"Maybe a month or two?" My nose threatens to wrinkle because I don't want to be in this town any more than my car wants to be dead in it. But I need to make some money and get another car before I try to figure out where the hell I'm meant to be and how in the world I'm going to straighten out my life. I allow myself a fraction of a second to contemplate asking my ex, Hank, for the money back, but no. No. Absolutely not. I owed it to him for the way I ditched him with the apartment lease and, well, everything. No. I can figure this out.

Zeb nods back at me before anchoring the cigarette in the corner of his mouth and pulling a phone from his back pocket. His grease-streaked thumbs type as he talks around his cigarette. "Stop by Roasted. It's a popular hangout for locals who can afford a cup of decent coffee but can't stand Starbucks. Lots of postings on the wall there for things like local services, short-term rentals, and rideshares. You can probably hook up with someone looking to rent out a room. You know, cash deal. Avoid fees and taxes and shit." He finishes typing and asks for my number to forward the listing.

Setting aside for the moment that this guy assumed I'd be cool with an under-the-table arrangement and I'm not, say, an undercover cop or something, I immediately (and shamelessly) pull out my phone.

"If anybody asks for a reference, I'm happy to oblige." He winks and exhales a cloud of smoke from the side of his mouth. I can't help but wonder if Zeb's seal of approval would be to my benefit or not.

"Thanks, Zeb." My smile lacks the flirtiness this time, but it's genuine. "I'm Jill."

"A pleasure to meet you, Jill."

"You too." I almost start walking to my car when I remember the damn thing is dead. "Uh, you guys have Uber here, right?"

Zeb shakes his head like he's clearing out cobwebs. "Oh, right. No need for Uber. One of the guys can drive you, and I'll shoot you a text when I find someone to take your car off your hands."

I beam at him. "That would be amazing. Thanks." Tilting my head toward my traitorous vehicle, I ask, "What do I owe you for the tow and looking at the car?"

"Don't you worry about it. Consider it a 'welcome to town' present." Zeb's smile is downright devilish. He's probably a few years younger than me, and I'm guessing his manager won't like him throwing me this freebie, but I'm at the point where I need any help I can get.

"Wow. That's really cool of you. Thank you, Zeb. You're a prince."

He winks again, further proving how on point his flirting game is. "Don't give it another thought." He drops his cigarette and grinds it with the toe of his boot before ushering me to the garage office to arrange a ride.

Twenty minutes later, I'm in a rusted, once-white truck with a mechanic named Navin who prefers singing off-pitch James Taylor classics to small talk. My phone pings with a text notification, and a glance down tells me it's my sister.

Jenna: *Do you know yet if you're coming back for Thanksgiving? The girls were asking.*

My eyes roll, and I can't help but grin. She's a horrible liar, but I'll give her points for using my nieces to try manipulating me.

The truth is I miss them all like crazy and most of me would love to go home for the holiday, but I just can't. If I do, I'll never leave. And it's not time yet.

Me: *I'll keep you posted, but don't get their hopes up.*

Me: *Or yours.*

The ellipses flash on my screen and then stop. I know Jenna is trying to form a response, and a ribbon of guilt curls in my gut.

Me: *Tell the girls I'll text them later. I love you.*

The ellipses are back, and then her message appears.

Jenna: *I love you too, sis. So much.*

This is followed by about seven hundred heart emojis, and I can't help but laugh out loud in the passenger seat of the truck. Navin pays me no attention, so I shift my gaze to the passing shops and restaurants. Traffic is light as we breeze through stoplights and past the practically deserted beach motels along the coastline of Carolina Beach. I know the locals prefer the offseason and the absence of the flocking tourists with their mini-vans full of kids, bucketloads of trash, and pasty-skinned drunk guys strutting shirtless down the sidewalks. But it's foreign to me. I've only ever been here in the summer at the height of the tourist season. This feels wrong in so many ways.

I'm distracted so it takes me a moment to realize the truck has stopped in front of my destination and is not just pausing at a light.

"Oh, thanks, Navin. I really appreciate it." I shift to the door and give him a half-wave before stepping down onto the sidewalk. The sound of a butchered rendition of "Fire and Rain" fades as the truck pulls away and turns at the first light.

Roasted doesn't appear to be anything special from the outside. In fact, the only signage is a tiny copper plaque with its name and a small logo on the front window with HOT COFFEE in block letters under-neath. But the scent of freshly ground beans draws me in, nonetheless. This door is blessedly lacking a music box and instead chimes with a simple ding when I pull it open. I'm also pleased to note the absence of goats.

Several pairs of eyes turn casually my way, and I nod while fixing a polite smile to my lips. My nod is returned by one patron, and any halted conversations and internet surfing soon resume. But my eyes are now on the giant paper-littered bulletin board occupying almost half of the far wall. Jackpot!

My joy is premature, however, as I peruse the offer-ings and find that most of the rental options are either out of my price range or appear to just be horny dudes seeking thinly veiled hookup arrangements. I may have better luck trying to strike a deal with one of the crappy deserted motels. Ugh.

But then, a hastily scrawled listing on plain white paper catches my eye.

The words are hand-written in black pen. "Room for Rent. Cheap. Shared kitchen and living space. Quiet tenant only. No pets. No messy assholes. No assholes, period." This is followed by a local phone number.

I whip out my phone in a nanosecond, a grin overtaking my face. Negotiation just happens to be my specialty, and I'm fairly confident I can manage to not be an asshole. It's only for a month or two, right?

CHAPTER THREE

MILO

I'd be lying if I said I didn't know exactly where Sherry and Felicity got their stubborn streaks because I got mine from the same source. My old man used his bull-headedness to burn his way through six marriages, sending just about every one of his wives sprinting for the horizon as fast as humanly possible. Not too many people on this earth can put up with a man who's incapable of being wrong, among other things.

My mother is the exception. She was wife number three, but 'til the day the old man died, she conducted her surprise check-ins on him at the beach house every few weeks, always bringing some frozen meals or coffee cake she claimed she'd made too much of. Morris, her current husband, never let it bother him on account of him being a man who can not only admit when he's wrong but who knows a good thing when he has it.

Mom claimed her visits were out of old habit, but I

knew better. There was something she couldn't let go of —either that or her innate human decency made it impossible to abandon a man who specialized in alienating everyone.

"He wanted you to have it. What you do with it is entirely up to you."

My boots come to a halt on the sidewalk, and I pinch the bridge of my nose before responding into my phone, "Your inner psychic is way off kilter, Mom. You may want to balance your chakras or whatever it is you like to do."

"Deny it all you want, but I know the real reason you called." She sounds way too self-satisfied, despite being completely off base.

"I called to see how you're doing, not to talk about the house." I stride forward once again, checking behind me for traffic before crossing the street.

"I'm fine. I'm always fine, and you know it." Although I do know this to be true, I feel the need to protest. But she cuts me off before I can. "Who was it this time? That Trent person? He's particularly odious, isn't he?" I swear she knows everyone in the entire Wilmington metro area and beyond.

Her choice of words makes me grin despite myself. Odious about covers it, but I'm not talking to her about Trent or any of the other dozens of assholes who keep knocking on my door. My dad once told me about the mouse traps and bang snaps he'd set out for the pain-in-the-ass realtors who couldn't take no for an answer. I thought he was nuts at the time, but I'm beginning to reconsider.

"It's nobody, *odious* or otherwise. How are you doing? Morris treating you okay?"

"What do you think?"

Yeah, stupid question. "Maybe I should be calling him to ask how he's being treated," I tease.

"Maybe. But he's going to tell you the same thing I'm telling you. You can sell the beach house if you want to. I know it's not your plan to stay here, and that's fine. You need to do what makes you happy."

Happy. Like it's that simple.

There's no understating how shocked I was to learn my dad had transferred the house to my name before he died, and I've spent the last six months trying to work it out in my mind with little success. I suppose he didn't want wife number six—a cantankerous delight named Monique—to get her hands on it. But surely there were other options. He of all people knew I never intended to come back here, aside from a brief visit to my mom a couple times each year.

And then there's the simple yet glaring fact that he never liked me much. He wasn't one of those abusive assholes or a deadbeat or anything; he just didn't take an interest when I was around—which, thankfully, wasn't that often since I lived with Mom and Morris until I graduated high school. The only time he talked to me was when he was drinking, and even then, he never said much. That man loved two things: the ocean and his rundown house. And now, here I am squatting in his legacy—for the time being, that is. This town doesn't feel right in my bones. We're practically strangers to each other after all my time away.

"Mom, I'm not selling the beach house." The truth is, I still haven't decided on a plan. "At least not right now. Maybe when Felicity graduates." I pick up my pace and spare a glare for a bike rider who's ignoring traffic laws by riding on the sidewalk.

"She could come stay with me. It would be nice having someone young around here for a change."

The cyclist flips me off and keeps going. Shithead is going to kill someone. "She's staying with me. I'm her uncle, and it's no big deal. Besides, you can't get rid of me that easily." I don't mention that Felicity would go nuts in their small house with my mom nosing her way into everyone's business.

"Well, maybe if someone would give me my own grandchild, I wouldn't have to go around poaching other people's."

Sherry and I have different mothers. I may be no picnic, but there's no way on earth my mom could ever be responsible for unleashing that disaster on humankind.

"Sorry, I think you're breaking up." It's just like her to tell me to go travel the world in one breath and tie me down with a wife and kids in the next. The impossible is never off the table with her.

"Liar." I can hear the smile in her voice. "Just promise me one thing."

"What's that?" I'm certain I'll regret asking.

"If you do sell the house, make sure you use the money for something you love, okay?"

My steps slow again, and I close my eyes for a second while her words try to sink in. "Yeah, Mom. Okay."

By the time we hang up, I'm running late for my

appointment at the bank, so I haul ass. My guess is I'll have better luck getting my loan if I don't piss the suits off. I even combed my hair and wore a collared shirt, an occasion that caused Felicity to choke on her cereal when I walked into the kitchen this morning. She didn't even give me a hard time if you can believe that.

"Milo Papatonis for a ten o'clock appointment."

The middle-aged teller in a crisp blue shirt smiles politely and asks me to have a seat, but I'm hard-pressed to stay still. Nerves have me shifting on the hard sofa and drumming my fingers to the tune of "Carry On Wayward Son" on the armrest. I've been on a Kansas kick lately.

By the time I'm finally led back to the semi-private office, I'm ready to call this whole thing off and go grab a liquid lunch instead. Why are banks so fucking hot?

"So, you said over the phone you're interested in a loan." The loan officer, William something-or-other, takes his seat across from me, unbuttoning his sport coat before rolling his chair closer to his desk.

"Uh, yeah." Why the hell am I so nervous? I've never given one single shit what someone thought of me—well, almost. But I've never needed a stranger's help the way I find myself needing it now. It's not something I'm anxious to repeat anytime soon. "I want to find out what my options are."

"All right." He smiles and uses his index fingers to hunt and peck on his keyboard. Something about that causes the buzzing in my hands to relax, and I take my first easy breath since walking through the bank doors. "I took the liberty of checking out your account before you came in this morning, and I have to say, you're in an ideal position for a loan."

Excuse me? I do my best to hide my surprise. "I see." I manage to lean back in my chair like he didn't just shock the ever-loving shit out of me. It seems all that worry was for nothing. I'll just get a small loan to give me a cushion until I figure shit out.

"Well." William chuckles, turning his computer monitor in my direction and leaning forward in a conspiratorial manner. "It's not so much about your account, but your assets. Have you thought about selling the beach house?"

Fuck me running.

"What's crawled up your ass?" Bran drops his backside in the chair next to mine and lifts his sunglasses to eye me.

"Nothin'. What's crawled up yours?" My focus remains on the incoming tide.

"Well, excuse me, but you seem to be even more pugnacious than usual tonight."

"Look at you using fifty-dollar words. You been reading or something?" I take a swig of my beer, knowing I'm being an asshole and not caring.

"Case in point." Bran leans back in the deck chair and crosses his ankles like he's got nowhere to be and nothing to do but stick his nose in my business. "I can't help it if I'm smarter than you."

Hell, he's probably right. Shit.

For reasons I don't understand, I decide to offer something other than bullshit. "I went to the bank today."

"Ah. Now it's making more sense. I keep telling you we can use a hand up at the shop." Bran works at an auto shop up the beach—has since we were in high school, except now he's in charge of the place.

I consider letting it go there and not sharing any more, but I'm even starting to annoy myself with this raincloud I've hung over my own head.

"I wanted to get a loan. Was hoping I wouldn't have to use the house as collateral, but it's a no go."

His laugh sounds like a wheezing hyena. "Yeah, 'cuz you don't have a job, genius. They want to see income."

I turn my head and pin him with a glare. "Well, why the hell did I go to the trouble of hauling ass all the way down to the bank when I could have just had a beer with you on the deck instead?"

"You know, sarcasm is a sign of impotence."

"It's a sign of intelligence."

"It's a sign of an asshole is what it is." He grins at me, and I throw my bottle cap at him. It hits him square in the forehead and bounces off.

"I know I need income to get a loan. I was gambling on my last few paychecks from Hobbs to smooth the way."

"I take it that didn't work."

I nod and turn my attention back to the water, relying on the rhythmic ebb and flow of the surf to fix something in my head.

"Hell, your last check had to have been months back,

wasn't it?" Bran leans forward in his chair and inspects the rolling tide next to me.

"Fuck. I don't know." Hobbs was never all that reliable when it came to paychecks—or anything else for that matter. Back then, in what seems like another life now, it didn't matter. All I needed was a place to rest my head and an ocean to swallow me up. Running pop-up diving charters with Hobbs all over the globe was a perfect fit. Until dear old dad kicked the bucket this spring, and I had to haul my ass back here.

"You know what you need?"

"I'm sure you're gonna tell me." I allow myself the smallest of grins. Pity parties never help anyway.

Bran points the mouth of his beer bottle at me and grins back in his easy way. "You need to get laid."

Hell, maybe Bran and Felicity have a point. My mind flashes back to the brunette at the SWiN before I can stop it. The electricity is back, but this time its location is farther south. "Yeah, maybe you're right."

Felicity emerges from her room the next morning without the accompaniment of her usual racket.

"Hey, check this out! I didn't even burn the house down." I grin over at her from my spot in front of the new-to-me range where I'm cooking an egg and cheese sandwich with the last of our eggs—and bread. Her expression makes me do a double-take. It's one I'm not familiar with, but it spells trouble, of that I'm positive.

"Nice." Her tone is cheerful.

Yup, trouble.

"What are you up to?" I switch the stovetop off and slide my sandwich onto the waiting plate, pausing briefly to cut it in half.

"Nothing much." She's playing with the skull ring on her right index finger.

"Is that so?" I approach and hold out half of the egg and cheese. She shakes her head.

"That's okay, I'm not hungry." This is followed by a forced smile and a series of furtive glances around the kitchen. It's nice to know my niece will never be able to pull one over on me.

Just as I'm about to call her out and put an end to this, there's a knock on the aluminum storm door out front.

"I'll get it!" Felicity races off before I have a chance to pin her down.

"If it's another one of those damn vultures, tell them I'm busy loading my shotgun!" They don't need to know I don't have a shotgun.

No response comes, and all is quiet at first. It's probably our friend Ted dropping off another of the countless comic books he supplies my niece with. But then I make out the sound of two female voices so I follow, planning on ushering this latest realtor right back out to her car.

My entire body locks up when I get a glimpse of the woman standing in the doorway talking to Felicity. It's not a realtor—at least I hope the hell not. It's the ghost that's been running through my mind the last four days, the very one I had to travel half the world to forget and the same one who always managed to catch up with me sooner or later.

She hasn't seen me yet, which is a good thing because I no doubt have a dumb fucking look on my face. It takes all my willpower to shift my stance to a casual one, my shoulder leaning into the entryway wall and arms crossed over my chest.

"Hello, Jill. Long time, no see."

Felicity's head jerks my way, and then it's a ping pong match between me and the blast from my past.

"You guys know each other?"

"No." Jill's uncertain voice matches the creases in her brow. She's wearing a pair of tight jeans and a red shirt with a neckline that plunges right down between a set of perfectly formed tits. Her hair is long and wavy, just like I remember, but her body is a little more rounded than the last time I set eyes on her. One glimpse is all it takes for my dick to perk up. She parts her full lips again, and I hold back a groan because Jill Holloway has always had a knack for driving me nuts. "Do we? How do you know my name?"

I don't respond, partly because my brain is still stuck on how gorgeous she is and partly because the possibility that I'd be so forgettable to her never once crossed my mind in any of the twelve years since I've seen her.

But in the next second, recognition dawns, and Jill is smiling her brilliant sunshine smile—the same one that's woken me up too many nights to count. It's a hard punch in the gut.

"Milo?"

CHAPTER FOUR

JILL

Twelve Years Earlier

"I can't believe by this time next year, you'll be married." I make a barfing noise because I know it will bug Jenna.

"Gross." She rewards me with a curl of her lip and a toss of her new straight bob. I'm still not used to the style. She's always had long hair just like mine. "And what exactly is so wrong with being married?"

"I don't know. It just makes you sound so... *old*." A shiny purple shell catches my eye and I pluck it from the sand before hurrying to catch up with her again.

"Gee, thanks. That's just how I love seeing myself— old, crusty, and, *gasp*, married." She pulls on my ponytail, and I step sideways into the surf to get out of range. At twenty-two, she's six years older than me, but it still feels too young to tie yourself down.

"I just mean, don't you want to, I don't know, see what else is out there?"

My sister's responding headshake either means "*no*" or "*you're too young to understand, you poor little child, you.*" Regardless, I hand her the shell because the purple ones are her favorite. I bend to pick up another one, and when I straighten, she's wearing that secret smile I'll never understand.

"There's nobody out there half as good as Mike."

Yuck. I throw my new shell as hard as I can out into the waves and bound ahead of her on the sand. "God, Jenna. Talk about old." Turning back to her, I begin to tread backward, kicking up the white sand with each step. "I meant seeing what's out there *besides* guys. Don't you want to travel the world? Climb a mountain? Jump out of a plane? Sing on Broadway?" Here comes that headshake again, and it makes me want to scream.

It's not that I don't like Mike. He's... fine. But Jenna is way too good for him on her most annoying day. I mean, the guy listens to talk radio instead of music, eats his pizza with a knife and fork, and uses the word "indeed" way too often. "*Indeed, Jill, I'd love nothing more than to marry your sister and turn her into a total snore like me.*"

"I'll leave the Broadway thing to you. I know how much you love being the center of attention." She shoots me a wicked grin.

She's not wrong, and I know it's no use, but I still need to try. "But there are so many things waiting out there to be discovered, Jenna."

She takes me by surprise with a tackle-hug, and we both fall onto the sand in a heap, her body on top of me and my boobs no doubt threatening to pop right out of my bikini. I shriek with laughter.

"And who says I can't discover things and be married at the same time?" Jenna lets out a breathless laugh and grins as she pins me down with her butt on my thighs.

"That's different. Now get your big, juicy J-Lo butt off me!" I flip us over again while she tries glaring at me, but her laughter makes it weak at best. "See how you like it!" I taunt and make a show of dropping down hard on her thighs, guffawing at her tortured expression.

"What the hell?!" A sharp male voice breaks through our laughter, and my hold on Jenna's arms drops in a flash.

It's only then I realize I've rolled us practically onto a stranger's lap—and right into his lunch.

"Oh shit!" I clap a hand over my mouth as Jenna rolls to the side, the bread from this poor guy's sandwich sticking to her arm, everything powdered in sand. "Oh my God. I'm so sorry." I turn to the guy and feel my face flush. For probably the first time in my life, I'm stunned into silence.

Jenna jumps to her feet, brushing off sand and holding the droopy piece of bread out in front of her like she's half expecting him to take it. "We're sorry. Please, let me buy you another sandwich—whatever you want."

His mouth is a hard line as he grunts through his teeth. "Forget about it."

Before we can say another word, he turns and trudges off, leaving his ruined lunch and faded beach towel behind. But I can't stop watching until he ducks past the boardwalk and out of sight, uneven steps making the journey take a lifetime.

Next to me, Jenna is clearing the lunch trash and folding up the guy's towel. When she sees me still staring in the direction he's gone, she tsks at me. "Jill, you know it's not polite to stare. Come on. Help me with this trash."

I know it's not polite, but I can't help it.

It's clear Jenna thinks my reason for staring is the series of gauze bandages lining the exposed parts of his right side, starting at his hand and extending up his arm and neck to the shaved skin above his ear. From the labored way he walked, I suspect they even continue down his denim-covered leg, but I'll never know for sure. The one thing I do know, though, is that this guy with the grim expression and countless wounds might just be the most beautiful boy I've ever seen.

I bend to help my sister and try to swallow down the sudden lump that's lodged itself in my throat.

"Jenna Holloway?"

My heart lurches, and I barely stop myself from searching around in a panic for my sister. *Deep breath, Jill. You can do this.*

"That's me!" I call out with a cheerful wave and my best superstar smile. I'm going to totally nail this.

The woman holds out her hand from behind the folding table. "I.D."

I whip out Jenna's driver's license and hand it over with another smile.

She inspects it from behind her glasses and glances up at me a couple times before handing it back along with a clipboard. Yes! It worked! "Go ahead and fill this out, then wait for your name to be called again." She barely pauses before calling out the next name.

I hug the clipboard to me until I find a concrete pillar to lean against and scrawl my responses to the questions. *Name*, *Birthdate*, and *Address* are easy enough, but I haven't a clue what to put down for *Phone Number* so I leave it blank for now. Maybe I can borrow some money from Jenna and get a disposable phone. *Acting Experience*. I bite my lip and glance at the growing groups of girls around me. They range in age, size, ethnicity, and style, but we all have one thing in common: we'll do just about anything to get a part on *Brothers of Moon Bay*.

"Oh my God!" A chorus of excited female voices echoes across the courtyard, with several girls whispering, "It's Noah!" My heart beats double-time in my chest, and I start to get tunnel vision. I mean, I've dreamed about being on this show for the last two years, but the reality of occupying the same space as Noah Chandler and Tyler Lazos is as surreal as it gets.

"Damn, that boy is sex on a stick," a brunette on the other side of the pillar says to the girl next to her.

"This time tomorrow, we could be sharing a screen with him!" Her friend grabs the brunette's arm, and they both crane their necks to get a glimpse of the star of the CW's hit show.

"Wait your turn, bitches," I mutter under my breath as Noah finally comes into sight. He is indeed sex on a stick with his flashy smile and deceivingly innocent eyes, not to mention the muscle-wrapped body he obviously knows sends girls straight into daytime fantasyland. But I'm not here for him. I'm here to launch my career as Hollywood's next big thing.

I send a silent thank you out to my parents for agreeing to spend our (*sigh*) "last summer vacation with our Jenna" as they put it, here in the Wilmington area. Not that it was that hard. The beaches are super charming, and Mom and Dad have already been raving about all the seafood restaurants, shopping, and golfing in the area. I pretended to be drawn to the same big boats and quaint boutiques, but my real reason for coming here was because I knew *Brothers of Moon Bay* would be filming a two-hour special this summer. And I'm destined to be a star.

Almost as quickly as he strolled into sight, Noah Chandler disappears through the doors of the main building across the courtyard. Sighs and whines can be heard all around, but I refocus on my paperwork.

Acting Experience.

Well, here goes nothing.

"OH MY GOD, OH MY GOD, OH MY GOD! I GOT A call-back!" I squeal into the phone three hours later, possibly rupturing my friend Madison's eardrum.

"Are you serious? Oh my God. What am I talking about? Of course you're serious! You wouldn't dare joke about the *Brothers*! Oh my God, Jill! Promise you'll take me to L.A. with you after graduation!"

"Duh!" A quick peek over my shoulder confirms that Jenna hasn't followed me out to the sidewalk. She let me borrow her cell phone to call my bestie, but I don't want her to know about the audition. I can't risk her telling our parents. "I wouldn't go anywhere without you."

"Awww." The sound of crunching fills my ear as Madison continues over what sounds like a mouthful of chips, "Now tell me all about it."

I proceed to share every last detail of my fabulous audition, from the part where I nailed the climactic line of the scene (*"Are you sure you don't want mayo on that?"*) to the part where the casting director told me I have a nice complexion. I knew all those hours of exfoliating would be worth it someday!

By the time we hang up, my jaw aches from smiling so hard and my chest is overflowing with excited anticipation. I've been asked to report to the set—*THE* set—tomorrow afternoon for some camera blocking, as they call it in the biz. I'll just tell everyone I'm going to a local gym—Jenna won't want to come because she says working out is boring. Which it totally is, but I need to work on my tone if I'm ever going to compete with Hollywood's elite. I'm totally going to pull this off.

The midday sun is high in the sky, turning the sidewalk into a cooktop and drawing beads of sweat from my scalp. I take a chug from my water bottle—because good hydration is very important for your skin—and decide to run to the corner store a couple blocks down and get a bag of saltwater taffy to share with Jenna. It'll be sort of like sharing my good news with her, right?

The store is tiny and quaint with some beachy

souvenirs, snacks, and a broad selection of ICEE flavors. I bypass the cold drinks for the colorful confections wrapped in wax paper and take my loot back out to the hot sidewalk. As my steps turn north, a voice calls from behind me.

"Mind if I take those and dump them in the sand?"

Before thinking better of it, I turn, knowing exactly who I'll find yet not adequately preparing myself for the impact. My stomach tries to drop right down to the concrete. It's the boy from yesterday. He's wearing the same uniform of ratty jeans, plain black t-shirt, and white gauze bandages along his right arm. There's a tear in the shirt hem but it looks like it belongs there on him. A dark mop of hair falls over his forehead, long on top and cropped closely on the sides, highlighting a red gash reaching up past his ear. There's no gauze hiding it this time, and I make a point not to stare at it, zeroing in on his face instead. His features are even more angular than I remember, with carved cheekbones and a prominent nose. But his mouth is what draws my attention. It reminds me of a wild animal snarling before a predator. Or maybe the other way around.

"Excuse me?" I manage, hoping to God I misheard.

No such luck.

"I just figured, you ruined my lunch, I should ruin yours."

And to think, I found him beautiful and tragic less than twenty-four hours ago. I don't even want to let my brain acknowledge the stupid daydreams I had trouble keeping at bay yesterday. God, I am such a cliché!

I firm my tone and lift the bag of taffy for him to see. "It's candy, not lunch."

His shoulders lift in a shrug, and I catch the barest wince of pain before he covers it.

But I'm not about to feel sorry for him. "And, besides, not only was it an accident, my sister offered to buy you a new lunch. You could have taken her up on it. You snooze, you lose." Take that!

"Whatever. You tourists are all the same, walking around here trashing the place with your entitled noses in the air." He rakes me over with his sharp eyes, and I can't remember ever feeling this exposed or self-conscious. I want to crawl out of my skin, and I hate him for it. This guy—this jerk—just took what was one of the best moments of my entire life and took a giant stinky-ass shit on it!

My belly is right back where it belongs in the center of my body when I hitch my hip to the side and cross my arms over my chest. "And what is that supposed to mean? You don't know anything about me."

He scoffs. "I know you're a spoiled kid whose only responsibility is working on your tan and spending Mommy and Daddy's money."

"Are you serious right now?" A reluctant grin pulls at the corner of my mouth, further easing the over-exposed feeling from his scrutiny moments ago.

"Couldn't be more serious." He, on the other hand, stiffens, his uninjured arm bunched tight at his side.

"Because you sound like an idiot. No, you sound like an idiot from some eighties high school movie."

His shrug is more careful this time. "I can't help it if you can't handle the truth."

I laugh because there's no stopping it. "Now you sound like Jack Nicholson. So, which is it? Are you a *Breakfast Club* kinda guy or more of a military/dramatic-suspense guy?" I mimic his tense jaw and rein in my hilarity for the few seconds it takes me to shout, "You're goddamn right I called a Code Red!"

He startles at my outburst and then shakes his head like *I'm* the lunatic before turning his back on me. I ignore the pang that tries to work its way in when I see his spine tighten with each stilted step away from me.

And maybe, just maybe, I have lost the plot because I hear myself yelling after him, "Go make me a turkey pot pie!"

Crap.

CHAPTER FIVE

JILL

Present Day

This is not happening. Clearly, I'm still asleep in the motel/hooker-ring-headquarters where I've been washing myself with bleach for the last three days waiting for my new rental room to be ready. It's the only explanation, and it makes sense if you think about it. The last time I was in town, Milo Papatonis played a major role in my day-to-day, so it's only natural that my subconscious would summon the boy up. Only, he's not a boy in this dream. He's a man. A bearded, smolder-y man who's done one hell of a job growing into his clothes—and his nose. Holy shit, I have a talented imagination. *Go, me!*

My mouth stretches into a dreamy smile, and I step forward until the familiar swirls of silver, green, and blue are visible in his eyes. And then I reach out my hand.

"Ow! Dammit!" His voice is almost a growl, and I feel it right between my legs.

My mouth opens, but nothing comes out. I don't ordinarily get tongue-tied in my dreams.

"What was that for?" Dream Milo gets those little parentheses between his eyebrows, and I can smell coffee on his breath.

Wait a second.

I find my voice and mirror his expression. "What was what for?"

"You pinched me." He rubs a spot on his arm, and I realize I did just as he said. I pinched him. Hard.

"This isn't a dream, is it?" The wariness is audible in my voice, and I want to rewind five minutes and tell my Uber driver to keep on moving.

The corner of Milo's mouth turns up, and his features immediately relax like a reflex. "Well, it's nice to know you missed me."

"Oh for God's sake!" The girl who introduced herself as Felicity steps between us, hands on her hips, her nose scrunched like she just smelled something foul. "What is going on here?"

I take a step back, unable to process more than one thing at a time. "I didn't miss you. I hoped I was having a nightmare."

Milo's half-grin drops. "Aren't you supposed to pinch *yourself* to check if you're asleep?"

It's my turn to grin. "What fun would that be?"

"Hey!" Felicity puts a hand on Milo's chest and tries pushing him back a step. "Somebody please explain how you know each other."

We respond simultaneously, Milo with, "She's a

spoiled tourist who used to follow me around," and me with, "He's a selfish asshole who ruined my life."

"Kind of," I tack on weakly while crossing my arms.

"Ruined your life?" Milo snorts. "Aren't we being a bit dramatic?"

"Says the guy who used his boating accident to score free sandwiches. *Oh, poor me. I hurt myself by being an idiot and, by the way, that sandwich looks delicious, hint hint,*" I snarl.

Felicity curls her lip at Milo, sounding unimpressed at best. "Seriously? You did that?"

"No. Yes. It's complicated." Milo swipes a hand through his messy hair and brings his attention back to me. "Besides, that's rich coming from your spoiled little ass. Still letting Mommy and Daddy pay for your lobster dinners? Let me guess; you're staying at a quaint little bed and breakfast right on the beach."

"I didn't think it was possible for your assholery to keep reaching new heights. I'm out of here." I turn to go and feel Felicity's hand on my arm. I don't want to offend the girl, but we're going to have a homicide on our hands if I stay here another second.

Milo isn't done yet though. "Don't let the door hit you on your ass. Although it's hard to believe anything could make it any flatter than it already is."

Felicity's sharp gasp follows, but I'm determined to keep walking.

"Holy crap, Milo. That's low," she scolds.

"You want low? You just met her. This woman is so shallow she'd make a minnow suck on air."

And I just can't seem to help myself. I pause only for

the time it takes to yell over my shoulder. "Looks like those penis-enlarging pills are working miracles. You're twice the dick you were last time I saw you!" It's an oldie, but it still rings true.

I shove the storm door open and let it slam with a satisfying *bang* behind me.

There goes my shot at affordable housing.

To be fair, though, I should have known better. The situation sounded too good to be true right from the start. I mean, $125 a week for a fully furnished room in a beach house with a girl named Felicity? With a name like that, there was no possible way she could be a shitty housemate. And all I had to do was not smoke, be tidy, keep stray animals from following me home, and hide my inner asshole until I earned enough for a car and could split for Charleston.

I can't afford to get comfortable in this town.

It had all sounded so perfect—until I showed up on Felicity's doorstep only to discover that this poor young girl is dating the biggest nightmare on earth. I can put up with a lot, but there is no way my willpower has the strength to keep me from stabbing Milo Papatonis. No matter how perfect his girlfriend's spare room is.

Back to square fricking one.

"Jill! Wait!" Felicity's footfalls crunch on the gravel behind me, and I'm swinging around on my heel before I can stop myself.

"I'm sorry. I don't know you, but you seem like a nice girl. You can do so much better than that... that..." Crap. A degree of discretion is certainly called for here. You don't tell a girl you just met that her boyfriend is the devil incarnate. A sneaky, two-faced, son of a turd-eating viper. The douchiest of all douchebags in the universe. A shit stain on Harvey Weinstein's shittiest pair of underwear. A—well, you get the idea.

"Yeah, he can be a pain sometimes, but I promise he means well." She attempts and fails an encouraging smile.

He has this poor girl brainwashed. Not that I haven't seen this kind of thing before. A woman falls for an older guy and buys into all his bullshit, and before she knows it, she's lost her entire identity and let herself be slowly isolated from her loved ones...

Wait. I take a few seconds to examine Felicity more closely. She's tugging at the frayed ends of her long sleeves and kicking the gravel of the short drive with her black combat boots. There's not a trace of a wrinkle or line on her skin, and I can see a few pimples close to her hairline.

"I hope you'll forgive me for asking, but how old are you?"

Her spine straightens a little in a way that's so achingly familiar. I think I know what she's going to say before the words leave her mouth.

"Sixteen. Why?"

I'm stalking past her and marching back to that storm door so fast I wouldn't be surprised if I had wind in my hair and an accompanying bad-ass soundtrack. I don't bother knocking, and it's possible I bust the hinges on the door when I jerk it open and sail on through into the house.

"If you think I won't call the police right fucking now,

you are not just a filthy piece of shit, you're even more idiotic than I remember!" I'm careful to keep my tone loud and free of any trace of a tremble.

"What now?" Milo's head cranes around the corner from what appears to be the kitchen.

I get right up in his face and poke his chest with my index finger. "How dare you take advantage of a sixteen-year-old girl, you son-of-a-bitch! You're going to rot in jail, and I'm going to bake myself a freaking cake every time I think about your big, burly cellmate making you his bitch. Now, feel free to stay and wait for the cops to arrive, but I'm calling now!" I whip my phone out from my back pocket and poise my thumb over the emergency button, but he's too fast for me.

A hand swipes at my wrist, and I'm suddenly facing the other way with my phone gripped behind my back and Milo's hot breath against my scalp.

"Calm. The hell. Down." His voice is steel.

Self-disgust pours over me when a tingle rushes down my spine at his controlled tone and hot breath. I use my best self-defense moves to break his hold, but I can't get free. I make a mental note to request a refund for that useless Krav Maga class I tried out last summer.

"Get your hands off me!"

I continue to struggle, but all it does is put me in closer contact with this vile man, my ass practically grinding into his crotch behind me.

"Not until you listen to me, woman!"

Part of me hopes he leaves bruises so I'll have one more thing to show the officers when they get here.

"I don't want to hear anything you have to say, you pervert!"

"I'm not a pervert, for fuck's sake!" he growls close to my ear. Too close.

And then I feel it. He's actually hard. This man is so warped, he got wood while trying to keep me from turning him over to the cops. Gross! But genius strikes in the next moment, and I know exactly what I need to do.

I stop struggling entirely and arch my back the barest bit until my ass is just about nestled against his nasty boner. "Milo." I fake a whimper and try not to gag.

And just as I knew it would, it works like a freaking charm. Milo's grip on me loosens, and I don't hesitate. I bring the heel of my boot down on his foot, elbow him hard in the gut, and spin out of his grip as he doubles over in pain.

Without wasting another second, I hit the emergency button on my phone and hold it up to my ear with what I know is the devil's grin on my face.

"9-1-1. What's your emergency?"

I draw in a ragged breath, ready to unfurl all my righteous indignation into the phone when Felicity comes tearing into the kitchen wearing an utterly horrified expression.

"Stop! He's my uncle!"

Uh, say what?!

My words die on my tongue, followed closely by the spread of cold tendrils of horror winding through my entire body until they reach the tips of my fingers where I grasp the phone.

We all freeze, Milo with clenched teeth and a vicious

glare, Felicity with wide eyes and a gaping mouth that matches my own.

"9-1-1. What is your emergency?" the operator repeats, and I know I have to rein this shit show in. So I clear my throat and run a careful hand over my hair while I try to regain a tiny sliver of my dignity. "I'm sorry, ma'am, there seems to have been a misunderstanding."

Milo maintains his glare, and I can perfectly read his lips as they mouth, "Yeah, no shit, Sherlock."

After which I am thoroughly schooled in 911 protocol and the various humiliations it offers. Apparently, you're not simply allowed to say, "Just kidding," and hang up—on the off chance that there happens to be, say, a gun pointing at your head. No, even misunderstandings require a multi-car, siren-wailing parade to the front door, followed by private interrogations of each individual involved in said misunderstanding. I can promise you that admitting to a room full of police officers that you mistakenly thought an old acquaintance was boffing a teenager is almost as uncomfortable as it sounds.

By the time the last officer leaves, I'm wishing for a nice fat juicy crow to shove in my piehole.

"So, I thought that went well."

I can't even look at him. "Milo, I—"

"No."

"I—"

"No. You don't get to say anything." He steps in front of me where I'm perched uncomfortably on the edge of a kitchen chair. "I just spent the last forty-five minutes trying to convince a police officer that I wasn't, in fact, molesting my niece and that her mother was fully aware that she is staying at my house. Do you have any idea what that feels like?"

I don't even attempt a defense. "No. I can't say that I do." And despite my desperate wish to not look at him, my eyes snap to his face like a magnet. If an expression had the power to slice down to your veins, Milo's would have me bleeding out in seconds. But I've wounded him even more deeply than that. His skin is sallow, and bags have formed under his eyes in record time. There's no life to his eyes, which is a crying shame because Milo has the most beautiful eyes I've ever seen.

"No, you don't." His gaze drops to the floor. "Now, I don't know what brought you to darken my doorstep this morning, and honestly, I don't give a rat's ass. But it's time for you to go."

The chair squeaking on the linoleum floor is exceedingly loud as I push to standing. "I'm sorry. I don't know what else to say." I can't bear to watch him anymore, so I turn to go.

"Please, don't say anything. Trouble has a habit of hurrying close when you open your mouth."

Ouch. I try not to wince.

But he's not wrong. I make extra effort to tread as quietly as possible across his floor and through his entryway. I latch the storm door with a gentle pull and keep walking until I'm back out on the sidewalk with the bright sun in my eyes and still no place to stay.

There are more than enough negatives in my situation to dwell on, but my mind can't let go of the hurt Milo didn't have the energy to even try to hide. God, I'm an asshole.

CHAPTER SIX

MILO

That woman is like a panther—beautiful to look at, but she won't hesitate to claw out your insides and eat them for breakfast if the spirit moves her. It's beyond me how I let the memory of her temper mellow over the past decade to a degree that only conjured words like "feisty" or "spirited" instead of the much more accurate "completely bat-shit crazy."

"So, let me get this straight." Felicity leans on the deck railing next to me. "You guys used to hang out when you were teenagers?"

"Hang out is a bit much. We met a few times, that's all." There's no way I'm getting into this with her. I shift on the wood rail, snagging the front of my shirt on a splinter. Damn. One more thing to add to the list.

She raises a skeptical brow at me. "Uh, I'm guessing it takes more than running into each other a couple times to *ruin her life.*"

I'm not even going there. Drama queens, the both of them. "Are you going to tell me what she was doing here in the first place? How in the hell does she even know you?"

"She didn't tell you?"

My frown says everything I need to say.

"Right. Um, well, funny story." She avoids my eyes and focuses on the beach instead.

"Well, I can't wait to hear this." I'm not keen on admitting to anyone, least of all myself, that when I saw Jill in my doorway, for a split second I had myself convinced she'd come all this way searching for me. Thankfully, my mind hadn't had time to take that any further before she started in on the insults and I got my head back on straight.

Felicity drops her forehead to the rail.

"Hey, watch for splinters." I wedge my hand between her skin and the wood.

She lifts her head again and rests her eyes on my hand. "Do they hurt?"

There's no need to ask what she's talking about. "Naw." I dismiss her concern with the lie and draw my hand back to flex it. "Not anymore." I won't tell her about the incessant buzzing of my confused nerve endings or the night pains my scars still give me—it won't change it and it'll only make her feel bad. "Now, are you going to tell me what Jill Holloway was doing in our house, or am I gonna have to dangle you by your ankles over this railing?"

"God." She shakes her head and cringes. "I had it all worked out until the two of you went at each other like two hipsters fighting over the last bottle of kombucha."

"I didn't want it to end like this," My voice is solemn as I bend down to grab her ankles. She sidesteps me with a laugh.

"Fine. I'll tell you, you big jerk."

I lean back and give her a nod to prod her along.

"So, you know how I'm trying to get tuition money?" She doesn't wait for me to answer because neither one of us is stupid last I checked. "Well, I thought a good way to bring in some extra cash for you would be to rent out the guest room while I'm gone." She grimaces and eyes me warily.

I let this information sink in for a moment. "Let's see if I have this right. You're so desperate to not have me paying for your tuition that you attempted to have someone *pay* me to let them sleep in your room?"

"The *guest* room."

"*Your* room."

"Whatever. The point is it's going to be sitting there empty for three months, and we can pay for like a third of my expenses by letting someone—Jill—use it. Combine that with the money I already saved, and you'll only be out of pocket a small amount before I can pay you back the rest."

"I already paid it. You know this." I cross my arms over my chest and do my best to stay calm. I don't even bother getting into the fact that there's no way someone like Jill Holloway would slum it in a place like this.

"Yeah, and you can't afford it any more than I can."

Here we go again. "Shows what you know, Liss. I

start working for Bran next week." Now, where the hell did I pull that lie from?

"Fixing cars?" She's got that just-smelled-a-dead-animal expression again.

It's like I don't even know her today. "And what's so wrong with fixing cars?"

She cocks out a hip and mimics my crossed arms. "Nothing—for people who actually know how to fix them."

"Oh, aren't you just hilarious."

"You know what I mean."

Unfortunately, I do. I'm no slouch, but I wouldn't be doing Bran any favors by joining his team. Overhauling a boat engine is no problem, but I haven't worked on anything newer than a 1990 Mercury outboard, much less a modern automobile engine.

"Can we just forget about this? Tuition is paid, I'm not broke, you're going to school in a couple weeks, and your room will be here for you when you get back. Got it?" I brush past her, done with this conversation and afraid I'll get mad at her. I know she meant well, but I am not the kind of person who'd tolerate a stranger living in my house, much less someone who already hates me.

"But she's already checked out of her hotel and doesn't have anywhere to stay."

What kind of bullshit ride did Jill take my niece on? "Then she can check right back into her hotel. It ain't rocket science." I jerk open the sliding glass door, and it sticks. Dammit. "And you're not even leaving 'til the week after next so that makes no sense." My thigh tightens in protest when I bend to see what's wrong with the damn door.

"I'm leaving today!"

I turn sharply in my crouch, and my leg seizes, sending a jolt of pain across my thigh and up to my hip. I clench my teeth. "No. You're on break this whole next week, and then there's Thanksgiving after that."

She reaches around me for the handle and slowly closes the door before pulling it open again with ease. "You gotta do it slow or it sticks."

I stare at the door from my position on the ground and then stand carefully, giving my leg a minute to orient itself and stop cramping.

"I'm leaving today, Milo. My roommate and her mom are doing a college tour before the trimester starts, and they invited me to come along."

My brows snap together. "You don't even know these people. I'm not letting you go on a trip with some random strangers only to find your body chopped up in someone's basement ten years from now. And that's final!" Shit. This is even worse than *"because I said so."*

"I'm starting to side with Jill about your attitude," Felicity snipes back.

Oh, hell. This is just perfect.

"I'm not stupid, Milo. I've been online friends with Carmen for two years, and her mom is not a serial killer. She's a special ed teacher. Real scary. And before you continue with the creepy dismemberment scenarios, Ted already did a background check on her, and it's squeaky clean."

I'm going to kill Ted.

I grasp for straws, not even sure why I'm trying to prevent her from doing something she'd otherwise probably never have the chance to do. I suspect I won't like what I find when I examine it later. "There's no way Sherry will let you go."

"She already said I could."

Dammit. I'm batting zero today.

I take a few long, slow breaths and finally manage to get over myself. "All right. I just… I just wish you had told me."

"I'm sorry." Her anger has calmed as well. "I was going to tell you when I told you about Jill, but I didn't really expect a bomb to detonate in the kitchen like that."

"Well, at least I never signed a lease agreement." I huff out a mirthless laugh. "That's something."

Felicity doesn't respond, and when I glance over again, one of her eyes is squeezed shut and the grimace is back. "Um, about that."

It's safe to say I've learned my lesson and won't be signing anything ever again without reading it first. This could have easily blown up in my face.

If I weren't so pissed, I'd be impressed at the skill level in Felicity's whole cloak-and-dagger scheme here. Last night, while my attention was caught on the fourth quarter of the Panthers game, she dropped a small stack of papers in front of me saying she needed a couple signatures for some art contest. I remember glancing at the first page and seeing her school's letterhead, but I admit I didn't read past that before signing my name a couple times. In my defense, however, the Panthers were down by only two points and had just regained possession of the ball with fifty-four seconds to go.

But, so what, really. It's not like Jill is going to come back here with a signed contract and demand I let her stay in my tiny guest room. Besides its lack of turn-down service, I doubt she wants to go to jail for homicide any more than I do.

And being upset with Felicity is worthless anyway. The kid was trying to help, as usual. She just has a ways to go on technique. After we had it out on the deck, I ended up spending the next four hours driving to and from Chapel Hill to meet up with Carmen and her mom. It saved Felicity the bus money and allowed me to check out this so-called special ed supermom for myself. Turns out she also teaches Sunday school and went to Yale. My fucking bad.

So, with Felicity on her whirlwind college tour and nothing on TV until tonight, the house is eerily quiet. Even the wind and the meddlesome seagulls have chosen to lay low for the afternoon.

I pop the top on a beer, more out of habit than thirst, and sit my ass on the couch where I focus on the empty beach out my window. I have a task to do—one that's been an overweight monkey hitching a piggyback ride for some time now—and I've put it off for as long as possible.

I don't know if it's my past catching up with me or Felicity leaving, but I'm finally ready to admit I'm out of excuses. So I pick up my phone and dial the number from memory.

"Coastal Adventures Dive School, this is Luke speaking."

I clear my throat as quietly as possible and seal my fate. "Hey Luke, this is Milo Papatonis. Is Leah in?"

Too late to turn back now.

CHAPTER SEVEN

MILO

Twelve Years Earlier

May 10th: "Mobility shouldn't be too much of a problem. Most of the nerve damage was surface, thank goodness, but he'll have significant scarring even with the skin grafts. And probably a slight limp if we're lucky. The significant tissue loss to the thigh is our biggest concern. That and infection." The disembodied voice is followed with a matching one a second later. This one sounds oddly like my dad, but that's impossible. It's Saturday, and he's got back-to-back off-shore charter runs on Saturdays. I'm too tired to figure it out anyway. I'll ask about it when I wake up.

May 11th: I blink but the light is too bright, so I close my eyes again. My entire head is muddy even though I know I've been sleeping for a while now. Damn, I told Bran to get rid of that shitty weed. I think it seriously fucked me up. Leah's parents are going to kill me if I'm hungover on a Saturday in the busy season, and I can't afford to lose this job. Just a little longer and then I'll get up.

May 12th: Someone wakes me up with a chainsaw to my right thigh. This can't be right. I hear screaming and it takes me a minute to realize it's coming from me. Here are the voices again—and the sweet blackness.

May 18th: It's been over a week since the accident, and every day has been a living hell. They say I'm lucky to be alive, but the pain makes me question it. I've only seen the worst wound—the one on my thigh—one time, but it weeps with pus and makes me want to vomit, so I keep my eyes averted when they change the dressings. My right half is covered in long lines of stitches and my fingers are still in splints. Bran says women love scars, so my fucked-up head should score me lots of chicks. I don't care about girls, though. All I care about is the pain. And maybe Leah. She hasn't come to visit, and I'm starting to think she never will. I need to ask Bran to replace my phone so she can reach me that way.

May 26th: I was discharged from the hospital today, and my mom cried. I missed graduation, so at least that's something. My mom wants me to come home with her so she and Morris can take care of me, but I don't want the attention. I just want everyone to leave me alone. I told her I needed to hear the ocean, so she didn't fight too hard when I said I was staying with my dad at the beach house. He's giving up his room on the first floor, something that tells me exactly how close to dying I came. Leah finally called and fired me. She kept it brief and clinical. Part of me wishes I had died anyway.

"FRICKING PASTRAMI ON RYE?" I FINISH unwrapping my sandwich and consider I should probably stop talking to myself so much. But there's never anyone around. Bran's up to his eyeballs with the shop, and Rayna is off at culinary school already. And here I am sitting on my ass on the sweltering beach, fully dressed in jeans and a t-shirt. I still have another three weeks until I can get in the water, and I wish I could just sleep through it.

A group of girls a few years older than me strut by in their bikinis, not even sparing me a glance. A couple months ago, I could have had them eating out of the palm of my hand. Bran may think he knows what women like, but he forgets how they light up at the prospect of a free private diving lesson. All I have to do is mention the possibility of a dolphin sighting and they're putty in my hands. Or, they were. Now I'm just some guy on the beach eating a free sandwich and feeling sorry for himself.

I drop my lunch back down on the towel and direct my eyes north. Two girls are coming my way, deep in conversation. They're both brunettes with long legs and nice racks. One looks the same age as those bikini girls and the other appears several years younger. The younger one jumps in front of her friend and walks back-ward, heading directly for me. This gives me a nice view of her ass in her tiny blue bikini, so at least something is going my way today.

The older one suddenly tackles her friend to the

ground a few feet in front of me and, damn! Two hot girls wresting is the best lunch entertainment I've ever had. This totally makes up for the sandwich. But they don't see me, which is made clear when they reverse positions and roll right into my bad leg. My vision begins to blacken at the edges with the pain. Sometimes I start to forget how bad it can be, but it's always there to remind me sooner or later.

I don't even hear what the girls are saying, but I think maybe I mumble a few words. I don't know; I'm too focused on getting the hell out of here before I vomit. The walk to the boardwalk is a marathon, but I make it past before losing the contents of my stomach in a bush. Just as well I didn't get to eat my lunch.

THE DOC SAYS I NEED TO WALK EVERY DAY TO KEEP mobility and teach my muscles how to support the new configuration of my trashed leg. I start from the house every day and make my way up and down 421, rewarding myself with an ICEE from Bob's Corner Stop halfway through. Most days are Coke-flavored days, but I mix it up now and then with mango or blue raspberry if I'm feeling crazy. Yes, this is my life now. Walking on the beach is too hard, so I stick to the streets where the rows of condos and houses get posher and posher the farther north I walk. It's not unusual to spot a Corvette or even a Ferrari now and then, but people who rent these places have so much money they don't know what to do with it. I used to not mind the tourists so much, especially all the girls in bikinis, but they've lost their shine now.

Today is particularly hot, even for a June day in North Carolina, and my t-shirt is soaked with sweat by the time I reach Bob's for my ICEE. It'll hit the spot today more than ever. God, I can't wait until I can swim again for exercise instead.

I know it's her before I even see her face. Her ass is encased in the shortest pair of shorts I think I've ever seen, although they still don't show as much as her bikini did yesterday. She's in profile, swinging a bag of something colorful in her hand and smiling like the sun came out just for her. She's got a carefree set to her shoulders and a spring in her step that makes her tits bounce. God, she's fucking beautiful. I let myself imagine for one minute what it would be like to have her kind of sunshine in my life. Then I get back to reality and open my mouth to spew angry words she doesn't deserve.

She's not responsible for my darkness, but maybe if I dim her light just a bit, I won't have to see what I can't have.

"Go make me a turkey pot pie!" Her voice shakes with anger as I shuffle back in the direction I came, my leg protesting and the deepest scar on my shoulder burning. I'm skipping my ICEE today. God knows I don't deserve it.

A few blocks down, my phone rings in my pocket, and I pull it out to see it's Rayna calling. The new phone was my graduation present from Mom and Morris to replace the one I lost in the accident. They even sprang for the monthly bill, something I'm sure was due to their relief at me living long enough to get my diploma.

"Hey, Rayna. What's up?" I force a lightness to my tone.

"I'm calling to take requests."

My lips can't help but turn up in genuine pleasure at that. Last time she came home, she brought some of the amazing stuff she's been cooking at school. She claimed they were the "reject" batches, but you'd never be able to tell the difference.

"Oh, man, can you bring more of that brisket thing?" My stomach rumbles audibly at the thought.

"Sorry, we've moved on to pork."

"Anything then. Looking forward to it."

I'm not an idiot, despite my recent behavior, so I know she's not calling about food. She's checking up on me.

"So how are you doing, Milo?" She keeps her tone casual because she knows me.

"I'm fine. Tell Bran to stop apologizing, would you?" I wipe away the sweat that's trying to drip in my eyes and smile again at the pause on the other end of the line.

"What do you—I don't—Bran and I don't talk much." Rayna hurries on, "How's your mom?"

The two of them are so transparent, but at least Bran doesn't lie to me about it.

"She's good. Now, promise me you'll tell Bran."

"Fine. If I happen to talk to him."

I roll my eyes, glad one part of my body doesn't hurt when I move it. "Thank you. He doesn't listen to me. Just keeps saying he'll never touch weed again and offering to do everything but wipe my ass."

"Now that I'd like to—never mind. Eww." She laughs, and it makes my shoulders relax.

Rayna's always been one of the guys, so to speak, never shy about burping and farting and always up for a good dare. I'm pretty sure Bran's been in love with her since the minute she belched the alphabet in eighth grade, but she has yet to reciprocate. He hangs in there, though, always hoping.

Leah, on the other hand, is refined, an athlete, careful with her body and everything she puts in it. She even had me trying vegan food for a while there, but it didn't do a thing to make her fall in love with me, so I stopped. I've been after her for six months, but I'm pretty sure I'll never see her again. And I'm certain I'll never get another job guiding dives in this town. Not after what I did.

There comes that tension again and it spreads to my chest. Is eighteen too young to have a heart attack?

"What are you doing anyway? You sound out of breath."

"Just following the doctor's orders like the obedient patient I am. I've been walking so much I'm making a groove in the sidewalk." I glance both ways before crossing at an intersection at my warp speed of molasses.

"Good for you. I'm glad to hear things are improving."

I don't deny or confirm that. "Coming home this weekend, I assume?"

"Yup. Can't wait to see your ugly mug."

"Yeah, me too." I hurry on before she can give me shit. "Bran's having a party, so it should be a good time."

We hang up a minute later, and my feet keep their slow rhythm until I'm back at the house. This time, I purposely examine it with fresh eyes. It's more of a shack than a house, really. Nothing more than a foundation with some clumsily assembled clapboard and a few windows. It was built back in the sixties on this postage-stamp lot before all the hurricane regulations. It's taken a few hits but is somehow still standing with a few slapdash repairs and such. There's a bed for me and an ocean right outside, though, so what more could a person need? Combine that with the facts that I didn't die and I have a good handful of people who care about me, and I should count myself more than a little lucky. So why can't I seem to keep myself from being an asshole?

I think about trying to find the girl and apologize, but I don't have a clue which place she's staying at. It's probably for the best anyway. She's likely already forgotten I exist, just like I should forget about her. But I can't seem to get her sunshine out of my mind—or stop wondering why in the hell she told me to make her a turkey pot pie.

CHAPTER EIGHT

JILL

I'm on the phone with Jenna as soon as the Uber pulls from Milo's driveway. The wait was excruciating. I didn't dare turn back to the house as I stood stock-still on the gravel, afraid I'd see two sets of angry eyes glaring at me. It turns out my mother was right; I should take a page from Jenna's book and think things through once in a while before jumping in headfirst.

"You're never going to guess who I just ran into." I do my best impression of a non-crazy person.

"Considering I don't even know where you are, I'd say you're right."

"I'm in Wilmington—sort of." She'll know what I mean. The whole area is made up of the city of Wilmington and then little beach towns and land preserves stacked alongside and below it from Wrightsville Beach down to Kure Beach, with the Intracoastal Waterway winding in between. I hadn't planned on telling her my whereabouts just yet, but I need to talk to someone about Milo and she's not just my sister, she's my best friend.

"Wilmington? Oh, I love that place. That's where we spent the last summer before I got married—the same summer you broke your arm. Do you remember?"

I refrain from saying "no doi" and just go with a hum of agreement as I finally give in to temptation and peek out the rearview window at the receding row of houses. Granted, Milo's house isn't the most impressive on the beach, but it would be a giant leap up the accommodation food chain from the hellhole I've been staying in— and it sure would have been nice to wake to sounds of the ocean. Sigh.

Jenna's voice snaps me back to reality. "Oh! Did you run into Noah Chandler from *Brothers of Moon Bay*? Wait, are they even filming that show anymore? I remember you had a little crush on him back then. Or was that the other guy?"

Wow. Talk about simplifying a situation. But I didn't share everything with her back then or in the years since.

"No, not the *Moon Bay* guys. And that show's been off the air for years now, grandma." I turn back around in my seat and focus on the back of my driver's head instead. His name is Klint with a K. His car smells like peaches, and it makes me wish I'd taken the time to eat breakfast.

"Very funny. I'm way too young to be a grandma and you know it."

I hear her boyfriend Sam's voice in the background saying something about not knowing many grandmas who wear crotchless underwear. My sister gasps, and I snort into the phone. Damn, I miss them.

"I'm glad my misadventures amuse you people," Jenna says. "Now tell me who you ran into."

"Milo." I whisper it as if Klint and Milo are BFFs and I'm afraid he'll spill that I was gossiping about him at the lunch table.

"Who's Milo?"

"Milo Papatonis." I bring my voice back up to normal levels, rolling my eyes at myself. "That jerk from the beach. The one who came over for dinner and broke that pelican statue that summer."

"Wait, is that the guy who had that boating accident? Poor kid. I remember him."

I want to say he's no kid anymore, but she doesn't need to read into anything. And, besides, he never deserved anyone feeling sorry for him, then or now.

"Yeah, that's him." Klint takes a left, and I hold on to a couple of my bags so they don't fall on the floor. "I saw him today, and he was just as much of an asshole as he was back then."

"He remembered you?"

I huff. "Gee, thanks."

"You know what I mean. I can't believe you guys recognized each other. I mean, you hardly knew him."

Ugh. I keep forgetting how much I kept from her.

"Well, be that as it may, it didn't stop him from calling me shallow and telling me I have a flat ass within sixty seconds of saying hello." God, Klint deserves a huge tip for not even flinching at that one.

Silence.

"Jenna?"

"I'm sorry. I'm just... speechless really."

"I know, right? What a douchebag." Another turn and another grasp at my bags.

"No. I mean, yeah but..." She's using her cautious tone, which means I'm not going to like what comes next.

"But what?"

"Honestly, Jill, you're the only person I know who could elicit insults that personal within such a short period."

"Hey!" This time I startle Klint, so I whisper an apology and mentally tack on another dollar to his tip. Not that I can spare it now that I'm headed back to the nightmare motel. How they have the nerve to charge forty bucks a night for that hellhole is a mystery.

"You forget I know you too well. What did you say to tick him off?" I can just picture her perched on one of her kitchen stools shaking her teacher finger at me.

"I didn't say anything! Jeez."

"Liar."

"Okay, fine. I pinched him. But in my defense, I didn't really mean to."

She gasps. "You punched him?!"

"I didn't punch him. I *pinched* him. You really think I go around punching people in the face? It's like we've never met."

"Well, I'm sorry, but I'm having a heck of a time figuring you out lately. Cut me some slack."

We're both quiet for a moment. I know she regrets her last words and probably thinks I'm going to hang up, but this is my fault. I'm the one who quit my job, broke up with my perfectly good boyfriend, and ditched town without a word to the people I love most in this world. This is the closest we've come to acknowledging the elephant in the room since shortly after I ditched them a few months ago. Jenna has been so careful when we chat —apart from the first few times when she tried to get me to talk and I told her I needed space. She doesn't want to scare me away. But she deserves answers. I just wish I had the right ones to give.

A lump forms in my throat. "I'm sorry, Jenna. Really."

She sighs. "Me too. Now, get back to your story." God, she is the best sister in the universe.

"So, I pinched him and, I don't know, things just spiraled from there."

"Uh huh." She pauses. "I still don't understand. Is this pinching thing one of your flirting techniques gone wrong?"

"No!" For God's sake. Just because I happen to be talented at flirting doesn't mean I flirt with just anyone. "I'd never flirt with him." Total lie. I used to flirt with him like my life depended on it. It just never worked.

"Sounds like flirting to me."

"That's because you're awful at flirting. We've already established that." The woman truly is helpless. Good thing Sam had the situation under control from day one with her.

"Shows what you know. I'm an excellent flirt now. I've been practicing."

Sam's voice comes through loud and clear. "You better be talking about flirting with *me*."

"Of course I am," Jenna placates him and then whispers into her phone, "I got him to take the girls Christmas shopping the other day by telling him how sexy I find it when he flexes his parenting muscles."

Good God. "Nicely done, sis." Sam is a cop and a straight-up hottie of the most masculine variety, but he's a pushover when it comes to Jenna and the girls.

"Yeah, well, when you come home, I can give *you* some lessons for a change."

This is the boldest she's been regarding my return home. Part of me just wants to tell Klint to drive me all the way there right now. But I'm not ready. I made too many mistakes back there, and I can't afford to repeat them.

"It's a deal." After all, it would be hilarious to watch Jenna try teaching me a thing or two about flirting. Great blackmail material too.

It suddenly doesn't seem like such a good idea to tell her about my colossal screw-up with Milo and the police. I can actually hear her smiling through the phone, and I'd rather leave things there. Besides, she obviously won't be of much help if she thinks I was actually flirting with that vile man. Like I'd ever stoop so low. *Oh, shut up.*

As if to reinforce my decision, the sign for the Misty Motor Inn appears through the windshield.

"Hey, I gotta go. I'm in an Uber, and we're pulling up to my stop."

"Wait. You didn't tell me the rest of the story about Milo! And why are you in an Uber? Where's your car? Oh no. Are you drunk? It's eleven in the morning, Jill!"

A laugh spills out. "Slow your roll, freakatron. It's no

big deal, and I'm not drunk. I'm fine. Everything is fine. No need to call out the state patrol." I wince at that one and don't add on the word "again."

"Fine, but we're not done with this conversation. I'm calling you later."

"Okay, gotta go. Love you. Give the girls kisses for me."

"Love you, Jilly."

Yup, best sister in the universe.

I bid *adieu* to Klint and drag my shit into the lobby of the Misty Motor Inn. And by lobby, I mean the sweltering metal sauna housing the unhelpful manager and her cat. They're watching *The Young and the Restless*, and the cat is making a gourmet meal out of his own ass. Neither one spares me a glance.

"Um, hi. Me again." I go for a little self-deprecating chuckle, but I really don't have the energy, so it comes out as more of a groan.

The manager's eyes remain glued to the TV. "Tell your johns to stop pissing on the signpost. Damn thing is rusting out."

My jaw drops. "Excuse me?" I clutch my purse closer and, I swear, if I were wearing pearls, I'd be clutching the hell out of them too.

"You heard me." Her voice sounds like she's two days away from keeling over from black lung.

"I'm not a..." I clear my throat and start again. "Listen, I just checked out this morning from room sixteen and I've had a, uh, change of plans. So, I'd like to check back in."

"Room sixteen ain't available no more." She picks

something out of her teeth with a yellow fingernail, and I fight my gag reflex.

"But I just checked out literally... never mind. I'll take whatever room you have then." Anything that will get me out of this den of horror.

Her response is immediate, but she still doesn't tear her eyes from the TV. "I can give you one on the second floor. Ocean view. Gonna cost a little more though."

I pull out my wallet. "How much more?"

"Sixty."

My head jerks back. "For sixty, I could stay at a motel that doesn't have hookers."

"Suit yourself." She reaches over and pets the cat, and I half expect her to yank out a piece of its hair and start flossing with it.

Dammit. I'll have to call another Uber and drag my ass around in circles until I find a place. Or maybe... "Well, my pimp said he won't pay more than forty so..." I throw my arms out in a *what are you gonna do* position. Everybody knows you don't mess with a pimp.

She finally swings her eyes over to me. "Price just went up to seventy."

Crap. Crap. Crap.

The cat jumps down from the desk, apparently finished with his butt buffet, and curls himself around my leg. Well, at least someone in this town doesn't hate me.

I mentally calculate my bank balance and hold out my debit card, being sure to maintain my grip as the manager reaches out and grabs the other end.

"Fifty," I say and then raise a brow when she frowns at me.

"Fine," she gives in begrudgingly, and I release my hold. "But we got a trade show coming in town on Thursday, and I'm gonna need all the rooms."

"What kind of trade show?" I can't imagine who would stay here voluntarily. Do pimps have trade shows?

"Carpet and Flooring." The gadget on her desk clicks and rumbles as she runs my card over the carbon paper and hands me the slip to sign.

"And they're staying here?" It's out before I can stop it, but she just slides a pen over and squints at me like I'm two steps down from a moron. "Oooooh." The lightbulb finally turns on in my brain. "Eww." That slips out too, but there's no preventing it.

Soon I'm ensconced in my "deluxe" accommodation, which is an exact replica of my first one, except I can sort of glimpse part of the ocean around the two buildings between the motel and the beach if I crane my neck just so. Doing my best not to touch anything more than absolutely necessary, I strip the duvet onto the floor and replace it with a few pieces of my dirty laundry. Then I scrub my hands to within an inch of their lives and settle on the bed with the Schnitzel with Noodles menu propped in front of me.

My first shift is tonight, and I'm determined to do such an amazing job that I'll soon be promoted to a von Trapp child who's actually gone through puberty and doesn't wear braids. I had completely forgotten about the oldest sister, Liesl, the other day. She was kind of sexy with her secret boyfriend and all that—even if he did turn out to be a Nazi in the end. And she was a flirt, so it's a perfect fit.

I've almost got the menu memorized, and I already shadowed Maria and another server named Natalie this weekend to nail down the protocol and get a feel for the place. Maria did what she could to trip me up, but I gave it back in kind—it's not the first time I've been engaged in a turf war at work, and I'm sure it won't be the last. I'm actually looking forward to the shift, even if it means wearing braids and the ridiculous costume. Work will allow me to clock out of my mental turmoil and focus only on completing the tasks in front of me. And, besides, it'll feel good to earn money and talk to customers again. I've been waitressing since I can remember, and I'm damn good at it if I do say so myself. So, I'm getting back on that horse, and I'll worry about a place to stay tomorrow.

I'm just glad I won't have to think about Milo Papatonis ever again.

CHAPTER NINE

MILO

"Here's to you finally growing a set of balls." Bran holds his beer glass up in a toast, and I frown at him. Ted looks only slightly less repulsed than I do.

"You mind keeping your voice down, man?" I sip my beer without touching my glass to his. We're all belly-up to the bar at the SWiN, and Bran's still grinning like a fool.

"Hey, getting a job is always something to celebrate. Congrats."

Ted turns to me. "I didn't know you got a job. Excellent. Congrats, man." He raises his glass too. Of all of us, Ted fits in the best here at the restaurant. He's in his usual tweed jacket, complete with leather elbow patches, and his professor glasses I've been told make him something called a "hot nerd." These are Rayna's words—and Haley's, Ted's girlfriend, but she's obviously biased. All I know is he's a decent guy and some kind of comic book guru who takes time out of his busy life to mentor my niece, which makes him good people in my book.

I finally give in and clink my glass to theirs. "Thanks."

This day has lasted a good month if you ask me, but when Bran called and said he and Ted were headed out, it sounded better than sitting on the couch watching TV alone.

"So, where are you working?" Ted asks. While Bran and I go way back, we've only known Ted and Haley for a few months, so he's not privy to most of my past and all its various fuckups.

"A place called Coastal Adventures. It's a dive school."

"Oh, right. I imagine you'll be happy getting back to diving after this hiatus. Good for you."

I nod because I don't feel like admitting to Ted that I'll be spending most of my time in a swimming pool.

Bran sets his glass down with a clunk. "Don't know that I've seen you go this long without diving. Well, except for back... you know."

Oh, I know all too well. We both do. Doesn't mean we need to talk about it.

Bran keeps yammering on while I try not to relive my phone conversation with Leah. "I told you from the beginning Leah would give you a job, but *noooo*. You had to exhaust every last possibility before picking up the phone to call her. Waste of time if you ask me. You could have been working for months by now."

I drop my beer back down to the bar top. "See, I don't remember asking you, now that I think of it."

He grins and takes a healthy swallow of his ale before quickly wiping his mouth with the back of his hand, class act that he is. But his actions are explained when Rayna pops her head between us in the next second to drop a kiss on my friend's cheek. "Hey boys." She turns to me and smiles, her perfect white teeth standing in contrast to the deeper tone of her skin. "Heard about the job. Congrats, Milo."

I scowl at Bran, but he just laughs and says, "Dude," like the one word is adequate explanation for sharing my business. Ted must agree because he's now grinning around his beer.

Since I'm not a complete asshole, I thank her and then try to change the subject. "What's the special tonight?" If there's any surefire way to distract Rayna, it's by talking about food.

"Oh, you guys picked a great night to come in. It's leg of lamb with roasted pumpkin salad and mixed greens." She continues to describe the dish using words like succulent, gorgeous, and ripe. You'd think she was talking about a naked woman from the way she's going on. But it does sound delicious. "I'll have the new girl run a few plates out to you guys."

"Are you sure? I don't want to be an imposition," Ted says with his usual politeness, but Rayna waves him off.

"Not at all. I live to feed people."

"Thanks, babe. You're the best." Bran kisses her, and my attention returns to my beer.

"And don't you forget it." Rayna laughs and pats me on the shoulder before dashing back to the kitchen.

Bran can't wipe the stupid smile off his face. Him

sitting there, arms folded, swiveling his bar stool side to side like a little kid makes it impossible for me not to laugh. "You're an idiot, you know that, right?"

"Oh, yeah," he acknowledges, completely unbothered, smile still firmly in place while he picks up his beer glass and raises it again. "You should be so lucky." He doesn't wait for me to toast this time, instead clinking glasses with Ted and maintaining his grin as he takes another sip. Ted's unabashed smile tells me he speaks the same language. I shift my attention elsewhere because I can't watch these assholes anymore.

Not being in ownership of vaginas, we're all content to sit quietly at the bar, each in our own thoughts for a while. The décor in this place is a bit on the horror-movie end of the spectrum, despite the fact that it contains nothing of an outright violent nature. Marionettes hang limply from hooks, surrounded by shelf upon shelf of porcelain figurines and snow globes, with dusty signs I can't interpret lining the moldings above. And then there are the dolls which, I admit, make me more than a little uncomfortable. It's the frozen expressions that do it. A menagerie of dead-eyed Austrian children in their Sunday best watching me drink my stout. Combine all that with the dim lighting and dark wood, and it harkens back to a bit of the creepy/obsessive collector vibe I remember from the classics. Hitchcock would have a field day with Camille and her collections. She's lucky for the award-winning food, or she'd be out of business and most likely locked up somewhere to save her from herself.

A glance at Ted tells me he's mulling over some work issue, while the expression on Bran's face reveals he's still thinking about Rayna because, let's face it, when isn't he? I can't even remember the last time I went on a date. Had to have been almost a year back. Yeah, that hotel clerk in the Virgin Islands. Although, I'm not sure you could call that a date. Before that, hell... there really hasn't been anybody apart from a few brief connections that had expiration dates before they even began. That's one perk of moving around. No strings to tie you down, and nobody in your business.

I roll my neck, trying to relieve the ever-present tightness. What I wouldn't give to head back out there and lose myself in the deep with nobody to worry about besides me and my diving tank. Not that living with Felicity is a hardship. I'm the one who made that choice, and I like having her around. I had to stay in town for a while anyway, dealing with my dad's estate and all the bullshit involved there. It's not like he had anybody else besides my mom who he could trust as executor of his estate. Although, the word "estate" is a bit of a stretch. It took me three months and all my savings to clean up both his debts and the piles of trash he'd accumulated around the property.

Then there's my mom who claims she doesn't need me, but she and Morris are getting older. They're not going to be around forever, and I don't even have a clue about their financial situation or their plans. So I'll put the outside world on hold for a bit and take care of my own for a change. Something which, I can finally admit, requires me to have a paying job to avoid being a complete bum.

Which reminds me again of my painfully uncomfortable call with Leah this afternoon.

It was, hands down, the strangest interview I've ever had. I don't even remember how the conversation started, but I know it involved exchanging awkward pleasantries before I bit the bullet and got to the reason for my call.

I almost choked on my words. "Listen, Leah. I know I have no right, and I swear to you I have no expectations."

"Milo—" she tried to interject, but if I didn't say my piece, I was going to crawl right out of my skin. It took me six months to make that call.

"Let me finish. As I said, I'm back in town and I'm staying here for at least a year or two before I can go anywhere. And I need a job. Believe me, I've applied everywhere else, but this town has a long memory. I'm not a dumb kid anymore, and I'd like to apply for a position. But, like I said, I have no expectations, and lord knows you don't owe me anything."

Fuck. I should have just gotten a job stocking groceries or thrown my application in at the marina—although those folks used to know me too. Hey, the state park must have jobs to fill. Diving isn't the only thing I can do. I remembered then why I despised asking anyone for anything. It felt like I was spiking a fever and developing hypothermia at the same time.

Her smooth voice interrupted my self-flagellation. "I assume you've been keeping up to date with your licenses and logbook."

I didn't dare breathe any more than necessary to keep me alive. "Absolutely. Been diving since I left, working with one outfit or another. Pretty much traveled half the world."

"Damn, now you're making me jealous." The lilt of her tone sparked old memories, and the tension in my shoulders loosened the tiniest bit.

"Some of it defies description. I swear, Leah, it's another galaxy down there." A silence settled but it wasn't awkward.

I heard her sigh. Us dive junkies are all the same. "I've got a part-time instructor position if everything checks out. Purely pool-based and recreational instruction," she clarified, telling me I'd be teaching nothing but basics to newbies in a swimming pool.

"I'll take it." I didn't care if it was teaching snorkeling to five-year-olds in a kiddie pool. It was one step closer to peace.

"Not so fast."

My heart began to plummet. I swallowed hard. "Okay."

"I'm willing to put the past in the past, Milo, but that means I have to treat you like any other new employee. You'd be on probation for the first month, and, to keep everything transparent, you need to know I may never have an open-water gig for you. I've got a good crew who have all earned their positions. That said, I feel fairly confident you could go full-time off-water during the season, but again, I can't make any promises."

I'd have been lying if I said I wasn't a bit deflated at that, but it was something. And something is almost always preferable to nothing.

"I understand. And I appreciate you giving me another shot, Leah. Not everybody would do that."

"Well, I always did have trouble saying no to you."

That had me scratching my head because it wasn't how I remembered things at all. But hell, I'd have agreed with just about anything she said if it meant I didn't have to stock groceries or shovel shit. I finally had a job teaching diving.

So why wasn't that fat-ass monkey off my back?

"Three lamb specials, compliments of the chef." I catch the waitress in my peripheral vision making her way behind the bar, and my spine straightens like a piece of rebar. I'd recognize that voice anywhere. And, sure enough, my ears haven't deceived me. Although my eyes threaten to because I expect to see long wavy hair falling over delicate shoulders and coming to rest on the best set of breasts I've seen in years. It should all be topped off with make-up just this side of seductive and probably a mini skirt revealing long legs that make a man's mind go places it's hard to return from.

I swear, I have to look twice, but she still hasn't lifted her eyes from her tray. It's Jill all right, but her hair is pulled back in some complicated braid things, and she's got an ultra-conservative lace number tied up to her chin, highlighting a face with only a touch of lip gloss and maybe a swipe of mascara. She looks younger than Felicity in her flower and lace dress and fresh face as she comes toward us and finally sets the tray down.

"Oh, and Camille asked me to tell whichever one of you is Brandon that she—Oh, Jesus Christ!"

Ted visibly jumps in his seat while Jill clutches her

neck and tries catching her breath as a flush of pink washes over her face.

I wondered how long that would take. Luckily the tray is resting mostly on the bar, so our dinners are probably out of danger.

Ted and Bran fall all over themselves in response to Jill's panicked reaction. "It's okay. I'm Bran. You must be the new girl." My buddy assumes a tone I've only heard him use with small children and zoo animals while Ted tries helping with the tray and repeatedly apologizing for his very existence.

I'm waiting for her to start in with an insult or maybe even hurl her body over the bar and finish me off with a tackle to the ground, but she just stands there like she's paralyzed. I decide to go for civil, or somewhere in that neighborhood. We are in public, after all. "Brandon, maybe you should apologize for scaring the young lady with your ugly face," I suggest.

Bran narrows his eyes and volleys them between Jill and me a few times. "What's going on here?"

"Bran, Ted, meet Jill. Jill, this is Bran and Ted." I know I should still be pissed at her, but sometime during the course of the longest day in recent memory, this morning's episode lost its impact. Felicity is happy, I've finally got a job, and I don't have to share my house with anyone. And, besides, it's hard maintaining a good fury at someone who looks about fifteen and just brought you a lamb dinner that promises to impress on a scale akin to a naked woman.

Jill sets both hands on the bar deliberately and takes another breath before shaking her head and coughing out a laugh that's two parts honey and one part the devil himself.

"Hello, Bran and Ted. Nice to meet you." The guys nod confused hellos, and then Jill's eyes flash to Bran again. "Wait. You're Bran? Wow, I mean... this is a surprise."

"How do you...?" Bran's still got the look of someone trying to wrap their brain around the end of *Planet of the Apes*, and then a lightbulb switches on. "Wait a minute. You're *Jill*? As in, *summer-break Jill*?"

"Uh..." Jill's peering at Bran like she's preparing to ask a lot of inconvenient questions. I've had enough drama for one day, so it's time to nip this thing in the bud.

I throw out the first words that come to mind. "I didn't know you worked here." Dammit. I should have figured that out the minute I saw her talking to Rayna outside the kitchen last week. I'm losing my edge, that's for damn sure. "You're just full of surprises, aren't you?"

Her eyes come to me again, and they're still missing that hostility I was expecting. Maybe it's because her boss is just across the room, not that Camille would ever argue with anyone about giving me a hard time. But Jill doesn't know that.

"Yeah. Tonight's my first night." But I'm not out of the woods yet because her gaze switches back to Bran. "I've heard a lot about you, Bran. It's nice to put a face with the name after all this time."

"Likewise." Bran smiles like a cat who just caught a whole flock of canaries. Shit.

Jill's lips spread in a smile to match his. "Although I

had it on good authority that you resembled a Wookie and your balls weren't ever going to drop."

Ted chokes on his beer, and Bran's smile drops like a brick before he punches me hard enough in the arm that my bar stool swivels halfway around. "Asshole."

This pulls a full-throated laugh out of Jill, and I can't help but stare while the air around me does its best impression of a vacuum and steals all my breath. It's just like before. Not a thing has changed, and I'm drowning in familiar waters without so much as a warning or a life vest.

But Jill's safe on dry land without a care in the world, it seems, because she winks at Bran and Ted and sets our plates in front of us. "As enjoyable as this is, I can't afford to get behind on my first night. Anything else I can get you boys?" She flips the empty tray under her arm and smiles at us expectantly.

She's acting like this morning never happened and we just met for the first time. I'm not really sure how I feel about that.

"No, this looks unbelievable. Thank you so much," Ted responds for all of us.

"All right then. Enjoy." She turns to go, and I open my mouth to say something. I haven't the first clue what, but something is trying to crawl its way out of my throat. What is she doing working here? What is she even doing in town? Where has she been for the last decade, and why does she need a place to stay? She pauses and looks over her shoulder. "Milo, you have time for a word later? I've got my break in thirty."

Ted's already digging into his meal, and Bran's

sporting an evil grin which Jill can't see, but I do my best to ignore him while I croak out, "Sure," and then watch as she hurries back to the kitchen and disappears through the galley doors.

"Well, well, well."

No use staring at the doors all night, so my eyes flick back to Bran. "You don't have the first clue what you're talking about. Eat your dinner."

Which he does, but he does it while snickering under his breath.

I'm going to need another beer.

CHAPTER TEN

JILL

I flatten myself against the kitchen wall just inside the door while my lungs search for air. Oh my God. My head tilts back, and I close my eyes for a second, silently asking God what the actual fuck he's thinking!

Milo was... not horrible to me. He even kind of flirted with me. Well, maybe *flirted* is the wrong word, but something. It was so... friendly. Although, I guess I was nice to him too. But I had to be—I'm at work, it's my first day, and I did call the cops on him after all. But what was I thinking asking him if we could talk over my break? Bad idea. Bad, bad, bad idea. I know myself too well. I'll start trying to apologize, then he'll piss me off, and I'll end up yelling at him and losing my job. Either that or I'll go rogue and start flirting with the bastard.

Would it be bad form to ask around for a Valium on my first day? Yeah, I thought so.

"Did you get to meet Bran?"

My eyes fly open, and I unstick myself from the wall with an awkward lurch forward. "What? Oh. Yeah. I met him. He's super nice—and cute. Good job." I force myself to wink at Rayna, who's multitasking like a mofo with one hand stirring a large pot and the other flipping sliced pork tenderloins in a pan. She's my top prospect for a friend in this town, and the best way to screw that up would be to show too much of my crazy. An assistant chef and three kitchen workers race around the space along with two servers running out with hot plates. I do my best to stay out of the way. Camille only gave me three tables since it's my first solo shift, and I just got through checking on all of them before running the specials to the bar.

Rayna's laugh is cute as hell. "Yeah, he's one of the good ones. And it doesn't hurt that food is the way to his heart—and just about everything else."

I smile at her, willing the drum set in my chest to quiet down. "Well, I'd say you've got it made then if the rave reviews of your food are anything to go by." I throw a thumb over my shoulder. "The customers talk about you like you're Emeril in lederhosen."

"They're sweet. I mean, of course my food's amazing." She grins. "But we've got a ton of regulars, and Camille sells the hell out of this place. Don't let her batty-old-lady act fool you. She's a shark when it comes to the business and marketing."

I nod. "Well, I'd better get back to it." I turn to head back to the dining room, but Rayna calls after me.

"Hey, did you meet Milo?"

I force myself to keep on walking. "You could say that." Ugh.

The couple at table thirteen is completely sauced by the time my break rolls around. I ask Kip, the bartender/food runner/unidentifiable movie extra, what their policy is in these situations, and he explains that the couple are old friends of Camille who come in every so often to get drunk and then go to karaoke down the street. He assures me they take a cab home after, so I file the info away in my mental rolodex where I keep all pertinent customer information and go serve them their third bottle of wine.

But I'm dawdling. I'm dawdling because Bran and Ted are no longer at the bar and Milo is counting a tip from his wallet and sliding off his bar stool. I'm out of time. And I'm being a big whiney baby about the whole thing. *Just apologize to the man and then get your ass back to work, Jill. Do not take any bait he throws out. Do not raise your voice. Do not look directly into his eyes—or his package.* Wait, what? Great, now I'm arguing with myself.

Yanking off my apron in the kitchen, I brief Natalie—who has the unfortunate role of the eldest von Trapp son, Kirk—on my tables in case they need anything during the next fifteen minutes. Then I straighten my posture and walk as casually as possible back into the dining room. Milo stands just outside the kitchen doors, and I almost run right into him. His hand snakes out to steady me, and the place where his palm comes in contact immediately warms.

"Sorry," I mumble and step aside, away from his

touch. "Uh, let's go outside. I'm not supposed to take breaks in the dining room."

He runs a hand through his hair, and I wonder for a second if he's as nervous as I am. But why would he be? Unless... Unless he's about to tell me he's suing me over the whole police thing! He wouldn't, would he? No. That's crazy. Or is it? Shit.

I'm practically sprinting by the time we get out to the sidewalk, and my heart isn't far behind in the race. Words start spilling out before I even turn around to face him.

"Look, I wanted to apologize again for this morning. I really hope this doesn't cause you and Felicity any problems with the authorities or with her staying with you. And I hope you guys find a good housemate who won't call the cops on you." Crap. *Not the time for jokes, you idiot. Say something else. Anything!* "And just because you were a jerk way back when doesn't necessarily mean you're the same way now. I mean, you're letting your niece live with you, so that's got to count for something."

"Uh, thanks?"

I finally turn around. His dark hair is mussed, thicker than it used to be, and that damn beard only highlights his half-smile. I would have thought a beard would hide so much of what made his face beautiful at eighteen, but it doesn't. If anything, it enhances his best features, all of which have evolved into a more rugged handsomeness now. It's sending me off-kilter, and I don't like it. My go-to move would be to flirt with a guy to regain the upper hand, but I can't flirt with Milo. He's too dangerous. And even though I wronged him today, it doesn't change the fact that he was a real asshole this morning before I took things too far.

And he still hasn't apologized.

I cross my arms and pretend to give him an unimpressed once-over. "Although come to think of it, you still act like a bit of a snob if you ask me." I just can't seem to help myself.

That sends his neck back. "*I'm* a snob?"

"You told Felicity I was shallow and, let's face it, you don't have any basis for that." My voice stays even like I'm simply reading him the specials. "You just assume anybody who didn't grow up in your precious town is somehow lacking real values and goes around demanding to be served hand and foot. Which is completely off base."

"Think whatever you like, but you've got some nerve calling me of all people a snob, and you know it."

"Snobbery goes both ways, SCUBA boy. Do you think me and my flat ass wear this insane get-up for laughs?"

He doesn't respond, but I catch the telltale twitch at the corner of his mouth, and my head threatens to explode.

"God, you're an asshole!" I knew it all along. Whatever cease-fire he was working inside the restaurant is long gone.

But any trace of humor fades at my insult, and the tendons in his neck pop as he steps closer and points a pissed-off finger in my face. "You are unbelievable. You seem to forget all the help I gave you that summer—you just turned around and threw it all back in my face before you trotted on back to your charmed life. And that was a decade *before* you called the cops on me for no reason!"

"I did not!"

He throws a hand out. "I believe I have a copy of the report on my kitchen table, Sunshine."

Oh, hell no! I step even closer. "Don't you call me that! And I meant I didn't throw anything in your face because there was nothing to throw! You were always out for yourself and you know it. You didn't care about me one bit!"

He steps back and laughs in response. *He laughs.* It's a bit maniacal, but it's a laugh for sure.

I'm left standing with my fists on my hips and a half-empty bottle of rage in my belly. "I always knew you had a screw loose."

"You should know. You're the one who loosened it." He's smiling, but it's not a nice one.

"Are you drunk? God, this is ridiculous. I'm going back inside." I stalk by him to the door. "Have a nice life!" It's time to get back to work and forget this man ever existed.

"You too!" His voice follows me, but I don't look back. "Don't forget your pitchfork when you go home tonight."

Crap. It's just like that asshole to remind me I only have one more day to find a place to live.

"You did well tonight, Louisa." Camille nods

in my direction as she settles the cash drawer. "Tomorrow, you get your own full section."

I don't miss the glare from Maria before she stalks to the back hallway. Girl needs to chill out. I'm only going to be here for a few weeks.

"Thank you, Mrs. Blume." I hitch my purse on my shoulder. I'm still wearing the dress, but the braids came out the minute the last customer left. They were starting to cut off blood flow to my brain, or at least that's what I'm blaming for the craptastic headache forming between my ears.

"Please, call me Camille. We're family now." She smiles and goes back to counting.

She really is sweet, but being included in her "family" makes me a bit nervous based on evidence to this point. Nevertheless, she gave me an awesome job, so I'm grateful. Tips were killer tonight. Unfortunately, very few of them were cash, and the restaurant pays credit card tips out on payday—which happens to be more than a week from now.

"Okay, Camille. I'll see you tomorrow." I pull out my phone to call an Uber and step outside onto the sidewalk. It's a beautiful fall night and I wish I could walk, but the Misty Inn is a few miles away. I push the power button on my phone, but nothing happens.

No, no, no! I press and hold the button, hoping I just powered the whole thing down earlier by mistake, but it's no use. "Dammit!"

"What's wrong?" A familiar voice comes from the other direction. It's Rayna, and she's got her hand in the crook of Bran's elbow. They must have come out the side door.

"Stupid battery died." I hold up the phone. "I was trying to call an Uber."

"We can give you a lift," Bran offers without hesitation and Rayna nods.

"Oh, you don't have to. That's really nice, though." I offer them a smile. I've always been a resourceful person, so I'll figure something else out.

Bran beckons with a tilt of his head. "Oh, come on. We insist." Rayna nods next to him, and they stand there like the quintessential storybook couple. Bran with his tall frame and fair good looks and Rayna with her petite curves, killer dimples, and head of curly black hair.

"Maybe I can just use your phone to call Uber?" But I immediately realize that won't work because the accounts are tied to phone numbers. "Ugh."

"Come on," Rayna coaxes. "Bran doesn't bite."

"And Rayna only does when she's hungry, so you should be safe."

I smile my appreciation, and we all walk down the sidewalk together. "Thanks, guys. I swear I'm getting a car soon."

I can practically see Bran's ears perk up. "What are you in the market for?" We end up talking about cars as we hop in Bran's truck and I direct them south on Lake Park Boulevard. Turns out he's an auto mechanic and runs a whole shop. My buddy Zeb comes to mind, and I wonder if maybe I should've had my car towed to Bran's place instead. It's still sitting at Zeb's waiting for me to deal with it.

Rayna chimes in, clearly done with the shop talk. "I know you're new in town, but I didn't ask. Do you have family here you're staying with or did you get your own place already?"

"Oh, I'm still working on that. Just staying at a motel for the time being, but I've got some feelers out." Total lie. "And no family here. I just like the place." I decide to leave it at that. The last thing I need is her telling Camille I only plan on staying for a little while. I need that job.

I'm holding my breath waiting for Bran to tell Rayna about Milo and me knowing each other, but he doesn't, thank God. That man is the last thing I want to talk about right now.

"Which motel? We've both lived here our entire lives, so you don't need to give us directions." She laughs from the front seat.

"The Misty Motor Inn," I say as quietly as possible.

"I'm sorry, what?" This comes from Bran.

I repeat the name a little louder, not daring to look at Rayna because if they know this town so well, they probably know the Misty Inn in all its shady glory. God, this is humiliating.

His face isn't visible from my position, but Bran practically growls behind the wheel. "Oh, no. I heard you the first time. What I mean is what the hell are you doing there? You're gonna get yourself killed staying at a shithole like that!"

"Bran," Rayna tries to interject, but he's on a roll.

"Don't 'Bran' me. If she manages not to get shot, she's gonna get hepatitis or tetanus or... or Ebola staying at that place." He turns in his seat and pins me with a frown. "You're not staying there."

"Gee, Dad," Rayna drawls. "Can she at least stay out 'til curfew?" She smiles back at me, and I appreciate her trying to make me feel better.

"It's just for a couple days," I offer, not liking where this is going. I mean, I know the place is a nightmare, and it's always nice having someone in your corner, but I'm a grown adult.

"Absolutely not! We'd never forgive ourselves if something happened to you." Bran's head is shaking like he's got water in his ears. "And *Milo*!"

Oh no.

"Shit. Milo's gonna blow a gasket when he finds out you're staying there!"

I lean forward. "No!" My voice is louder than I intended, but this has utter catastrophe written all over it.

"Wait. Why would Milo...?" Rayna is as confused as every other damn person I've come across who knows that dickhead.

Bran turns to her and hooks a thumb back at me. "This is Jill."

Rayna rolls her eyes and tucks her hair behind her ear with what tolerance she has left. "I know, genius. I work with her."

"No, I mean, this is *Jill*." He leaves it at that, and Rayna glances back at me—like I'm about to help her out with this one? Nope.

"What do... Ooooh!" Her eyes go wide. "You're *Jill*?"

Oh my God. This is not happening.

What in the hell did Milo tell these people about me?

"No. I mean, yes. Of course I'm Jill. But I'm not *Jill* or whatever that's supposed to mean."

Rayna eyes me. "I'm confused. Do you know Milo or not?"

"Uhhhh, yes?" I try to hide my grimace.

"Oh my God. I can't believe this. What a small world." She's smiling and staring at me like she's never seen me before.

"Utterly microscopic," I murmur, my eyes straying to the window.

The buildings start to look familiar, telling me we've almost reached the motel. Thank you, baby Jesus.

I gather my purse and phone and scooch toward the door. "Okay, um, we don't need to involve Milo in this at all, okay? I've got things under control, and I swear once I leave the inn, I won't ever go back. Deal?"

But Bran isn't slowing down. Aaand there goes the inn.

"Hey! You missed it!" I gaze almost forlornly—if you can believe that—out the rear window as the sign gets smaller and smaller.

"No, I didn't. I know exactly where I'm going." Bran adjusts his grip on the steering wheel like he's about to challenge someone to a drag race.

"But my stuff is there," I protest. "Look, it's nice of you to try and take care of me and let me sleep on your couch or whatever, but I swear I'm fine. Please, just turn around. You guys must be exhausted. I know I am." I keep blathering on, hoping something sticks.

"We'll get your stuff tomorrow when it's daylight and we're less likely to be shot."

I get the feeling he's not joking, and I swallow hard. Well, it looks like I'm couch surfing until I get a place of my own.

But Bran's not done. "For tonight, you're staying at Milo's"

Hello, baby Jesus, we need to have a word.

CHAPTER ELEVEN

MILO

"What now?" My feet hit the floor, and I push myself up from the couch, feeling the burn from the stretch in my leg. Who in the hell is knocking on my door at 10:45 at night on a Tuesday? Shuffling to the front door, I scratch my beard and try shaking off the sleep that almost had me under while the news rattled from the TV.

I open the door without checking who's there, which just goes to show how damn tired my brain is, and I'm not all that surprised to see Bran standing there. I am, however, surprised to see the expression he's wearing.

"What's the matter? Did you have a fight with Rayna?" He's spitting mad, which, in my experience, is usually caused by either a shitty client or a woman. And since Bran didn't work today, I can only assume it's a woman—*his* woman.

He lets himself in and stalks toward the kitchen as the door bangs shut behind him.

"Make yourself at home. Can I get you a beer? Maybe a four-course meal?" I follow him at a much slower pace. I need to stretch my leg out after he leaves.

"That woman is so damn stubborn."

"I hate to be the bearer of bad news, man, but you've known that for twenty years, and you still put a ring on it."

He looks up like he just realized I'm in the room. "Not Rayna."

I back up a step. "Whoa! Is there something you need to confess here? I never took you for that kind of guy." I'm half joking, but something's got him worked up.

"No, jackass. I'm talking about your little friend." He's pacing now, and I'm even more confused, which I didn't think was possible.

"What little friend?" I consider for a split second that he might be talking about Felicity since he's as familiar as I am with her stubborn nature. But my niece is hundreds of miles north, hanging with her friend.

"Jill."

And here I was thinking this shit show of a day was over.

"What about her?" Honestly, it could be anything. I wouldn't be the least bit surprised if she were perched on some rooftop claiming to have grown wings at this rate.

He pauses and looks me straight in the eye. "Tell me you didn't know she's been staying at the Misty."

My body locks. "What did you say?"

"She's staying at the Misty. At least she was until I drove her ass here. Now she won't get out of the damn truck."

I don't care how she ended up in the backseat of my friend's truck, but I've never been more grateful to Bran for anything. That woman may be a pain in my ass, but that doesn't mean I want her dead or attacked—or worse. What in the hell is she doing at that shithole?

My boots are headed for the door before I can think twice.

Rayna jumps down from the front seat of the truck as soon as she sees me barreling down. "Now, Milo, just calm down. She's fine. For whatever reason, she doesn't want to stay here and that's her business, so I say Bran and I take her to our place, and she can sleep on the couch."

I've slept on their couch. One night when Bran and I were overserved, I passed out on the miserable thing, and I don't think my neck has been the same since.

And, besides, I need to see her. Check with my own eyes that she's okay. It makes no sense, but there it is.

I yank open the back door of Bran's extended cab and there she is, that caged panther ready to claw my freakin' eyes out. Her hair is in a wild halo around her face, free of the confines of that ridiculous hairdo from earlier. I can see the deep blue of her eyes even in the weak overhead light of the cab, and if I didn't know better, I'd say they were burning.

"Don't be stupid, Jill."

"I am not stupid!" Oh, yeah, there's a fire all right.

"I didn't say you were. I said don't be stupid *now*." I gesture to the ground, knowing she gets my meaning.

"I'm not staying here." Her arms cross, and I'm about two seconds from hauling her ass out of the cab and spanking it red. It takes everything I have to rein in my temper.

"Now is not the time to be all self-righteous and shit, Jill. You know I've got the room, so get on out of there and let everyone get a good night's sleep." There's plenty of time later to figure out what the hell has her so broke she's risking her wellbeing for a night's sleep.

Her eyes dart to Rayna who's climbed back in the cab —probably to protect Jill from me. I can see her wavering.

"It's too late to go looking for another place, and Bran and Rayna's couch is no picnic," I continue.

Rayna shrugs. "It's true." Then she tacks on, "But you're welcome to it if you want." Solidarity among stubborn females. Jesus.

I jerk my hand toward the house. "In sixty seconds, I'm locking the door of my bedroom and going to sleep. Either you come in and sleep in a real bed, the couch, or the damn porch—doesn't matter to me. But you're not going back to that motel."

I'm done with this. But before I can move another muscle, Bran pushes past me, reaches into the cab, and pulls Jill out in a fireman's hold. She's too shocked to resist at first, but when Bran turns and bends, her upper half comes flying toward me, and I barely have time to react. I catch her and pull her entire body to my chest, legs bent over one arm and back against the other.

She yelps and starts squirming, but Bran tosses her purse on her lap and slams the door shut. "Stay!" He shouts like he's talking to an unruly dog, and I'm tempted to laugh out loud if I didn't think it would get me two black eyes. Five seconds later, the truck is spewing gravel as he pulls out of my drive.

Rayna leans out the window and waves. "I'll see you tomorrow! Get some good sleep!" And they're gone.

There's no telling what Jill might do if I set her down, so I stride to the house the best I can with her still in my arms and somehow manage to get through the doorway without dropping her. It's like a caveman carrying his feral bride over the threshold.

"Welcome home, Sunshine," I say, and then drop her on her ass in my entryway.

THAT WAS, QUITE POSSIBLY, THE WORST NIGHT OF sleep I've had in a decade—and that includes more than a few nights crashing on a beach with nothing but the moon and sand fleas to keep me company. I pull on my t-shirt and a pair of sweatpants and wander out to the kitchen, my face splitting in an enormous yawn. Apart from its usual noises, the house is quiet, but I can still feel her lurking somewhere within its walls.

I meant what I said last night about going to bed in sixty seconds—even if good sleep never found me. After dropping Jill on the floor, I didn't pause on my way to my room, tossing only a few words over my shoulder as I went.

"Felicity's room is up the stairs."

Jill didn't respond, to my relief, and I shut my bedroom door behind me. My phone pinged with a text from Rayna, but I only glanced at it before sinking down on the bed, ready for the day to finally be over.

But I've never been a particularly lucky guy, as was evidenced by the knock on my door five minutes later.

"What?" I shouted from my pillow.

"She's not there." Jill's voice had lost a little of its petulance.

"Who's not where?"

"Felicity. She's not in her room."

I was not getting up. "I know. Go to sleep or whatever you want to do, but don't wake me up."

"Aren't you going to wait for her to get home? She's only sixteen." I could picture Jill standing outside my bedroom door, hands on her hips and a disapproving frown taking center stage.

For Christ's sake.

I pinched the bridge of my nose and pushed to sitting before getting to my feet and going to the door. I opened it just enough to see Jill standing there in that crazy dress with the expected frown, but not enough that she could barge in and punch me in the nuts.

"That'd be a hell of a long wait considering she won't be back until Christmas."

"What?! This is ridiculous!"

"Calm your ass down. What do you care? The sooner you go to sleep the sooner we can be rid of each other. Goodnight." I tried closing the door, but she wedged her shoe in the crack. "Dammit, Jill! What now?"

She took a breath and relaxed her posture, which just served to make me even warier. "Do you have a phone charger?"

"Maybe."

"Well, can I borrow it?" She tried for a smile and… was she batting her eyelashes at me? Nice try, sweetheart.

"That depends."

"On what?" Yup, she was definitely giving me flirty eyes.

"If you're gonna use it to charge your phone and call an Uber."

She gasped, and I held up my phone. "Rayna texted."

The smile and doe eyes were long gone as Jill swiped her hand out to snatch my phone, but I shoved it down the front of my jeans before she could grab it. *What?* It was the easiest place to reach. Her hand grappled for it out of reflex, and then she jumped back like a startled cat when she realized where her hand was going. I took the opportunity to shut the door and lock it.

"Goodnight!"

I heard some grumbling and muttering, but it soon faded, and I was left to toss and turn until the sun coming through my window woke me up for good.

"You don't have any food."

Jill's voice scares the crap out of me from the corner of the kitchen.

"Jesus. Warn a guy, would you?" I reach up to scratch my beard as I glance over. And I almost swallow my tongue.

Standing in the corner of my kitchen is a goddamn goddess. Her hair is sleep-tumbled where it falls around her shoulders and face, and there's not a trace of make-up on her. Instead, her skin is dewy and fresh with full pink lips pouted and laced with dampness from what could only have been her tongue dragging across them.

My dick goes hard in my sweatpants, and I can't help the sweep of my eyes down the rest of her body. She's wearing one of those flimsy white camisole tops that barely contains her breasts, and it's paired with hot pink boy shorts that show off her long legs and the swell of hips to perfection.

I'm rendered entirely stupid. I know the moment she glances down she'll see the tent in my pants, and I really don't give a shit right now. It's all I can do not to close the space between us and bite her full lower lip before taking things way too far on the kitchen floor.

But Jill is unfazed. She doesn't even look at me, just turns and rifles through the cabinets on a hunt for breakfast. I almost lose my shit entirely when she bends to examine the lower half of the fridge and sticks her ass out so I can see the exact spot where the backs of her thighs meet the swell of her ass cheeks. Nothing flat in sight here. I actually need to lift the crew neck of my t-shirt to wipe my mouth.

"I'll uh." I clear my throat to get the horny frog out of it. "I'll make coffee."

She finally turns my way, but I hurry to the counter where the coffee maker stands, pressing my hard-on against it before she sees it and gets violent.

"Okay."

I busy myself with the coffee and don't dare peek behind me to see what she's doing. Hell, she could be doing yoga in her underwear on my kitchen table for all I know. Damn. I'd like to see that. But nope. I'm getting her coffee, and then I'm checking her into a decent hotel before Bran and I go grab her shit from the Misty and get to the bottom of this.

I do everything but drum my fingers on the counter as I wait, willing my boner down and the damn coffee to brew. I finally get desperate enough to make an attempt at conversation.

"Been meaning to go shopping but haven't gotten around to it. We can go through a drive-thru on our way to your new hotel if you need to."

"Where's Felicity?" she asks from the direction of my table, and the yoga images pop up again in my mind before I shut that shit down.

"She's off looking at colleges, and then she's going to art school in Virginia for three months."

I hear her give a half-laugh. "I thought the *two* of you were looking for a housemate. I didn't realize you were looking for someone to take her room."

"*She* was looking for someone to take her room. Not me." What is taking this coffee so damn long?

"Doesn't play well with others. Check."

My jaw tenses. "It's not a character flaw to prefer living alone."

"If you say so."

"I do—never mind." Damn, she gets my back up. "I'm not fighting with you this morning." What I need is my morning swim and this damn coffee.

"Oh, and just when I was looking forward to it so much." She snaps her fingers in what I assume is an *oh darn* expression. Brat.

The coffee finally finishes dripping, and I pull two

mugs from the cabinet before filling each. Now that my dick is back where it should be, I grab my dad's old sugar bowl and take it to the table with the coffee, careful to avert my eyes from the temptation sitting in the chair in her underwear.

"Sorry I don't have any milk. I know you like your coffee white and sweet, but the sugar will have to do." I take a seat across from her and pull my coffee toward me.

She doesn't say anything, and I glance up at her by mistake to find her watching me with an unreadable expression.

"What?"

"You remember how I like my coffee." It's not a question.

I open my mouth to protest when I realize she's right. I hadn't even given it a thought. "Yeah," is all I can say.

We're both quiet as we sip our coffee, but it's a heavy silence loaded with so many unsaid things. I should ask her why she's here and, further, why she's broke, but do I really want to get involved? I start to tap my foot and wonder what the hell is wrong with me. And then the words are out before I even know I'm going to say them.

"You know, you can stay in Felicity's room for a while if you want. I'm starting a new job, and I won't be around much anyway." What the hell am I doing? I'm supposed to find out why she's staying in a shithole and fix that in whatever way doesn't have her living under my roof—and my skin.

Jill opens her mouth, and I'm not sure if I want her to accept my offer or tell me to go to hell. But a phone chimes. It's not mine.

Jill immediately bites her lip and jumps out of her chair. She's back in two minutes, her ridiculous dress from last night covering her hot body, and her purse slung over her shoulder. She tosses something at me, and I catch it. It's my phone charger.

"Sorry. My Uber's outside."

Then she turns to go but pauses in the doorway to the kitchen, not looking back at me. "Thanks, Milo."

She's out the door a second later, and it closes gently behind her. I continue to sit with my coffee and my charger until the crunch of gravel silences and it's only the groans of the house to keep me company.

CHAPTER TWELVE

JILL

Dammit. Dammit. Dammit.

The plan was simple. Since the subtle flirting bombed last night, I was supposed to strut around half-naked this morning so I could steal his phone charger while he was struck stupid, letting his little head do the thinking. Then I'd slip out to catch my Uber and get back to the motel and be rid of him for good.

But I miscalculated the teensiest bit. I didn't plan on *his* getting turned on making *me* get turned on. I thought my nipples were going to bust right through the fabric of my cami, for God's sake! Milo Papatonis first thing in the morning is a sight to behold. Milo Papatonis first thing in the morning with a giant pipe in his pants? Come to mama! Ack!

I probably could have talked myself down from that one, so to speak, but then he hit me with the coffee. How does a man not see a person—whom he hates, by the way

—for twelve years and still remember how they like their coffee? It was a wonder I didn't swipe our mugs to the floor and crawl across the table to mount him like a sex-starved soldier returning from war.

Thank God my Uber came, or I might have even taken him up on his offer to stay before I ripped off my clothes. Which would have been a complete disaster. The only reason he offered was because he had boobs on the brain. He wasn't thinking clearly at all, and neither was I. I'm going to tip my driver a gazillion percent for rescuing me from that close call.

Oh, but I can't. Because I'm broke.

Which brings me to my next problem. I'm due at work in two and a half hours, and I still need to check out of my motel, find a new place to stash all my shit, and take a shower.

I honestly hadn't realized exactly how bad the Misty Motor Inn was until everybody flipped their ever-loving shit last night. I mean, hookers are never a good sign, but people need to make a living, right? Although, now that I think about it, the bent spoon and syringe I spied on the railing the other day should have perhaps given me more pause. Hmm.

I ask the driver to wait when she pulls into the parking lot and then go grab the first load of bags. She doesn't offer to help, which is understandable. I wouldn't leave my car unattended here either. It takes three trips before everything is loaded safely in the roomy trunk, and then I'm in the back seat catching my breath.

"Where to?"

"Oh. Um." Crap. "Do you know of any cheap motels where I won't get mistaken for a prostitute?"

She takes in my crazy get-up, and I inwardly cringe. She either thinks I'm a fetish hooker or an escapee from a fundamentalist cult.

I gesture down to my dress with a pained smile. "Work uniform."

She glances at my dress again and back to my face. "Uh huh." And then she starts driving. *Nice, Jill.*

We only drive for about five minutes before she pulls into a Days Inn and puts the car in park in front of reception. "Not sure what the rate is right now, but it's decent during the season. Bound to be a fraction of that now."

"Thanks," I say. "Do you mind waiting another second while I make sure they have a room?"

She nods, and I take my purse with me as I head for the doors, saying a silent prayer as I go. I inquire about the rate and vacancy and go grab all my things when both answers turn out in my favor. They only have two rooms left, but the clerk is saving one for me. It's sixty a night plus taxes and fees, but she assures me it's a bargain with the carpet and flooring people coming in today and tomorrow. I'll figure out a way to swing it until I can get a minute to find something else.

But when I go to check in, it seems fate has other plans. Again.

"Declined? But I just used it."

"I don't know what to tell you," the clerk says, not entirely void of sympathy. "Do you have another card?"

"No." I bang my forehead on the counter.

What is wrong with me? I mean, seriously! I left a

good job, a loving family, a tolerant boyfriend—one who, okay, maybe I wasn't *in love* with, but he was fun and nice—to do what? Go wandering around squandering my savings in some ridiculously clichéd journey to find my "purpose?" What kind of person does that? Correction. What kind of *adult* does that? A stupid one, that's who. A spoiled idiot who thinks she deserves more than a nice, normal life and a perfectly fine boyfriend. A raving lunatic who thinks something is waiting out there that's going to feel like fireworks in her chest and electricity in her veins and rain-showers of joyfulness on her skin. It's foolish. *I'm* foolish.

In fact, I'm no smarter than I was at sixteen.

Twelve Years Earlier

"Thank you so much for this incredible honor. I wouldn't be here without the constant support of my family and friends—and, most of all, my fans. So this is for all of you." I kiss my palm and extend it out to the moon's reflection on the dark water before I wipe a tear from the corner of my eye. A real tear, not some fake one from eyedrops or menthol like some of those hacks use. I'm a *real* actress, after all.

I take a deep breath and start again, clasping my driftwood trophy with both hands in front of me. "Wow. I really didn't expect to win. I didn't even prepare anything to say." Pause for laughter and applause. "This is an honor, truly."

"Who are you talking to?" A voice startles me, and I

drop the driftwood to the sand, my palm flying up to cover my mouth.

"Oh my God! You scared me!" I almost pee my pants when I recognize the guy from the beach and the corner store. "What are you doing here?" It's almost an accusation, but I can't help it. He caught me making a fake acceptance speech—talk about embarrassing.

He glances meaningfully around at the empty beach and, even with just the light of the moon and some condo lights, I can see the inflamed red marks on his head, neck, and arm. There are no bandages tonight.

"Last I checked, the ocean is fair game." The comment is sarcastic, but his tone is missing the contempt from our last encounter. It's almost... playful this time.

"Sorry. I just meant... I mean, I just thought I was alone." Duh.

"I gathered that." He shoves his hands in his jeans pocket and studies the spot where his boot is toeing the sand.

"How much did you hear?" My fingers tuck loose strands of hair behind my ears, and I mentally cross my fingers he didn't witness the entire thing. I know it's ridiculous to practice an Oscar speech after getting *one* paying gig, but I can't help it. I got my first real acting job, and there's no one to celebrate with. My parents would freak if they knew what I was up to, and Jenna would disapprove, saying I'm too young and that I shouldn't hang out with strange adults.

"Was there more before you thanked Meryl Streep for the honor of being nominated alongside her?" His eyes meet mine. He's wearing a half-smile, and it transforms his face, so much so that I forget to be embarrassed for a minute.

"You're smiling." The words are out before my brain catches up. His smile drops, and I want to smack myself.

When he turns his head, I'm afraid I've scared him away. "Sorry," he mumbles for some reason.

"I like it!" I nearly shout. *Smooth, Jill.* But he stops turning and glances back at me. "I mean, it's better than the scowl, that's all." I smile so he knows I didn't mean anything by it. This boy is so different from the angry one I met before.

He nods but doesn't smile or look at me again. There's a silence where all we can hear is the rhythmic lapping of the water on the beach. "So, what are you doing out here in the middle of the night?" he finally asks, and I'm happier than I should be that he didn't run off.

"I couldn't sleep. You?"

He shrugs and kicks at the sand with his boot again. "I was at a party at my friend's house and needed some air. Thought a walk on the beach might do the trick."

"Oh yeah? Where does your friend live? Our condo is right there." I point to the darkened three-story beach house where my family rented the second-floor condo.

He studies the building with its cheerful white shutters and American flag flying from the stand on the wide back porch. I expect him to make some comment about me being spoiled again, but he doesn't. Heck, if his friend lives in one of these houses, he obviously befriends some wealthy people.

"His apartment is a few blocks in, not one of these." It's like he's reading my thoughts.

"You don't really seem like the party type," I tell him, feeling a little defensive and not wanting to lose my footing. But I don't want to fight with him.

He huffs out a quick breath and it almost sounds like a laugh. "Oh yeah, what gave it away?"

"Oh, I don't know." I watch him for a few seconds before pointing to his shirt and sweeping my finger up and down. "Maybe the black clothes. Or maybe because you spend a lot of time looking at the ground with your hands in your pockets. Or maybe it's that you don't seem accustomed to talking much." His eyes flash up to me and he frowns like he wasn't expecting me to say so much and he doesn't like it. "Or the general grouchiness," I tack on, but I do it with a smile so he knows I'm teasing. I don't want him to leave. I don't like being alone.

"You're pretty observant."

"Well, I have to be." I straighten my back and strike a pose with perfect posture. "All good actors are acutely aware of the people around them. That way we can feed off their energy."

"Can't say I've ever met an actress before." I can't tell if he's making fun of me or not.

"I may not be famous yet, but I will be one day."

He nods thoughtfully. "And then I can say I knew you when." He's still too hard to read, but I choose to give him the benefit of the doubt.

"It would probably help if you knew my name, then." I hold out my hand. "Jill Holloway, future EGOT winner."

He pauses before grasping my hand. "What's an eegot?"

"Emmy, Grammy, Oscar, Tony," I rattle off and send him my most dazzling smile.

He takes my hand in his and shakes it. I feel a warmth spread from the place where his fingers rest all the way up my arm and into my body where it settles at the base of my belly. My smile threatens to waver, but I force it to stay firmly in place.

"Milo," he responds. "Milo Papatonis. It means bad-ass guy."

PRESENT DAY

"Camille?" I knock on the back door of Schnitzel with Noodles for the second time. I smell like stale sauerkraut and day-old sweat. Super attractive.

After the Days Inn fiasco and my ensuing pity party, I managed to take a whore's bath in a fast food restroom across the street, but it could only do so much. I scrubbed my pits to within an inch of their lives and raised a stick of deodorant to my former Misty Motor Inn working girls before getting down to business hunting online for Craigslist postings while I sipped a cup of cheap coffee and tried not to fall apart. There wasn't much to speak of in my price range, and I knew I had maybe one more Uber ride left before my debit card would be declined by them as well.

So I gave up and headed into work.

All I need is my paycheck and tips and then I can breathe again, so I decided to ask Camille for an advance —or at least my tips from last night. If that doesn't work,

I'll throw in the towel, call Jenna, and go back to Sunview with my tail between my legs. If the universe is pointing me there, maybe I should listen.

There's still no response to my knocking, and when I press my ear to the door, I don't hear a thing. It's only 9:30, so I suppose it's possible nobody is in yet. I sink down on the concrete steps and survey my various bags and belongings. I wonder if Camille would let me ditch my stuff here, and I could sleep in my car tonight. Damn, I never should have had it towed. It should worry me that I'm disappointed I don't have a car handy to live in, but we've reached that point in the dark comedy that is my life, now haven't we. Le sigh.

I kick my pink backpack with the red lips printed all over it. "What are you looking at?!" Obviously, it doesn't respond, so I kick it again. The paisley overnight bag catches my eye, and I give it a kick as well. "That's for costing me fifty bucks!" It skids to a stop a few feet away from me, and I'm on a roll. "You want a piece of that?" I ask my rolling suitcase before knocking it over with a solid foot to the front. I've pretty much lost my mind, I know, but it feels good to get some aggression out.

I realize my purse hasn't gotten in on the action, so I hold it out in front of me, ready to drop-kick it and see how far I can launch it, but it's snatched out of my hands before I can release it.

"You mind telling me what your luggage did to deserve this kind of treatment?" If the scarred hand didn't give him away, I would have known it was Milo from his voice—and possibly the millions of hairs standing up on the back of my neck. Damn the man!

"I have my reasons." I try grabbing my purse back, but he holds it out of reach. "Give it back. I think I can hit the garbage can down the way."

"Not until you tell me what's going on." He's the picture of patience standing there in the alley with my purse in his arms and a stupid black beanie that makes him look way hotter than is strictly necessary.

I sigh and give up. "Just killing time until someone shows up to unlock the door. And before you ask, yes, I've already tried the front door."

Milo turns without pause and bangs so hard on the metal door it echoes back and forth down the alley, pinging off the brick walls and making my ears ring. "Her hearing's not all that great."

"Neither is mine after that." I work my jaw like that's going to help.

Sure enough, five seconds later, the door opens and Camille pokes her head out. "Oh, Louisa. Good morning."

I gave up yesterday on reminding her of my real name, so I smile my hello and glance around me at my scattered bags. Crap.

"Good morning, Mrs. Blume," Milo greets her, stepping forward to hold the door open.

"What are *you* doing here?" she asks without so much as a hello. Well, isn't this interesting?

"Just helping Ms. von Trapp with her bags."

The sarcasm is completely lost on Camille, and I don't have the energy to tell him I've got it covered.

"I'd advise you to check your bags, dear." Camille turns to me. "This one has light fingers if you know what

I mean." She turns and disappears from the doorway but tosses another comment behind her. "You're a good girl. Don't get mixed up with him."

I raise a brow at Milo, thankful I'm not the only one scraping bottom today. "My, my, my, it seems you have an even darker past than the one I knew about." Just goes to show my initial instincts were spot on.

"It was a misunderstanding," he mumbles as he pushes my purse at me and bends to pick up my back-pack and paisley bag.

"Isn't that what all criminals say?"

"I wouldn't know."

I give him the side-eye, and his shoulder drops in resignation.

"Okay, fine. When I was a teenager, me and a couple guys might have broken into her friend's food truck for a midnight snack—just a couple roller dogs and some chips. I happened to be the only one who got caught."

"And now she hates you." I can't hold back my smile.

He throws a chin out, indicating I should grab the suitcase handle, and steps into the hall. "Hate's a pretty strong word."

"Goodbye, Mr. Papatonis!" comes Camille's shout from inside. "There's no cash in the drawer, so don't bother!"

I laugh, my first genuine one of the day, and follow. "Oh, she hates you all right."

"In." Milo scowls and opens the door to the storage room.

It seems we're both on the same page. I'll just stash my stuff in here and go roll silverware or something until my shift starts. But once we drop my bags off, he doesn't leave. In fact, he blocks the door to the hallway.

"You know I can call for Camille, right?" I'm more amused than I should be by this new insight into Milo. If I'd known he was *persona non grata* around Camille, I would have Velcroed myself to her from day one.

"Just a second." His forearms rest on the doorframe, propping him up. It's a disturbingly good look for him.

I'm suddenly way too aware of not just how small this room is, but of every spot where my clothing touches my skin. Why does this happen to me around him? It's more than a little inconvenient.

"What?" I motion for him to get on with it, hoping to God my nipples have forgotten about the sight of his erection this morning.

"I've been looking all over for you."

My swallow is audible. "Why?"

"I haven't the first clue."

"Okay, well thanks for clearing that up."

The corner of his mouth turns up and, damn, does he give good grin. "I don't know. Maybe I was worried about you."

I need to get my act together. There's an advance to ask for and more tips to be earned. "Well, I'm fine."

"Yeah, tell your luggage that." And there goes that chin toss again. Good God, it's like he's been watching YouTube tutorials on how to use body language to get into girls' pants.

"I was experiencing a moment of frustration." I go for light and breezy.

And then he drops a lead weight on it. "I didn't like the idea of not knowing where you were."

I let that settle for a minute. It decides to settle in my panties. Dammit! I can't do this right now. I can't do this *ever*!

"I hate to point out the obvious, but you haven't known where I was for a single day of the last decade, and I've gotten along fine. Thanks for the concern, though." Not that it isn't nice having someone care whether you're dead or not, but coming from him, it's way too complicated.

He scratches the back of his neck and shakes his head like he's trying to work it out as well. "I know. It doesn't make sense, but I don't like it."

Did he just double down on his two-ton, panty-incinerating proclamation?

I decide to return to breezy and motion in the direction we came from. "Well, now you know where I am, so you can put your mind at ease and go to work or whatever you're doing today." But when I move to go past him, he steps in to further block me.

"Where are you staying? Please say you're not going back to the Misty."

"I'm not going back to the Misty."

His eyes bore holes through me. "Are you just saying that, or is it true?"

"Why do you think I have all my shit with me? I just haven't checked in anywhere yet." I skirt around the truth. If he'd just leave, I could ask Camille about the tip money and the advance. "But I will. I don't want to be rude but…" My words trail off, because since when have I not wanted to be rude to Milo? It makes me smile despite myself and despite our uncomfortably intimate proximity.

He coughs out a laugh, clearly thinking the same thing. "Since when?" Gah! I can see the multicolor swirls in his irises again, and they're on the move.

"All right, funny guy. I need to get to work." And I need to get away from him before I become the naughty von Trapp child who introduces teen pregnancy to the franchise. I motion to the door, and this time he steps aside. My arm brushes his leg when I pass, and I swear he stiffens. Well, maybe that's a poor choice of words, but it's nice to know I'm not the only one affected. I need to screw my head on straight. "Bye." I don't dare look behind me as I wonder like I've done before if this will be the last time we say goodbye. And for the first time since he popped back into my life, I don't want it to be.

CHAPTER THIRTEEN

MILO

Twelve Years Earlier

"Are you sure you don't mind?" The girl I now know as Jill asks from her spot on the cool sand beside me.

I shake my head and toss a shell in the water, trying to follow its path in the moonlight. "Naw. No big deal."

"Okay, now repeat it back to me so we can make sure it doesn't get messed up." She's got her hair tucked behind her ears and her knees pulled up to her chest.

"You mean so you can make sure *I* don't mess it up."

"Whatever, bad-ass." Her smile is almost a physical punch it's so stunning.

I don't know why I said that stupid thing about my name meaning "bad-ass guy" except that my dad said it one night when he was lit on vodka. And for some reason, I wanted to impress this girl. I don't think it worked.

I clear my throat. "Fine. When the production

assistant calls, I say you're out and you'll call back. Then I call your sister's phone, ask for you, and tell you to call."

She gives my good arm a playful swat. "You forgot the part about telling them I'm out running because I take fitness seriously. I heard running on the sand makes your butt perkier, and I can't afford to have a flat butt."

"I'm not saying that." I grin at her. It's impossible not to. But I manage to keep from telling her I already saw her butt and it's more than perfect the way it is.

"Ugh. Fine." She does a shit job pretending to be mad before dropping the pretense. "Thank you so much, Milo. You're saving my ass." I like the way my name sounds coming from her lips. But this is a bad idea.

"I already said it's no big deal. Everybody does stuff they don't want their parents to know about."

"I usually tell my mom and sister everything." She sighs and rests her cheek on her knees while she considers me. "Do you have any brothers or sisters?"

"Uh, I guess."

Her smile is back, and I'm ridiculously pleased to be the one who put it there. "What does that mean?"

I weigh how much to tell her. "Well, I have an older half-sister, but we don't get along very well."

"That sucks."

"Believe me, it's better for us to keep our distance." I throw another shell and think about my last encounter with Sherry. She and Felicity came to see me in the hospital and brought Sherry's new boyfriend. Some douchebag named Ricky. The guy asked her for money for the vending machine and didn't even see if she or Felicity wanted anything. Fucking barnacle. She and I got into it when I asked if he was living with them.

"Well, maybe that will change someday." Jill says it like she really wants that for me. The asshole part of me wants to tell her that not all families are perfect like hers, but a bigger part of me wants her to keep her naïve side.

"Maybe. She has a daughter."

When her worry lines disappear, I know I made the right choice. "You have a niece? I'm so jealous."

"Technically, I think I have about a dozen, but I only know Felicity."

"What? How?"

"My dad's been married five times, so I have a bunch of step-siblings I've only met a few times."

Her eyes go wide. "Five times? Sounds like a soap opera."

"I guess."

She peers out at the dark water and then back at me. The breeze picks her hair up. "Can I ask you a question?"

It's not like I didn't know this was coming. I just don't relish the idea of sharing my idiocy with a pretty girl who seems to have forgotten I was an asshole to her. "I was in an accident."

Her brow furrows, and I assume she's preparing some follow-up questions. "What? I mean. No. I didn't mean..." She shakes her head. "I was going to ask why you're being nice to me."

Her words register, bringing relief with them. I could ask her the same thing. "I don't know." I shrug. But I kind of do know. It's partly because I was such a dick before and partly because she's pretty as hell and, as much as I'd like to be immune, I'm not. "Anyway, all I'm doing is answering the phone a couple times. You don't have to get all mushy on me."

She laughs, and it sounds like birds singing. Damn, she's turning me into a sap. "I'm not. Don't worry. What I meant was, you didn't like me—like, *at all*—the last two times we met. In fact, you were a real jerk."

I wince a little at that. "Yeah, that happens sometimes."

"Well, I guess I yelled at you too."

I turn to her again, reminded of something. "About that. Why did you ask me to make you a pot pie?"

Her head sinks into her hands and she laughs again, louder this time. "It's from *The Breakfast Club*."

"Never seen it."

She bounds to her feet and perches her hands on her slim hips. It startles the hell out of me. "You've never seen *The Breakfast Club*? It's a classic!"

"Uh, sorry?"

She shoos my pseudo-apology aside. "I mean, it's super old, but that's part of its charm. John Hughes is like the godfather of high school coming-of-age comedies. Parts of it are super awkward, but it's hella good."

"If you say so."

"No, I mean, okay." She starts talking with her hands and babbling on about some chick named Claire and a dude named John, and there's something about a peanut butter sandwich, but I mostly just watch her talk. She's joyful and animated and full of that sunshine I remember from the other day—even though it's the middle of the night. When she finally finishes, she lets her hands drop to her sides, and I can tell she's blushing, even in the sparse light. "Anyway. It's a good movie."

I don't want her to be embarrassed, so I search for the right thing to say. "I'll definitely have to watch it some-time." The lie is worth it for the smile I get in return.

"Well, I guess I should head in before Jenna wakes up and goes calling the police."

"Yeah, I guess." I don't want her to go, but we've been talking for a couple hours now, and the last thing I need is more cops in my business or another set of rich parents coming after me. I only narrowly escaped the last time. My thigh pulses, as if to remind me.

"It was nice to meet you, Milo." She's twisting the hem of her t-shirt in her fingers, and it soothes me.

I stand up and shove my hands in my pockets. "You too, movie star."

"From your lips to God's ear."

I don't think I've ever heard anyone under seventy say that phrase, and I'm finding it cuter than is wise.

"I'll call you," I say.

Her eyes widen in surprise and she blushes again. And damn if it doesn't make me entertain a whole lot of what-ifs.

"Your sister, I mean," I clarify, and I can see the second it registers because she shoos the air like she knew what I was talking about all along.

"Yeah, I know. Thanks again." She turns and runs to the darkened condo, kicking up sand behind her as she goes.

I wait until she disappears behind the porch door and then make my way back to Bran's apartment.

Present Day

Now that I know Jill's not hanging out with hookers and junkies anymore, I should be able to breathe easy. Sure, she didn't confide in me what's going on, but why should she? Hell, maybe she was doing a social experiment and writing some op-ed on life in a small-town prostitution ring. I don't want to admit to myself that the more likely reason is she's just plain broke. It hasn't escaped my notice that the woman doesn't appear to own a car, which has me even more curious as to how she ended up here and what she's been doing for the last twelve years. I figured she'd be in New York or L.A. living the good life.

But I need to put her out of my mind and get to my first day of work. I've been back in town for a few months, but I've been laying low—as in, gutter level. I'm not sure why, exactly, apart from maybe a sense of denial that I'm staying put for the time being. In some ways, it's like I'm in a completely new town and I'm the tourist.

A lot has changed in the last twelve years. Multibuilding condos and hotels have sprung up on sites that used to house independent variety stores, mom-and-pop restaurants, and family neighborhoods. My favorite pizza place is gone, and so is Bob's Corner Stop. Streets have been rerouted, the boardwalk has had a facelift, and my dad's house is just about the only one left on Kure beach that hasn't been torn down and replaced with something grander. This explains the near-constant stream of real estate vultures to my door since he died. I have no doubt my old man threatened bodily harm to each and every one of them who showed up trying to get him to sell over the years—and let's not forget the mouse traps and bang snaps. Even though he left the place practically a run-down hovel, it was *his* hovel, and he always said he'd never budge. The man was born and raised on the ocean, worked his whole life on it, and died on it—just how he wanted.

Even Camille's restaurant is new since I left. She used to run a Bavarian bakery with her husband, but I heard he died and she got some idea in her head to start the SWiN. She still does all the bread and desserts, from what Rayna told me. And Jill's right. She still hates my guts, but that's no surprise. She should probably get in line.

One thing that hasn't changed much is Coastal Adventures Dive School. It sits a couple blocks off Carolina Beach with the same three buildings, a handful of equipment and transport vans, and the small training pool. But Leah has taken over the entire business from her parents, something I learned from Bran as soon as he hunted me down the week after I got back to town. I'm not surprised. The woman was always driven, and she loves the water just as much as I do.

I park my bike out in front of the utility building and grab my bag before making my way to the main entrance. I don't want to presume to use the side door, at least not yet, so I weave my way around the unfamiliar racks of branded clothing and equipment until I reach the front desk. And then I see her.

Leah Musgraves looks exactly the same as the last

time I laid eyes on her. Blond hair pulled back in a tight ponytail, work polo fitted to her athletic frame, and an expression of fixed concentration parked on her face. A staff member asks if I need help, but I wave him off, preferring to stand where I am until she notices me. It doesn't take long, and I'm surprised by both the warmth in her smile and her move around the counter to hug me. Eighteen-year-old Milo would have sprouted a boner and tripped over his tongue, but the adult me is just happy to have a job.

"Look what the cat dragged in." Leah pulls back and tugs on my beard like we just saw each other yesterday. "This is new. You dive with this thing?"

I reach up to smooth my beard, feeling slightly discomfited by her playing with it. I don't really know what I expected, but it wasn't this sort of instant familiarity on her part. She's always been just a little standoffish, and it suits her serious personality. But I'm unsure what to do with this version of Leah, so I just nod and push on.

"Took a little adjusting at first, but I'm going on four years now."

"It looks good. *You* look good." Leah props her hands on her hips and smiles up at me. Small talk has never been my forte, and now that it's veering in an unexpected direction, I have an instinct to get the hell out. I need to get my head in the game.

I take an involuntary step back and shift my bag on my shoulder. "So, uh, what does it feel like running the place on your own?"

She doesn't even seem to notice my retreat. She just

rolls her eyes good-naturedly. "Please. Vicky and Bill check in on me daily. *'Don't forget to do the cash drop off, Leah. Don't forget to call the Tourism Board, Leah.'*" She waves a hand in front of her. "I'm used to it. But business is great."

"Cool." I rock on my heels and nod.

"So!" She claps her hands together, maybe sensing my discomfort. "Welcome back." She gestures for me to follow, and we head to the staff area that's mostly the same as I remember. "You can familiarize yourself with the place and then sit in on Luke's class at one. Locker room has moved to the other side since you were here." She keeps walking until we reach what used to be her parents' office but is now obviously hers. "I just have some paperwork for you to fill out, and I'll need to make copies of your licenses and logs." It's back to business as usual, and I'm more than a little relieved.

The hard part is over, and now it's time to get swimming.

I'VE JUST CHANGED BACK INTO MY STREET CLOTHES when my phone buzzes with a text from Rayna.

Rayna: *Don't let Bran talk you into coming in tonight. We're completely slammed with the first wave from the trade show. You may need to entertain him.*

I hold back a chuckle. I'll bet it's the flooring trade show. It's good to find one more thing that hasn't changed. Morris used to book contracts to cover half his annual business when that thing came through town each fall. I wonder if he still does. Which reminds me, I probably owe my mom another call or stop in. I used to go months without so much as dropping her an email and now look at me. Checking in like she's my parole officer.

Me: *I'm on it.*

Rayna: *Thx*

I still need to get my daily swim in, since I was too busy searching all over town for Jill this morning to do it, but then I'll give Bran a call and take him off Rayna's hands.

My mind should be light after my first day at work, but something is nagging at the back of my brain. By the time I'm on my bike and weaving through heavier-than-usual traffic, the nagging gets worse, and I try concentrating on it to jog my thoughts. The car in front of me slams on its brakes and sends me swerving sharply to the side where I nearly wipe out. And then it hits me.

The traffic is from all the new arrivals in town for the trade show. Sure enough, as I slowly make my way down along Carolina Beach, inching forward with the cars, there's nothing but No Vacancy signs at the beach motels. Which means Jill will need to go north into downtown Wilmington or Wrightsville Beach to get a hotel room. And that's gonna cost her.

I take a quick right and make my way home through neighborhood backways. I only go inside long enough to grab the keys to my beater, and then I'm heading for the SWiN before the reasonable part of me can think better of it.

CHAPTER FOURTEEN

JILL

I'm calling on every one of my ten years of waitressing experience to make it through the lunch and dinner service. You name it, and I've dealt with it today. The "can I just change my order one more time?" lady, the "my steak is underdone even though you told me not to order rare" guy, the "I'm not drunk even though I just fell off my chair" buffoon, the classic "you've got to *earn* your tip" douchebag, the "oh, how did my hotel keycard get in there instead of my credit card?" sleazebag, as well as all the general running around and perma-smiling one does during a busy service.

The tips are mostly great, but the majority are charged to company credit cards. I can't even allow myself to think of how many more tips I might have gotten if I didn't look like I was posing for a PSA on child labor laws. My feet are killing me by the time the last guests exit and the door locks. Even Maria is too tired to be rude to me.

It turns out the hookers aren't the only ones booked up with this trade show. Table reservations are full for the next four days straight, and Camille is baking up a storm in the kitchen. Rayna handles the entire thing like a champ, and I'm in awe as usual.

But I can't wait to sink my head into a pillow and pass out.

It's only when I'm halfway to the door that I remember my stuff—and the small fact that I don't have a place to stay tonight. Shit! I couldn't get Camille alone before my lunch shift to ask about the money, and then we were all completely slammed until just minutes before closing. I can't ask her while she's elbow-deep in strudel—and with Maria lurking around, no less.

Maybe I *will* have to go back to Zeb's garage and sleep in my car. It wouldn't be that bad. It's not like it's the middle of summer or winter. It'll probably only get down to fifty tonight.

I've all but resigned myself to calling Zeb and begging for a ride when I open the door to the storage room and stop short. My eyes dart to every shelf and corner of the space, but it's no use. My bags are gone. Even my purse. What the hell am I going to do? Thank God I at least have my phone in my bra.

I feel the telltale sting in my nose and tilt my head back to stave off the tears as I blink at the ceiling. It's over. It's all over, and I have nothing to show for it besides an empty bank account and absolutely zero gained wisdom or insight. My journey to find myself has hit a dead-end in Losertown, and I'm the town's new mascot. A brief image of Hank flashes in my mind, and I wonder if he'd laugh if he could see me now. But no. Hank was never vindictive. Yet another reason I was crazy to dump him.

Nobody here needs to see me cry—or overhear the conversation I'm about to have with Jenna—so I trudge to the side door and open it to the dim light of the alley.

And then I scream.

Not a delicate little yelp. Not a startled "Oh!" But a blood-curdling scream the likes of which Wes Craven himself would rise from the grave to applaud.

"Jesus!" Milo shouts, bringing a hand to his right ear where I've likely just rendered him deaf.

My heart is beating like it's keeping time with a Gloria Estefan classic, and I'm surprised I haven't torn the lace of my bodice clean off with how hard I just clawed at my neck.

There's scrambling in the hall behind me, and I hear Rayna call out, "She's fine. It's just Milo," before retreating to the kitchen.

"You scared the absolute shit out of me!" I smack Milo on the arm and suck in a breath. "What in the hell are you doing lurking out here in the dark like a creeper?"

He takes a step to the left where the hallway light lets me make out his features. "I was waiting for you."

"Hasn't anyone told you women don't like being stalked—or attacked in alleyways?" I'm still breathing hard. All I need to top off my day now is a little cardiac episode and an ambulance ride I can't afford.

Milo scowls, and it makes his eyebrows almost touch

in the middle. "I didn't attack you, and I'm definitely not stalking you."

"Then why do I feel like Jamie Lee Curtis?"

"What?"

"Never mind. I forgot you don't watch the classics." I slide past him onto the concrete and let the door close behind me. "So, wait. Why were you waiting for me?"

"Because you don't have anywhere to stay." He crosses his arms over his chest, clearly ready for a fight. It seems he's met me a time or two.

"I told you I'm getting a hotel." It's technically not a lie. I did tell him that. I'm just not actually *doing* it.

"Not here you're not." His tone is too self-assured for my liking.

"What do you mean?" This conversation is useless. I just need to get somewhere private to call Jenna and arrange for her to come to my rescue. Like the child I clearly still am. Then I need to call the cops and report my things stolen—unless Maria is to blame. Maybe that explains why she wasn't rude to me. Hmm.

"Places south of Wilmington are all booked for the trade show." I can't make out his features anymore, and I think that's a good thing.

"Then I'll get one in Wilmington." Why does he care?

"Just how long do you intend to keep lying to me?" He's got a bit of that growly impatience that makes me want to pick a fight with him for some reason I'm not willing to explore right now.

"I'm not lying," I lie.

"Okay. So, where's your purse?"

Dammit. My lips firm, and I fix him with a glare he probably can't see.

"That's what I thought. Come on." He throws a thumb over his shoulder, and I hear faint sirens in the distance. Maybe they're chasing my robber as we speak.

When I don't move, Milo gestures again with his stupid chin.

Then something occurs to me, and I narrow my eyes at him. "How do you know my purse is missing?"

"Because I'm the one who took it, Sunshine," he says as he turns and walks his ass to the end of the alley, casual as can be.

What the actual...? My mouth gapes as I chase after him. "You stole my stuff?"

"Simmer down. I didn't steal it. I put it in your room." For a guy with a limp, he sure does walk fast.

My feet grind to a halt on the sidewalk. Why am I following this guy? "My room?"

"Well, Felicity's, but it's yours until you don't need it anymore." He glances over his shoulder and when he realizes I'm not following him anymore, he stops and turns.

"I'm not staying with you." I reset my glare in case he missed it before.

He throws his arms out, a bit of that familiar frustration bleeding through. "Then tell me, where exactly are you planning on staying?"

I can't admit to him that my plan had been to call some dude named Zeb to whisk me away to my broken-down car to sleep—before I discovered my purse had been stolen, that is. And the call to Jenna. I should still make it. I fish my phone from the top of my dress with awkward hands and hover my thumb over her contact. I know Milo is watching me, but I try to ignore him.

"You don't need to read anything into it." His voice drops along with his hands like he's tired of fighting with me. "I've got the room, you need a place to sleep, and you don't have to stay any longer than you want."

It's the tone that gets me, and I finally raise my gaze to him again to see him eying me carefully. My teeth tear at my lip while I try to decide what to do. "Why are you doing this? Being nice to me, I mean."

A half-smile breaches the dark hair on his face, and I have the sudden urge to sigh and lie down on the sidewalk by his feet for a ten-hour nap.

"Maybe I have a soft spot for stranded movie stars."

My smile feels broken.

"I'm not a movie star, Milo."

He shakes his head, almost imperceptibly. "I wouldn't count yourself out yet. I've heard lots of movie stars wait tables until their big break."

We both know my big break isn't ever coming. The one shot I had blew up in my face. And Milo was the one to light the ignitor. But I'm too tired to be mad about old wrongs. And I know full well if I was really meant to be an actress, I wouldn't have let a couple failed endeavors make me quit so easily.

"I'll have to take your word on that."

I drop the hand holding my phone to my side, and we stand in silence for a few seconds before I find my voice again. "If you're still offering, I think I'll take you up on that good night's sleep."

Milo throws his chin to the side, and I follow him down the sidewalk.

"THAT WAS THE BEST SHOWER OF MY ENTIRE LIFE." I sink onto the couch cushion and fold my feet under me. We haven't said much of anything to each other, first because we were on his motorcycle and couldn't hear anything, and then because I retreated to the shared bathroom (the one Felicity failed to mention) to shower the ten hours of sauerbraten off myself the moment we walked in the house. But while the hot water pelted my back and did its thing, I resolved to be kinder to Milo—and less suspicious of his motives. Maybe he's turned into a regular old nice guy who just happens to hurl insults now and then.

Milo glances my way from the other end of the couch, and a little part of me—way, way, way deep inside —is disappointed he doesn't let his eyes linger on my bare legs. *What is wrong with you, Jill? You accuse the guy of stalking you, and then you're bummed he didn't check you out? Nice.*

Not that I'm dressed anything like I was this morning when I was executing my phone charger plan, but I think I still look cute in my "This nap ain't gonna take itself" t-shirt and sleep shorts.

He still hasn't said anything, so I take it upon myself to lead the conversation. "Who's playing?" I nod to the TV where some football game is on.

"Nobody. It's just the news wrap-up." His eyes stay glued to the TV.

"Oh." I scan the room, taking in the sparse furniture and walls that could use a good paint job. There's nothing homey in the least about the place—no family photos, no knickknacks from favorite destinations, not even a few measly seashells to pay homage to the whole beach-house thing. It's a little depressing. "So, how long have you lived here?"

Truthfully, I know little about the man besides the fact that he drives a motorcycle and he used to put Cheetos on his sandwiches.

"A while," he responds in the most unhelpful manner possible.

"A while like a few months or a while like since we met?"

This has him finally turning my way. "Look, can we not do this?"

"Not do what? Have a civilized conversation?"

"No. Yes. The small talk."

"Sorry. Just trying to be polite. Sheesh." I shake my head and look around the room again.

I can see him shift in his seat. "Forgive me if I'm too tired to interpret all your mixed signals."

This sets my head back. "My mixed signals? I wasn't the one lurking in the alleyway outside your work asking you to come stay with me."

"I knew this was a mistake." He gets up and limps to the kitchen, leaving me to stew in front of his stupid football wrap-up thingy.

"So freaking cranky," I mumble under my breath.

"What's that?" His voice comes from right behind me, and I jump.

"For crying out loud—quit scaring me! Jeez."

"You should be more aware of your surroundings." I can't see his face, but the tone adequately communicates the sarcasm all on its own.

"Sorry. I didn't think I'd need my Krav Maga skills in your vacation home. My bad."

"It's not my vacation home."

Now he wants to talk? I don't bother turning my head to give him my attention. "Fine then. Your non-vacation home."

He comes back around and takes his spot on the couch again, holding his left hand out with a cold beer. I grab it like it's made of diamonds. "Thanks."

We quietly sip our beers while the guy on TV drones on and the screen's reflection paints moving colors on Milo's face. Not that I'm watching him or anything.

The man is utterly mercurial and impossible to figure out.

"It was my dad's place. He left it to me when he died."

"Oh." Then I tack on, "I'm sorry for your loss," because, manners. I remember he wasn't close to his dad back when we met.

He waves me off. "The truth is I haven't lived in this town in over a decade. I didn't want to move back, but here I am."

He takes another sip of his beer, and I don't try to hide my watching him. I do hide my surprise, however. I assumed he'd been right here all these years, running a local dive outfit and swimming in his home waters. I had every reason to believe it was true, and I want to ask what happened. Why he left when he had all he ever wanted at the expense of a sixteen-year-old girl's happiness. But if I ask and he answers, I'll need to leave this house. And I don't want to leave. Not yet. So I ask a different question.

"Why don't you want to be here?"

He shrugs like most guys when presented with a question requiring more than a one-syllable response.

I try from another angle. "So, where were you that was so hard to leave?"

"Everywhere. Nowhere." He shakes his head and finally looks over at me. His eyes are tired. "Worked a pop-up diving operation with this guy Hobbs for the last seven or eight years. A couple other people before that. We'd set up shop in coastal towns in South America, some of the Caribbean islands. All over the place. Spend the first week scoping out local diving spots, then hang our sign and book diving tours until the local authorities kicked us out for one reason or another. Made a decent living. Got to see the world. What more could you ask for?" The words are carefree, but the tone misses the mark.

"Sounds amazing." In fact, it makes my little journey look like peanuts in comparison. "I can see why you'd want to get back out there." I'm not lying. It sounds incredible, but it also sounds damn lonely. What happened that I don't know about?

"But shit happens." He sighs and takes a longer pull on his beer, a clear indication that his sharing portion of the evening is over. I'm amazed he spoke that much as it is. "You finally going to tell me what you're doing here?"

Who said it was my turn? "I thought you didn't like to talk."

"I said I don't like small talk."

I remember that from before—from a million years ago.

I have a choice between telling him everything and being coy. I choose coy. "Let's just say you and I might be more alike than you realize."

He raises a brow at me and thumbs the label on his beer. "Oh? You've been diving in South America?"

"Nope. But I've been on the road quite a bit recently."

He nods and watches me for a minute. I pretend it doesn't make me uncomfortable.

"Running away from something or toward something?"

Clever bastard. I stall by drinking more of my beer while thinking of a good response.

"How about neither. Can't a person run for running's sake?"

He leans forward and sets his bottle on the warped coffee table. "Now, that, I don't know." Which tells me he was most certainly running for a reason himself. Curious. I want to know more, of course, but he's done sharing.

Milo stands and stretches, the movement pulling his t-shirt up just enough to expose a slice of bare skin above his waistband. It makes me swallow hard and question my sanity.

"It's late. I'm heading to bed."

I watch him wander over to the bathroom and stand up myself, still gripping my bottle. "Goodnight. Thanks again for letting me stay."

His only response is to throw up a hand in a backward wave before the bathroom door shuts behind him.

I take my half-empty beer bottle upstairs with me and, despite being dog-ass exhausted, I lie awake for the better part of the night, letting my memory take over.

CHAPTER FIFTEEN

JILL

Twelve Years Ago

Milo and I agree to meet at the pier where he's going to teach me how to fish. His dad has a deep-sea fishing charter, and Milo thought it was a crime that I'd never even held a pole or rod or whatever. I didn't lie to my family this time. I told them I'd met a local who wanted to take me fishing—in a very public and populated area—and they thought it was "adorable." Gag.

But being open about Milo does give me a ready excuse to use when I'm needed on the *Brothers* set. So far, I've only had one scene and it was a silent part, but I did get to meet Raven Yang, who's even prettier and nicer than she seems on TV. My speaking part is coming up in a few days, and I've been rehearsing nonstop. My only hope is that my voice will work when I'm face-to-face with Noah Chandler. Eek!

I spot Milo's dark head through the crowd and put a

hand up to wave at him. He nods when he sees me but doesn't wave back. I guess he's too cool for that, but it doesn't bother me.

"We're never catching anything with so many people here," he says when he reaches me. "There are plenty of other spots, you know."

"I'm sure there are, but isn't this like one of the classic things to do at the beach? Fish off the giant pier?"

"If you say so." He shakes his head like I baffle him, but I can see a half-smile in there somewhere. "Come on, Captain Ahab."

"Ooh! Are there whales around here?" That would be kickass.

That little crinkle forms between his brows, and I resist the urge to press my finger to it. "No, dummy. They'd fry up in water this warm."

Oh, right. Note to self: research whales and memorize fascinating tidbits to impress boys.

"I knew that. Just testing you."

He rolls his eyes at me and continues down the pier, so I follow along on the evenly-spaced planks. "Now, don't get your hopes up. It's unlikely we'll even get a bite, but I can at least teach you the basics."

"Awesome." And it is. My mom and dad aren't really the outdoorsy types, so there are a lot of things I've never done. Fishing, water-skiing, camping—you know, the classic stuff. Not that I've ever minded. Shopping, singing, dancing, museums, off-Broadway shows—those are more my style anyway. And since my parents are both college professors who get time off in the summer, we've never had a boring time.

But this is different. It's new, and I like an adventure as much as the next girl.

"That's a long way down." My flip flops settle on the bottom rail and I lean over the top one at the end of the long wooden pier while Milo sets up our gear.

"Probably forty feet, give or take. It won't feel all that great if you belly flop, so get on down from there."

"I can swim, you know." My arms extend outward as I lean into the railing like I'm Kate Winslet at the bow of a ship.

"I'd rather just trust you on that than get a demonstration right now. Besides, the rip currents are brutal. Get down."

I grin at his overly protective tone and hop back onto the wood slats. "You must be a good swimmer if you're a diver."

"I do all right." His fingers twist the fishing line into a complicated knot.

"Look at you being all modest. I'll bet you were star of your high school swim team or something."

"Uh, no." I don't miss the self-deprecating grin.

"What, too mainstream for you?" Admittedly, it would be hard picturing him in a speedo and swim cap, snapping towels in a locker room.

"No."

"Then what?"

He holds out a pole for me to grab while he starts in on the second one. "Let's just say you needed a certain GPA to do extracurriculars. And I had my own version of extracurriculars." His grin turns sly, and my belly flips. I'll bet he's had lots of sex. Just the thought has my belly more tied up than the fishing line, not that I'm some prudish goodie-two-shoes. I've done stuff.

But, no! I'm not going to be one of those girls who finds underachieving attractive. That's how you end up giving up your dreams and having two babies before your eighteenth birthday. No thanks.

"So, what? You hung out by the dumpsters and smoked pot? Borrrring."

"You're just a kid." He scoffs, and it feels like an arrow to the chest. He's trying to be a jerk again.

"Well, then what are you doing hanging out with me, old man?" I prop my free hand on my hip, refusing to take this lying down. He's only eighteen, for Pete's sake.

His mouth opens and then closes again as he shakes his head.

"What?"

"Nothing."

"Liar," I challenge again.

"Fine." He squints up at me from his crouched position, shielding his eyes from the sun with one hand. "I was going to say that all my friends are working, and I'm out of a job while I play the obedient patient. But that would be cruel. And I don't really mean it anyway."

My heart drops. "That is cruel. You know, I have plenty of other things I could be doing."

"I'm sure you do. Wrightsville Beach has lots of sailing lessons and golf courses to keep you busy. Don't let me keep you." He's back to the boy I met last week.

"You know, you're a real jerk. I'm outta here." My rod hits the wood with a smack, and I don't care if it rolls into the ocean. Let him go diving after it and belly flop.

"Jill! Wait up." His voice is closer than I expect so I pick up my pace, swerving around tourists on the crowded pier. But he still catches up to me with a hand on my arm. "Come on. I'm sorry. I said I didn't mean it."

I whip around to face him. "Just what do you have against people with money anyway? I didn't ask for my parents to make a good living. What am I supposed to do? Eat bread and water and refuse nice things out of principle? Let it turn me into an angry jerk like you?"

"No. I'm an asshole. Look, it's not your fault."

I swipe at a traitorous tear trying to escape my eye. "My parents aren't actually rich, you know. They teach college and got a discount on a two-bedroom condo for a few weeks through a friend-of-a-friend. Not that I should have to justify myself to you—or anyone."

His fingers tighten around my arm. "I know. You're right. Like I said, I'm an asshole."

I stifle a sniffle and straighten my back. "Well, stop then."

"Okay." He tries to smile, but it comes out as a grimace instead, and he drops my arm. "I'm really sorry."

I glance down and see he's favoring his bad leg. "You're in pain."

"Well, I'm not quite up to running yet, and I kind of forgot." He tries putting his full weight on it and winces.

"You should sit." Grabbing his good arm, I scan the pier for an available spot, finally spying a small bench with some seagulls investigating it for forgotten food.

"No, I should explain."

I lead him to the bench, and we both sit, shooing the brazen birds away. "Explain what?"

Milo leans forward, massaging his thigh through his jeans. "Why I took my own shit out on you."

"Okay, then tell me."

He coughs out a half-laugh. "Well, now I'm not really sure where to start."

"The beginning is usually a good place."

He laughs again, but it doesn't sound entirely genuine. My back rests against the warm wood of the bench as I give him time to find his words.

"I fucked up."

It's my turn to laugh. "I think we established that already. Has the pot gone to your head?"

"Would you shut up for a second?" He sighs when he catches my sour expression at the *shut up* part, then leans back and stretches his denim-covered leg straight out in front of him. "I mean, I would like to tell you what happened if now is a good time for you," he recites carefully.

"Better." I nod. "Go on."

He takes a breath and studies me for a few seconds. His hair is caught in his eyelashes, and the red lines on his neck and jaw look especially angry in the bright sun, even through the sunscreen he's slathered on them. I can make out the individual dots left by the stitches and I want to ask him if the pain ever goes away. He releases his breath and lets it all out. "I stole a boat, took a senator's daughter out on an unauthorized dive, got high on some laced pot, and almost killed four people, including myself. All to make a girl jealous."

My jaw threatens to unhinge. "Wow." I let that marinate for a moment and shake my head. "I was totally wrong."

"What? You thought I fell down the stairs or something?" The corner of his mouth twitches.

I shake my head again. "No. I had you pegged as an underachiever, but it sounds like you went *way* above and beyond on this one."

"That's me." His lips curve into a real grin. "Go big or go home, right?"

"Yeah. I'd say that's one big freaking whale, Captain Ahab."

He laughs. "Aye aye." I'm guessing he hasn't had much to laugh about lately, and I'm glad for the sound.

A seagull chooses that moment to dive-bomb us, and I screech while Milo swipes the air to scare it away. He spends the next couple minutes making fun of me, but I give as good as I get until we're both out of insults.

I turn on the bench and tuck one leg under me. "So how much trouble did you get in?"

"Besides this lifelong trophy?" He gestures down to his body, and I tilt my head at him with a sad smile. "Some of it's still being worked out, but I think my parents are over it, for the most part."

"I still can't believe it was all about a girl." A pang of jealousy tries to wiggle its way in, and I do my best to push it back.

"You remember the part about the drugs, right?" He maintains his relatively casual air with a shrug. "Besides, haven't you ever done something dumb to get someone— or something—you wanted?"

"You mean like steal your sister's I.D. and lie to your family so you can get a part on a TV show?"

Another shrug. "Yeah, although that's arguably a little less risky."

"You've never met my parents." I level my gaze at him.

"Strict, I assume?"

"Well, Jenna's the perfect child, so they never had to give her so much as a curfew, but my dad is way overprotective when it comes to me."

"What about your mom?"

It's my turn to shrug. "She's cool—more in-touch and practical than my dad." I pause, not sure if I should continue with what I was about to say. Whatever. "Like, I told her right away the first time a guy got to second base with me. She'd never tell my dad."

Milo's eyes go to my boobs, and I kind of want to stick my chest out. If I know one thing, guys love boobs. And I'm not gonna lie—I've used this knowledge to my advantage more than a few times.

But if I thought he'd linger on the topic, I'm wrong. "But she'd tell him you want to be an actress, and you'd get in trouble? Why? What's wrong with being an actress?"

I sigh, not sure if I'm disappointed or pleased that my boobs weren't a huge distraction. "Nothing, *per se*, but they both want me to go to college and, I don't know, be a lawyer or a teacher or something. That's one of the reasons my mom isn't shy about talking about sex and stuff. She doesn't want me being stupid and ruining my life." *Wow, super sexy, Jill.*

But Milo just stretches his leg out again. "She should have talked to my sister a decade ago." He glances back at me. "What about your sister?"

"Jenna?" I laugh. "God, I'll bet she's still a virgin." A needle of guilt tries to poke through for talking about my sister like this, but I ignore it. I'm only being honest.

"You said she's getting married."

"I know, but I'd bet you a million bucks that Mike is the kind of guy who'd insist on a virgin bride."

Milo's nose wrinkles. "He sounds like an asshole."

"You said it, I didn't." I throw my hands up in defense.

"*She* must not think so if she's marrying him."

"She's too nice. She always sees the good things in people." It's true, and I know it's another thing I should aspire to.

But Milo surprises me. "I think you're that way too." When I glance up at him, he's smiling in that self-deprecating way again. "Otherwise you would have punched me and left me on the end of the pier."

"Ha! It's still early." I wave him off. "No. Jenna says I expect too much of people."

"And that's a bad thing?"

"I honestly don't know, but I gather she thinks it's kind of selfish."

Milo leans forward and rests his elbows on his knees, letting his eyes follow a few couples and families walking the pier. "Nobody has ever expected much of me at all. I kind of wonder if it would have made a difference." His eyes come back to me and his lips curve. "Or not."

I watch him. I don't know Milo well at all, and it's

clear he's got a lot of things to work out. But he's unlike anyone I've ever met. He hides, he fronts, he lashes out, and then he's an open book. And he listens. Real listening, not like when my friends only pretend to listen while waiting for their turn to talk. And, yeah, maybe he's judgy, but maybe he's earned it too. I wonder if he's like this with everyone, but I know to my bones he's not.

So I slowly get to my feet and stand in front of him. "Okay, then." He lifts his eyes and squints when the sun hits them. Why the boy doesn't own a pair of sunglasses is beyond me. "Milo Papatonis, I expect great things of you."

"Oh yeah?" I know he's going for dismissive, but he doesn't try very hard.

"Yes. I expect you to get over this what's-her-face chick, first of all." I put up a finger. "Then I expect you to do something that makes you happy while you're healing up." Another finger. "But it can't involve any more breaking the law or killing people. You can't accomplish all that much in jail."

"Noted." He fakes a very studious demeanor.

I hold up a third finger and pin him with my eyes. "Then I expect you to stop letting other people tell you what you can and can't accomplish."

"You make it sound easy."

I shrug. "Well, what do you want to do?"

He doesn't hesitate. "I want to have my own dive charter outfit. Right here."

"Okay, so do that." I throw my arms out like I've just performed an amazing magic trick.

He chokes out a laugh. "Tell me, oh wise one, how

exactly am I supposed to do that? I have no money, everyone in town hates me—except for Bran and maybe my mom—and I'm not even allowed to swim."

"All technicalities."

"You're insane." His smile is back, and I like it too much.

"No, I'm not." I take a step closer. "I'm a believer."

"Then I've got a bridge or two to sell you, Sunshine."

My pulse jumps at the name, and my chest gets warm. Nobody has ever called me anything but Jill or Jilly. Not even my parents. It feels special and somehow intimate—even if he didn't mean it that way. It takes me a few seconds to continue. "People will forgive and forget, Milo. And if you work hard and be smart with your money, you can start your business. Maybe not tomorrow, but one day. And you said yourself the no-swimming thing is temporary."

"You make it sound easy," he says again. His fingers spike through his hair, exposing his forehead. It makes him look younger and maybe a little vulnerable.

"Not really. But what's the point in having a dream if you're not willing to work for it?"

He shakes his head, but I can tell it's not in disagreement. "You know, there's going to be a day when I turn on the TV and see you staring back at me, the star of your own show."

I preen a little at that, just to make him smile. "And I'll be utterly fabulous."

"Without a doubt." I get the smile I was after.

"Come on." I put a hand out.

"Where are we going?" He stands but doesn't take my hand.

"You can be my date for the Oscars."

He frowns but steps forward and bends his arm for me to loop my hand through. So I do.

"Just so you know, I'm not wearing a tux," he says.

I laugh at that and steer him back toward the end of the pier and all his fishing gear. "There you go being a rebel again."

"Always."

CHAPTER SIXTEEN

MILO

The minute I heard that shower turn on last night, I knew I'd made a horrible mistake. There was no wiping my mind of the mental image of Jill Holloway standing under a stream of hot water, hands running over her tits and steam billowing around her. Even thinking about it now gets me half hard.

Honestly, I feel like a first-class idiot, which explains why I lost my shit last night and barked at her. Not only did I get Rayna to let me into the SWiN so I could confiscate Jill's belongings, I followed that up by going on a ridiculously thorough grocery run and tidying up the house. Then I all but kidnapped her on my bike and brought her back to my lair where I listened to her shower and shouted at her.

It was only a matter of days ago that my life was quiet, simple, where the biggest wrench in my routine was an odd thunderstorm during my morning swim. Now look at me. I'm running around town like an asshat, abducting women who hate me.

I sip my coffee and flip through the news on my phone. There's a voice message from my mom that I'll bet money has something to do with the Thanksgiving holiday coming up, but I'm ignoring it for now. Without Felicity here, there's no reason for me to put myself through a dinner with Sherry and Brix or Brox or whatever the hell her boyfriend's name is, so I imagine I'll be heading to Mom and Morris's place. I wonder for a second what Jill's doing for the holiday and then I shove the thought aside.

"Morning." And speak of the devil. Jill greets me on a yawn, and I'm relieved to see she's wearing clothes this morning. An encore of yesterday just might kill me at this point.

"Mornin'," I respond around my coffee mug. "You sleep okay?"

She sighs. "Like the dead."

That makes one of us.

"I'm done in the bathroom, so it's all yours," I tell her. It's ten in the morning, and I've been up since the crack of dawn. I already swam two miles, and this is my fourth cup of coffee. I'm pretty certain I could power a small watercraft at this point.

"Coffee first." Her voice is practically a groan as she pours herself a cup, and I clench my teeth at the sound.

"Listen, I gotta head into work. The fridge is stocked so help yourself, and I'll leave a key so you can lock up. Not that there's much of anything to steal, but some people are stupid."

"Okay, cool. I need to head in soon too." She turns from the counter. "Um, so this is super awkward, but do you have time to drop me off if I take a really quick shower?"

This would be the perfect time to ask her what the hell's going on, but I'm starting to think it might be better for me if I don't know after all. It's clear that my brain does stupid shit when she's around, and the last thing I need is to place myself in the middle of someone else's drama. I need to take a page from my dad and Hobbs on this one and just focus on myself.

"Here." I toss the keys to the beater on the counter next to her. "It ain't pretty, and the clutch sticks, but it'll get you where you need to go."

"Wow. Thanks, Milo. That's really nice of you." She smiles and dumps an ungodly amount of sugar in her coffee.

"No big deal. It's Felicity's really, and she's not here to drive it." I can't afford for her to think I'm going any further out of my way for her.

"First the room and now a car. I'm beginning to feel like I have my very own sugar daddy." She laughs, and then I can see the cringe. She clearly recognizes that even though I'm the one who put myself in this situation, I'm less than comfortable with it. "Anyway, thanks. And you don't have to worry. I'll be out of your hair ASAP."

I don't respond since I'm liable to invite her to move in for good if I open my mouth. It's becoming harder and harder to recognize myself. Since when has a pretty woman done such a number on me?

Right. Ask a stupid question...

When I get to work, I have a text waiting from Felicity.

Felicity: *Forget the rest of high school. I'm going to college NOW. Just thought you should know.*

I stash my helmet and work my thumbs across my phone screen.

Me: *Then it's a good thing I got a job. Glad you're having a good time.*

Felicity: *Tell me you're not working for Bran.*

Me: *I'm not working for Bran. I'm teaching intro diving in Carolina Beach.*

Felicity: *Cool.*

I'm tempted to tell her not to go so overboard with excitement, but I manage not to.

Me: *You need anything? Money? Clothes? A bodyguard?*

Felicity: *As tempting as that sounds, no. I'm good. Just checking in.*

Me: *Things are exactly the same here. You're not missing anything.*

There's no way in hell I'm telling her about Jill staying with me.

Felicity: *Please tell me the new fridge has something besides beer in it.*

Me: *Don't you worry about me. I'm good. You sure you don't need anything?*

Felicity: *Nope.*

Me: *Okay. I gotta get to work.*

Felicity: *Have fun.*

My first lesson of the day is with a couple teenagers and their parents. They're going on a cruise over the holidays and want to get certified in SCUBA before they go. I've inherited them halfway through their certification, so they're almost ready for their first open-water dive. They're model students, even the teens, and the session flies by without a hitch.

My second lesson, not so much. It's a couple in for their first lesson, and the guy is clearly claustrophobic and too embarrassed to tell his girlfriend. They both pass the swim and treading tests just fine, giving each other shit and goofing around, but that all changes when we put the masks and regulators on. She's clearing her mask and regulator like a pro from her first try while he keeps surfacing and complaining that there's something wrong with his equipment. I try pulling him aside to talk out of earshot, but he's not having it. When I finally swap him for my gear to prove it's not the equipment, he inhales a lungful of water and taps out, coughing and sputtering into his towel while I finish the lesson with just the woman. I doubt I'll see them back again.

I want to tell the guy that his girlfriend won't give a shit if he can't dive as long as he's not an asshole about it, but it would be a waste of breath trying to get him to admit a weakness. We men will go to ridiculous lengths to hide our insecurities, even though we know everything comes out in the end anyway. I never said we were smart.

When Bran calls later in the day, I make a point not to pick up. His only reason for calling is to try coaxing me into a beer at Rayna's work so he can drink, play poker on his phone, and gawk at her every chance he gets. It's been the same thing since I moved back, and it has me wondering what is so damn captivating about a woman you live with that makes you unable to go eight hours without laying eyes on her? It's fucked up if you ask me.

But I suppose my reason for *not* wanting to go involves a woman I live with too, so I probably shouldn't judge.

Live with. That sounds way, way too complicated for my liking.

She's just staying in my spare room for a few days, that's all. The image of her bending over in her underwear surfaces in my mind, and I suppress a groan. I must admit, though, she sure did have my number with that fast one she pulled. I could hardly remember my own name, much less remember why it wasn't a good idea to let her wander around my house unsupervised. There's no stopping the smile pulling at my lips.

Since Jill won't be back to the house until after the dinner service, I decide to swing by the hardware store on my way home. There are more than a few things I've been meaning to fix, and there's no time like the present, right?

I manage to wrangle a bag of supplies and two cans of deck stain home on my bike and spend the better part of the afternoon sanding and staining the deck. I know I'm overdoing it with all the squatting and stretching, but I push through until long past the sun sets and the darkness makes it impossible to see where I'm staining. I'll have to touch it up in the morning light, but it feels good to have accomplished something productive for a change —even if I know my body will make me pay for it. I should think about getting a hot tub.

I hadn't realized the full extent of both my laziness

and my denial of it until just recently. I'd likely have rotted right into my deck chair if I hadn't finally gotten off my ass this week.

After gathering the drop cloths and closing all the lids, I go to the kitchen to wash out the brushes, but when I bend to pick up a dropped shop towel, my leg completely seizes, sending flaming arrows of pain radiating up and down my right side until I collapse under the agony of it. I grit my teeth and suck in shallow breaths, waiting for it to ease up, but it's a relentless beast. Fuck. I should have known this would happen. Every muscle in my body draws tight as I try fighting off the pain. I rasp and grunt into the linoleum floor, my sweat forming a slick pool where my skin touches the surface. My silent pleas for it to be over go unanswered for what feels like hours until finally—*finally*—the tension begins to unspool, and I pull in huge gasps of air as, muscle by muscle, the pain releases its grip. By the time the last spasm passes, I'm lost in the sweet blackness.

CHAPTER SEVENTEEN

MILO

Twelve Years Ago

"Dammit!"

A tourist on a bike darts across the sidewalk right in front of me, and I narrowly avoid going down on my face. My leg continues its screams of protest, telling me I'm an asshat and I'll pay for this act of stupidity, but I'm almost there and I'm not about to give up now—not after almost three miles.

To any passerby, I'm sure I look ridiculous with my half-run/half-stumble, but it's the best I can do under the circumstances. My dad is gone for the week on some trip he refused to talk about, and Bran is working on the old Yamaha I bought last summer—he's doing it as some act of contrition no matter how many times I tell him my fuck-up wasn't his fault. So the only way to get to Jill's is the old fashioned way. It's just too bad I'm under a deadline. Or, more accurately, she is.

The condo comes in sight, and I put everything I have left into the last hundred yards to the back porch and her window above it. *Don't fall now, asshole.* It's only been a few days since I last saw my doctor, and I'm not looking for a reason to go back anytime soon. I could just see him pulling my newly-earned ocean privileges and putting me back on bedrest if he caught wind of what I'm doing now.

"Jill!" It's more of a gasp than a shout, so I cup my hands around my mouth and try again. "Jill!" I hope to God she's here because I don't have it in me to drag my ass along the beach hunting for her.

"Milo?"

Her head pops out a second-story window on the far side. Thank you, God. I'm sucking wind and gripping my thigh at this point. The muscles are locking up, and if I don't massage it and get some heat on it soon, I'm in for a world of pain.

"Oh my God. Stay right there!" The window slams shut, and within five seconds, Jill bursts through the porch door and runs to where I'm doubled over. "What happened?" One of her hands rests on my sweat-soaked t-shirt and the other holds me by the side of my neck. It's the first time she's touched me other than our initial handshake and maybe a few fake punches, but I have zero energy left to enjoy it.

"Your sister's not answering her phone," I manage to say through clenched teeth.

"I know. She went to some foreign film with my dad. What's going on? You're scaring me."

"That production guy called." I suck in a breath.

"They want you on the set at four to reshoot some scene. Said they'd have to replace you if you didn't show." A shockwave of pain vibrates down my leg, and I grit my teeth against it.

"Oh my God. And you ran here to tell me? What were you thinking?" I don't need to see her face to know the expression she's wearing. I call it the scolding face. It's one of her favorites.

"It's pretty clear I *wasn't* thinking, isn't it?" I go for humor even though it hurts to breathe, much less move.

"Come on. Sit down." She tries gripping my arm, but I shake my head, sending droplets of sweat flying.

"No."

"Now is not the time to be stubborn and macho, you idiot."

"No, I mean, if I sit it'll just get worse."

She stops pulling, thank God. "Okay. Tell me what I can do."

I blink a few times and focus on my breathing. "You can go to that set." Honestly, the last thing I want is for someone—especially her—to see me looking so pathetic. The pain pulses again as my muscles constrict, and tears prick my eyes. God, I fucking hate this.

"I'm not leaving you here!"

And she's the one calling *me* stubborn? "Then why did I just run all the way here?" I growl, watching the gnarled muscle and skin of my leg constrict where it's not covered by my board shorts.

"Because you're crazy."

She's got that right. Why in the hell did I do this to myself? Just so she could stand in a roomful of people reciting a line about mayonnaise to some two-bit celebrities? But this isn't a question I really need to ponder right now.

"Give me your phone," she demands.

I hand it over without thought, and she snatches it up before stepping to the far end of the porch. She's back in less than a minute. I use the time to try slowing my heart rate.

"All fixed. Now tell me what to do to help." She's using her other favorite tone, the don't-mess-with-me one, and, really, I'm beyond the point where I can put up a good fight.

"Uh, you don't happen to have a bathtub up there, do you?"

Fifteen minutes later, I'm soaking in a giant whirlpool tub in the master suite of the Holloways' condo. Thankfully, her mom isn't home either, so it's just the two of us. I can't imagine her parents would be too excited to find a sweaty stranger taking a dip in their fancy tub. I massaged my muscles the best I could while Jill filled the tub with hot water and then helped me hobble in. The heat and the jets are doing wonders, and I'm about ten seconds from drifting off when she knocks on the door.

"Yeah?"

She cracks it open just enough to be heard over the jets. "You decent?"

I don't bother opening my eyes. "No. In the three minutes you've been gone, I've completely undressed because everyone knows how easy it is to remove a wet bathing suit."

"Ha ha. I'm just checking to see if it's working."

"It's the most incredible bathtub in the entire world, and I'm pretty sure I'm moving in. Your folks won't mind, will they?"

"As long as you don't mind sleeping in here too, I'm sure they'll be on board."

"Perfect." My voice is barely a murmur. These episodes completely zap my energy, leaving me a battered husk only good for bad jokes and propping doors open. But my eyes pop open when I remember the whole reason I ran over here like a moron. "Hey! What happened with the show? It's gotta be past four by now."

She waves me off, and I get my first lucid look at her since I showed up on her porch. She must have just changed for her acting thing because she's dressed up in a sundress that ties behind her neck, showing off her delicate shoulders and throat. Half her dark hair is piled on top of her head while the other half lies in shiny waves down her back. Her face has more make-up than usual too, bringing attention to her full lips and sky-blue eyes. She not only looks beautiful, she looks older than the sixteen I know her to be. I swallow hard.

"Don't worry. They said they'd wait for me." She busies herself checking her dress in the mirror.

"How did you pull that off?" I distinctly remember the guy's casual comment on the phone that Jill could easily be replaced. I'm pretty sure his bored tone was the very thing that sent me running my ass all the way here. This opportunity is important to Jill—in fact, it's everything to her from the way she's been talking about it for the last few weeks. It's always the *Brothers* this and the

Brothers that. Even in the middle of her lesson on clearing a diving mask, she had to surface from the water twice to tell me some "hilarious" stories about a cast pool party she'd snuck out for. Not my cup of tea, but whatever. And if it grates on me a little when she talks about those two actors who star in the show, it's only because I think a show about vampire siblings solving crimes is the dumbest thing I've ever heard. I'm not jealous. It's not like Jill and I are dating or anything; we're just friends. And being a part of that show makes her happy, so that's the important part.

Jill shrugs and lets her eyes skip around the room, completely avoiding my eyes.

"What did you do this time?"

She furrows her brow and finally looks at me. "Nothing. I told you they said they'd wait for me. No big deal. But we might want to step things up here 'cuz I need to be there in thirty or I really will get fired." She taps her wrist and then steps back. "How do I look?"

I want to say *fucking gorgeous,* but I don't. She's hiding something. "What did you do?"

She frowns and drops the act. "Fine. It's no big deal. I just told him I'd go out with him."

I sit up so sharply that my torso cramps and water sloshes over the edge of the tub. "What?!" Jill scrambles for some towels and covers the puddles before they can spread.

"Jeez. It's no big deal." She drops to her hands and knees on the tile to clean the mess. "He's been bugging me to go out with him, and I figured, what the hell."

I pull in a deep breath, and when it doesn't hurt too bad, I turn to her. "I'll tell you what the hell." I'm trying not to seethe, but know I'm failing. "That guy has got to be in his twenties, and you're sixteen!"

Her eyes flash up from the towels. "But he thinks I'm twenty-two, remember? He also thinks my name is Jenna but I prefer being called Jill." She rolls her eyes like this is one big joke.

I lean closer. "You need to call this off. It's dangerous, not to mention you didn't even need to do it in the first place. I was fine. You should have just gone in at four."

She snaps her eyes to me again, this time only a foot away. "You weren't fine. You looked like you were dying." Her chin wobbles, and a sheen of tears washes over her eyes. My chest immediately constricts, only this time it's not from my injuries.

I take pains to calm my tone. If she starts crying, I'm a dead man. That day on the pier when she wiped a tear away, I wanted to punch myself for putting it there—and I promised myself I'd never do it again. "It looks worse than it is, Sunshine. I promise." I don't mind lying if it will make her feel better.

"Are you just lying to make me feel better?" She completely calls me out.

Before I know what I'm doing, I reach a hand out and cup her chin with my thumb and forefinger, not caring that I'm dripping water on her pretty dress. "Never," I lie again, and then we're both leaning in.

The reality of what we're doing doesn't hit me until we're maybe an inch apart and my fucking phone rings, pinging the sound around the huge bathroom, taking advantage of its ridiculously awesome acoustics. We both jump back and Jill springs to her feet to grab the phone from the counter where we left it. I stand in the tub, letting the water drip from my board shorts and t-shirt I didn't bother to remove before getting in. I know I need to get out of here. What if her parents walk in? They'd probably call the cops on me. And what was I doing almost kissing her? She doesn't belong with me.

"It says it's someone named Rayna." Jill holds the phone out toward me with a frown. I open my mouth to tell her Rayna's just a friend and to let it go to voicemail, but then I watch as her eyes drop down my body. I realize too late that my shorts have ridden up, exposing almost my entire right thigh and the very worst of my wounds.

The doctors said the blades of the propeller took out probably a pound of tissue from my thigh. I told them it looked more like a shark attack than a boat accident. They didn't disagree. The blades shredded the skin of my calf, the right half of my torso and back, and kept on going up my arm, shoulder, neck, chin, and head. It was a miracle I didn't lose a limb—or worse.

Her gasp isn't at all unexpected; I'd just been determined to avoid it. I yank down the leg of the shorts to cover as much as I can and then do my best to exit the tub without falling. Jill comes toward me to help, but even in my peripheral vision, I can see she's reluctant to touch me. Hell, I'm actually kind of impressed she didn't pass out like my mom did when she first saw it.

"Milo." Her voice is quiet, so I fill the void for her.

"Hey, I gotta go. Thanks for the soak—it did wonders." I paste on a fake smile but still don't look at her. The leg isn't nearly as tight as I thought it would be, so I'm able to make it down the staircase alone. She doesn't come after me, and I don't even try to apologize for the trail of water I leave in my wake.

She's got a show to get to, and I don't belong here anyway.

CHAPTER EIGHTEEN

JILL

The lights are still on when I park the ancient Toyota Tercel in the gravel drive. Milo wasn't lying about the clutch, but it was kind of fun driving this old thing around town. It reminded me of a particular night halfway through my junior year in high school when I did some very naughty things in the backseat of a car eerily similar to this one. What was that guy's name anyway? Nate something. Nate Mathers. That was it. I told Jenna and my mom about it the very next day and almost got whiplash with the speed at which my mom hauled my ass to the gynecologist to get me on the pill. Jenna was home for some reason I can't remember and spent most of the following week either scolding me or just frowning at me, but I was happy to be rid of my virginity. I know she couldn't understand why I'd just give it away to some guy I wasn't serious about, but I didn't see it as a big deal.

If she and Mike wanted to hold sex up as some sacred

thing between soulmates, more power to them, but I didn't see the point of giving one person so much power over you that they could ruin you with a goodbye and there wouldn't be anything you could do about it. And I was right, as it turned out, because Mike almost destroyed my sister when he left her.

I switch the engine off and grab my purse before stepping out and heading for the front door of Milo's. I sigh in both pleasure and anticipation because, as predicted, waking up to the sounds of the ocean is incredible. And—bonus—Felicity's room has a window perfect for watching the sunrise. Well, I assume it is. I haven't exactly been up that early in the two nights I've slept here.

Hopefully, Milo is in a good mood tonight. I know I made him uncomfortable this morning pointing out how many favors he's doing me. From what I remember of him, he doesn't like any fawning. Like, at all. He also only likes to talk when it's his idea, which sucks for him because I'm a talker. Something he surely remembers about me. The thought makes me grin as I close the door and pass through the entryway. "Honey, I'm home!" I can't resist.

But there's no smartass comeback, I'm sad to say. He must have passed from the mildly annoyed stage to Captain Grumpypants already. I should really cut him some slack, I remind myself, resolving to just make myself scarce and head up to bed.

It appears Milo's already in bed and just left the lights on for me because the TV is off and he's not on the couch where I expected to see him. I turn to hit the bathroom when my heart rolls over in my chest.

"Milo!" I drop my purse on the floor and run the few steps to the kitchen where Milo lies motionless on the floor, one leg tucked under him and his cheek flat against the cracked linoleum. "Milo!" I shake him like an imbecile before remembering my basic first aid. Please, please, please.

He's breathing, thank God, and I can feel his pulse. So I go back to shaking him. This elicits a groan that makes me double down on the promise I made to God a few seconds ago that I'd never sneak candy into the movies ever again if he'd just make Milo wake up. I also promised never to lie or watch reality TV again, but let's be honest about human limitations here.

"Milo, wake up. Please." I cup his cheek in my hand and realize I'm crying. When he blinks his eyes open a few times, I do that awful snotty laughing/crying thing that has never in the history of the world been cute and bend down to kiss his head a couple dozen times.

"You're awake." I am a master of the obvious.

He sucks in a breath and rolls to his back, bringing his right thigh with him and holding it to his chest. "Fuck."

That is now my new favorite word.

"Fuck is right. What happened to you?" I cup his other cheek too, reveling in the warmth of his skin and the soft feeling of his beard against my palms.

"My leg." He groans again.

I release his face and lean back to take in all of him. He's wearing his normal uniform of jeans and t-shirt, but both are stained with something dark and he smells like turpentine, I just now realize. Which would explain the blue towels and paintbrushes scattered across the floor.

"What do you need me to do?" My mind flashes to a memory from years back. "A bath," I blurt out.

"Yeah." He grits his teeth, and I practically hurl myself to standing and over to the bathroom.

"Don't move!" I yell behind me because Milo is exactly the kind of man who would drag himself across a pile of broken glass just to prove he doesn't need anyone's help.

Good thing I'm exactly the kind of girl who would tackle him to the ground for trying.

It takes an eternity for the water to run hot in the tub, but as soon as it does, I shove in the plug and race back to the kitchen. Milo is in the same position as before, leg hugged to his chest and eyes squeezed shut against the pain.

"The water's running. Let's get you to the bathroom." I kneel beside him and try to figure out how exactly I'm going to maneuver him the twenty feet or so to the tub. He's quite a bit bulkier than he was at eighteen, and from what I've glimpsed, it's mostly muscle. He's clearly been keeping up with his swimming in the years since we saw each other last. "I'm afraid you're gonna have to help me out here. I haven't exactly been keeping up with my weight training."

He's in too much pain to laugh at my lame joke, but he manages to roll himself to his stomach and push up on his good knee. I quickly grab his arm to help him stand. We clumsily drag/walk him to the bathroom where he drops to the floor again, this time propped against the tub.

My hands work on his boots while he sheds his t-shirt, and then we tackle his jeans together. It's all very clinical and done in silence, punctuated by the occasional grunt or groan from Milo.

I shut off the tap and help him crawl into the steamy bathwater, where he sinks into it with a giant sigh. I'm practically panting from all the stress and exertion, but I need to keep busy, or I'll lose it. So I take his dirty clothes to the utility closet and shove them in the washer before pouring in way too much detergent and slamming the lid closed. Then it's on to the kitchen where I throw the paintbrushes in the sink and set to the task of scrubbing the dried paint off the old linoleum where the brushes landed.

My mind won't stop flashing back to the seconds before I saw Milo blink, when I thought he was dead or in a coma or something. His whole body was slack and lifeless. I breathe in deep, but it catches on a hiccup, and the next thing I know I'm sobbing into the skirt of my stupid dress.

I should have gone home to Sunview instead of staying here. Home means hugs and jokes and silly games with my sweet, funny nieces. It means heart-to-hearts with Jenna and ganging up on Sam just to see him pretend to be mad. It even means Hank with his taco Tuesdays and dumb video games and awful taste in music. There's no heartache there. No fighting. No horrific moments when you have to imagine never seeing or talking to someone again.

"Jill." Milo's voice calls from the bathroom. I take a

deep breath, then drop my dress and swipe at my eyes with my knuckles before jumping to my feet.

"Coming!" I dash to the bathroom doorway and take in the scene of a mostly naked, full-grown Milo stuffed in a tiny tub of steaming water, his eyes closed and head tilted back against the tiles. I can see the tension draining from his features, and I make a concerted effort to control the tremble in my voice. "Are you okay?"

His head lolls to the side like he's drunk, and he opens his eyes to gaze at me. "Come here."

I'm stepping forward and dropping to my knees before I know it. My palm cups his cheek again, and there go those swirling colors in his beautiful eyes as he scans my face.

"You make one pretty mountain girl," he murmurs.

My lips twitch. "Did you take some drugs I should know about?"

"Not yet, but I fully plan on doing that as soon as humanly possible." His mouth curves in a lazy grin, and my belly swoops and spins.

"I should have thought of that. Tell me where they are, and I'll get them." I move to stand, but he reaches out a wet hand to grab my arm.

"In a minute. Don't go anywhere yet, mountain girl."

I'm grinning full-on now, tears forgotten. "Okay, I won't."

He lets go of my arm and lifts his hand to run his fingers over one of the braids I've forgot are still in my hair.

"But you can call me Louisa since I've seen you mostly naked," I tease. My eyes immediately drop to the water, where Milo is lounging in just a pair of black boxer briefs. Crap. I deliberately shift my gaze up but that's not a whole lot better because now I'm staring at his bare chest and—is that a six-pack? That is so extraordinarily inconvenient.

"My eyes are up here, Louisa."

I can feel the heat hit my cheeks, and I'm on my feet in a nanosecond. "Be right back!" I dash out the door to hunt for his medicine. Granted, the bathroom would be the first logical place to look, but I go for the bedroom since I need time to get my shit together. I was just ogling Milo. To be fair, there's a lot to ogle there, but the man just collapsed on his kitchen floor, and here I am checking out his firm pecs and sexy stomach and—*stop it!*

I rifle through his bedside table, where I definitely don't notice the conspicuous lack of condoms, and then snatch the bottle of prescription pain killers before returning to the bathroom.

"How much are you supposed to take?" I ask, rattling the bottle and pretending he's fully clothed.

"Two," he responds.

I ignore his grin and dispense the pills into his waiting hand. He drops them in his mouth and swallows.

"How do you do that?" I frown at him.

"Do what?"

"Swallow pills dry. That's so unfair."

He shrugs and motions for me to kneel down again. I ignore him.

"I need half a glass of water to swallow one, and even then, I have to psych myself up for it." I drop the pill bottle on the sink.

"I don't know. You just need to open your throat and swallow."

My eyes go wide about half a second before his do, and then I'm out the door again, his guffaw following me all the way upstairs where I finally rid myself of my ridiculous uniform and even more ridiculous braids.

"OHMAGAW," I MOAN AROUND MY ICE CREAM SPOON.

It's a half-hour later, and I'm sitting with my legs crossed at the end of Milo's bed while I shove ice cream in my face and we both watch a *How I Met Your Mother* rerun on the small TV on the dresser.

When I returned downstairs from changing—and retrieving my remaining shreds of dignity from the floor—I helped Milo out of the tub and to his bedroom, averting my eyes the entire time and trying to keep both of us from slipping on our asses. Faced with the dilemma of wet boxer briefs and dry sheets, I ditched him at his dresser and made myself busy getting him a glass of water. It took a good ten minutes to get the ice to water ratio just right, and by the time I returned to the bedroom, he was blessedly secure under the covers with pillows propping his head up and a t-shirt covering those damn pecs.

He then declared it was time for ice cream, at which point I discovered that it takes exactly twenty-two minutes for Milo's pain meds to fully kick in. This explains why he's allowing me to command the remote and he's not making dirty jokes about my moaning—not that I could help it either way. This ice cream is *amazing*.

"Wait. Is that Doogie?" Milo asks from the head of the bed, taking pains to pronounce each word carefully.

I lick my spoon clean before answering. "No, it's Barney. How old are you?"

"What's wrong with Doooogie?" He sounds drunk, and I try not to laugh.

"That show is a million years old, and it was *terrible*."

"But you like classss-ics."

Another glance his way reveals him staring at his spoon like he's forgotten its entire purpose. I do a one-handed crawl to the head of the bed and set my ice cream bowl on the side table before grabbing his bowl and spoon from him.

"Hey," he protests but doesn't have the coordination to stop me.

"You're about to dump your ice cream all over the bed." I set his bowl next to mine. "And *Doogie* is not a classic. It's trash that belongs in a burning landfill alongside the *Dirty Dancing* TV show and the reboot of *Knight Rider*."

Milo leans forward like he has a secret. "He was a kid who was *also* a doctor," he whispers, and I can't help my huge grin. "That's awesome." He tries to do the fist-exploding thing and hits himself in the face.

"That's not awesome; it's embarrassing." I grab my ice cream again because there's no way I'm letting it go to waste. "Ask NPH. I guarantee he's on my side."

Milo watches my spoon as it disappears in my mouth, and he lets his head settle back on the propped pillows. "What's NPH? Where's my ice cream? Wait. Did I tell you about Doogie?" It's all a sloppy jumble of words.

I decide to go for a simple, "Yes," and extend my spoon toward him without thinking. "Here."

His lips close around the spoon, and his half-baked eyes meet mine as I withdraw it. Milo may be high as a kite, but I'm now on a completely different kind of buzz—one that has my toes curling and my nipples going tight. His lips are sensual enough on their own, but add in the sweep of his tongue across that full bottom lip and, damn, I might be the one needing resuscitation.

"Mountain girl," he murmurs, and I know I need to be the one in control here because he's driving us off a cliff.

"Not anymore." I straighten and increase the distance between us.

His hand snakes out and rests on my bare knee. "Did you find your goats?"

I have no idea what he's talking about, and neither does he, obviously. "Uh, yup." I try ignoring the heat of his hand and scoop up the last of my ice cream.

"Are you going back to your grandfather?"

He has completely lost his hold on reality.

"Absolutely," I reply.

"Can't you stay one more night, mountain girl?" His eyes close, and I watch the flutter of his lashes across his cheek. Despite his natural olive complexion, his skin is so pale in contrast to his dark hair and beard. I reach out and push the hair from his forehead without thinking. He sighs when I touch him, and my chest warms inside at the sound of him releasing the awful events of the night—right here, with me.

I bend to kiss his cheek. "I won't go anywhere, Milo."

His eyes flutter open right as I close the distance, and he turns his head so my lips land on his soft lips instead of the smooth skin of his cheek. I freeze, completely mystified as to what to do.

But Milo seems to know exactly what he's doing because he whispers the word "Sunshine" against my lips, and then his hand cups the back of my head and he's kissing me. Not some heated, passionate snogfest, but a sweet, slow, tentative kiss of just his lips and mine getting acquainted with one another. I can smell the ice cream on his breath and the lingering sweat from his hair, and I want to fold him in my arms and fall asleep right here, with his heart beating against mine and his lips warm and soft on my skin. I don't know how long the kiss lasts, but it can't be more than a minute before he sighs again and his head rolls to the side in slumber.

I'm left hovering over his sleeping form wondering what in the world just happened. Because if I didn't know any better, I'd say I just had my first kiss with Milo Papatonis. And it was the sweetest kiss of my life.

CHAPTER NINETEEN

MILO

I awake to a fuzzy head and an arm buzzing with pins and needles. The head I expected since the same thing happens every time I take those damn pain meds. But the arm thing is new.

The explanation, it turns out, is lying right beside me. The bed shifts, and a groggy voice mumbles, "Goat."

I tilt my head to see Jill sprawled out over the covers next to me, her head tucked in the crook of my arm and her wild hair spread out around her, half of it covering her face.

I can't say how many times I've had this exact same fantasy over the years—with the minor elimination of the t-shirt and leggings she's wearing, of course—but I never once thought it might actually become reality.

She mumbles again, and my chest vibrates with suppressed laughter at her nonsense.

Jill lifts her head a few inches and peers up at me

through a swath of her crazy hair. "Why are you laughing?"

I know I'm grinning like a fool, and I can't help it. "You just said, 'Come here, Mister Goat.' Am I to assume I'm this Mister Goat you're speaking of?"

She squints and glances around to get her bearings, but she doesn't jump up and run from the room—or punch me—like I anticipated. Instead, her head falls back down onto my arm. "No. It was an actual goat—or a dream goat, I guess." She groans and closes her eyes again. "It's your fault. You kept calling me 'mountain girl' and asking if I was going home to my grandfather. I think you got *The Sound of Music* and *Heidi* mixed up."

"Heidi's not in *The Sound of Music*?" I could have sworn.

"No, ding dong." And there comes the expected smack to my arm. It stings against the still-sleeping nerves, and I shift to restore my circulation.

"Ding dong?"

"Believe me, there are worse things I could call you after last night."

That has my curiosity piqued. "Do they have anything to do with you sleeping in my bed?" If something good happened and I missed it because of those meds, I'm flushing them all down the toilet.

"Rein it in there, Romeo. All you did was talk about Barney and eat my ice cream."

This all sounds potentially embarrassing. Maybe we should fast forward to part two of our morning. "The purple dinosaur?"

"Different Barney." This isn't helpful at all since I

don't know any other Barneys, but delving deeper sounds unwise.

"I believe it was *my* ice cream, Louisa. I distinctly remember buying some at the store yesterday."

Jill swipes the rest of her hair off her face, and I can make out the indentations from my t-shirt on her cheek. There's something oddly satisfying about seeing the evidence of her sleeping against me there. "Oh, speaking of, if I weren't so tired, I'd give you a standing ovation on that shopping trip. Well done."

I could tell her I made the trip with her in mind, picking out things I thought she might like from pretty much every aisle in the place, but I won't. It's way too revealing.

"Crap. What time is it?" Her brow furrows.

"No idea. I don't know where my phone ended up."

She rolls over and stretches her arm to the bedside table, causing her t-shirt to tighten over her tits and reveal the tight buds of her nipples underneath. I try tearing my eyes away, but it's impossible, so I attempt to shift my thoughts to something entirely unsexy instead. This only results in me picturing both the pope *and* me staring at Jill's naked breasts together. Shit. I'm going to hell for sure.

"Thank God. I don't have to be at work for another two hours." She rolls back, and I'm starting to wonder what exactly she's not telling me about last night. Because the Jill from the last week would never voluntarily lie in a bed with me, lean into me, or casually talk about groceries and dreams while doing so. I'm definitely flushing the meds just to be safe.

Both my cock and the area of my brain responsible for ignoring consequences want to tell her I can think of a lot of things we could do in two hours, but I don't for obvious reasons. I'm a guy and we're pretty good at separating sex from, well, everything else, but I have a history with this woman that tells me there's still a shit-ton left in Pandora's box where Jill is concerned. And I prefer my balls to remain attached to my body, thank you very much. Not to mention, hooking up would be a surefire way to send her running in the other direction, and I just got her to agree to stay here where I can keep my eye on her and put my mind at ease. At least for a little while.

But it's a moot point anyway because, thanks to my home improvement project gone wrong, she saw me at my most vulnerable last night. And that surely explains why she's not running from my bed like her hair is on fire. She's entered the realm of caregiver, which leaves me squarely in the "never gonna see her naked" realm. The only possibility now is pity sex, and I'd rather get hit by a bus.

So, as good as it feels to have her gorgeous body stretched out alongside mine, I've got to preserve what sanity I have left and put an end to this.

"I'll go make breakfast." I fold the covers aside and push to sitting, consequently breaking my contact with Jill. She sits up as well.

"No. You need to rest. Let me make it."

Yup, she's gonna try taking care of me from now until the minute she leaves. She'll probably even start agreeing with me and paying me compliments. It sounds like a living hell.

I swing my legs to the side a little faster than I should, but frustration is fueling me now. "I got it." My leg tries to buckle the second I put weight on it, but I adjust and do my best to limp toward the door.

"Milo, stop!" I hear her scrambling out of the bed and then her arm is around my waist and her shoulder is propping me up under my arm. "Here, let me help at least."

"I said I got it!" I snap. Shit.

Jill stills and silently drops her arm back to her side. God, I'm an asshole. But she already knows that so I don't say I'm sorry like I should and, instead, continue on until I reach the kitchen and the refrigerator full of all the things I bought with her in mind.

She doesn't follow.

Breakfast is a silent torture of runny eggs and burnt toast, but Jill doesn't complain. She keeps her nose to her phone for the time it takes to inhale the awful food and then takes her coffee to the bathroom with her. I don't see her again until she bolts out the door for work without so much as a goodbye, which is exactly what I deserve.

Thankfully, the lessons don't involve me doing much besides pulling on a buoyancy compensator and demonstrating equipment because I'm stiff as hell today. Granted, moving around is one of the best ways to recover from an episode like last night's, but only if it's balanced with a good amount of rest as well. I popped a few ibuprofen to tide me over until I can repeat my routine of soaking, massaging, stretching, and resting again, but by the time my last lesson is over, I'm beginning to wonder if I can get home on my bike without crashing. As I'm thinking out my options, Leah breezes into the staff room and stops when she sees me. Her khaki shorts and blue work polo are crisp and fresh as usual, giving her the appearance of head counselor at summer camp. I, on the other hand, pulled my clothes out of the hamper this morning, and even that was a chore.

"Oh, come on, you're not that old yet, are you?" She ribs me good-naturedly for my slow movements and accompanying winces. Back in the day, I would have pretended nothing was wrong and volunteered to stay longer for free. But that was a long time ago.

Today, I smile politely, hoping she'll keep on walking. "Just a little stiff, that's all."

She returns my smile. "I've been known to give a decent massage. I can help you out if you need."

I throw out a staying hand when she moves to set down her clipboard. Did my boss just offer me a massage?

"Raincheck," is all I can think to say as I grab my bag and make the split-second decision to try my luck with the motorcycle after all.

Leah doesn't appear put out, making me wonder if I'm just shitty at reading everyone these days. "Have a good one," she calls over her shoulder, ponytail swinging as she strolls through the far door and out to the pool deck.

What the hell is going on?

By the time I get out to the parking lot, storm clouds are drifting in from the east. I reckon I have about twenty minutes before I'm drenched, so I throw caution to the wind and get on my bike. If I don't make it home soon, my work on the deck last night will be a total waste.

I pull into my drive with just enough time to secure a couple old tarps over the deck before the skies open and everything, including me, is soaked to the bone. My leg protests again when I start walking toward the water instead of into the house, where a hot bath calls my name. But there's something extraordinary about these flash ocean storms, when the line between rain and sea is blurred and all you can see is a massive void before the skies magically clear again. My boots are soaked through in minutes, and the sand cakes to the leather as I get closer to the water's edge. I'm the only one out here, and it reminds me of the solitude of diving where it's just you, the ocean, and the sound of your own breathing.

The rain is coming down so hard I can't see the house right away when I turn around. I wonder for a second if it finally met its match and was decimated by the storm. In a lot of ways, that would make things so much easier. No decisions involved, no guilt, no messy emotions. No houseguest.

But it's still there. And someone is standing between me and the house. I already know who it is, even though I can't make out her features or hear what she's calling out to me with her hands cupped around her mouth. I don't even glance back at the ocean before hurrying across the sand to her.

"What are you doing out here?" I yell over the storm.

"What are *you* doing out here?" The rain plasters the cotton and lace of her dress to her skin, showing the outline of her body and whipping her braids around her head.

"Watching the storm. Why aren't you at work?" I close the distance to where she's planted on the sand, her eyes squinted at either me or the rain, I can't say.

"What?"

I shake my head and motion for her to turn around and head for the house. She pushes through the wind and rain, glancing back every few steps to make sure I'm following her. By the time we reach the house, the storm has picked up even more, and I all but shove her through the door before it slams shut behind me and the storm's volume is abruptly severed in half.

"Were you trying to get hit by lightning?" She scrapes strands of wayward hair from her wet cheeks and tucks them back. We're both dripping buckets of water onto the entryway floor.

"I was fine." I gesture for her to stay put while I limp over to the linen closet and retrieve some old beach towels.

"Why do you have to tempt fate like that?" She snatches one from my hand and wraps it around her soaked body. Her lips are turning blue, but I don't dare point that out.

"What are you doing here anyway?" It comes out sharper than I mean, and she pauses securing her towel to frown at me.

"The power went out, and Camille sent me home. I mean *here*." She shakes her head and bends to remove her shoes. They make a sucking pop when she pulls them off. "Great," she mutters under her breath.

"I was fine, you know. You didn't have to come check on me." But of course she had to check on her patient, didn't she?

"All evidence to the contrary." She pads in her bare feet to the stairs, leaving wet prints behind. "Give me a holler if you're dying."

"You'll be the first to smell the corpse," I call after her before shutting myself in the bathroom and finally getting to my hot bath.

Half of me is surprised she came back at all after this morning, but I suppose her things were still here, so she had little choice. It's not her fault that I'm a temperamental ass.

I know I should say something—do something—to smooth the waters and potentially apologize, but I have no desire to explain myself and earn even more pity. I guess I could go with option B and do something nice for her so she'll get the general idea that I know I'm a disaster and I'm sorry I took it out on her. Yeah, maybe that's the way to go. Because I might not want the kind of attention I'm getting from Jill, but I'm not ready for her to leave either.

CHAPTER TWENTY

JILL

God, he is such a colossal pain in the ass. It's as if he were raised on another planet where common decency doesn't exist and snarling is the only acceptable form of communication. I am never—I mean *never*—telling him about that kiss. And what was I thinking lounging around in his bed this morning like we were some long-time couple on a regular old Friday? I feel like spitting, if it weren't entirely socially unacceptable on my planet, that is.

It's not like I was all that anxious to return to Fort Crabbypants after this morning, but there was no way I'd go galivanting around town wearing this outfit. And when I spotted Milo out in that storm, I couldn't just ditch him without making sure he was okay. For all I knew, he was stuck in the sand with his bum leg and calling for help. What was I going to do? Let him die? Oh, he'd just love rubbing that in my face!

It takes about five minutes to strip the damn dress off because it keeps sticking to my skin. When it's finally off, I throw it by the door with a little more force than necessary, planning to wash it later. My teeth immediately begin chattering so I pull the blanket from the bed and wrap myself in it for the time being. It's soft and warm and covered in pink and black skulls, which perfectly matches my image of Felicity from our brief acquaintance.

I asked Camille today about a spare uniform and, to my delight, she told me I could pick one out—as long as it passes her approval. So I plan on upgrading as soon as possible.

With that in mind, I grab my phone and text Rayna, hoping she isn't still stuck in the kitchen. When I left, she was shouting about ice and begging Kip to please save her weisswurst instead of using the bar's ice to keep the beer cold.

Me: *Hey, did you rescue your wieners?*

She doesn't acknowledge my third-grade humor.

Rayna: *Yes! Bran brought a generator over from the shop so the kitchen is back. The rest of the place is still out of commission, so don't worry. No need to come in.*

Me: *Well, that's good because my uniform is currently functioning as an industrial-sized sponge.*

Rayna: *You need more clothes, girl.*

Me: *That's actually why I'm texting. Do you know any place around here where I can get a dress that'll work?*

I pull the blanket tighter to trap my body heat inside.

Rayna: *I do! I can pick you up in twenty if you want to go now.*

Me: *Really? You're a lifesaver!*

And, bonus, it will get me out of here.

Rayna: *Oh, don't thank me yet.*

I try not to read into that and instead focus on getting out of Milo's hair for the rest of the afternoon. I pull on a pair of jeans, some boots, and an old sweater I stole from Jenna and tiptoe down the stairs. Milo is nowhere in sight, and the bathroom door is closed. Based on his pronounced limp earlier, I'd guess he's soaking in the tub again. This immediately brings images of a half-naked Milo to mind, and I curse at myself until I hear a car pull into the driveway.

The rain has stopped as quickly as it started, but I still need to hop around to avoid puddles on my way to Rayna's car. She's dry and fresh as a daisy, as usual, and soon we're chatting away as she drives us north toward Wilmington.

"So what is it like living with Milo?" she finally asks after we exhaust both the topics of Bran and the nearly ruined weisswurst.

"Let me put it this way: you wanna trade?"

She grimaces and turns to me at a stoplight. "That bad, huh?"

"I don't know. He's just so... touchy. And grumpy. It makes it hard to remember he's doing me a favor."

"Ha. Well, the last part is no surprise. He's not exactly known for being a ray of sunshine."

My brain flashes back to him calling me Sunshine right before he kissed me last night, and I feel a flush working up my neck. It's been like this all day. I go back and forth, remembering both the sweet and sour moments of the last eighteen hours, and no matter what I do, I can't stop thinking about the damn man and his stupid soft lips.

I make a noncommittal sound of agreement because my brain-to-mouth nervous function is broken at the moment.

"I know it's none of my business, but what's the deal with you two?" Rayna's grin is sly as she pulls forward again.

I pretend to cough, but I'm fooling absolutely no one. She snorts out a laugh, and I flash her a dirty look, but I don't think she sees it.

"There's no deal. We're sort of friends, I guess."

Her expression brightens even more, making her dimples pop. "The fun kind? Or the 'can I borrow five bucks' kind?" Her face falls.

"Definitely not the fun kind. Although, I don't think I'd lend him anything after what an assface he was today."

"Damn. I was hoping there was at least a little sexual tension or something. Oh well. I guess I've got Netflix for that."

I immediately grasp onto the opportunity for a change of topic and ask if Rayna has seen *Russian Doll* yet. Because there's no way I'm admitting that the sexual tension between Milo and me might possibly burn the entire house down by the time I split town.

Twenty minutes later, we pull into the massive circular driveway of a house I believe was featured on the cover of *Southern Living*. Okay, I've never read *Southern Living* in my life, but if I had, I'm sure I would have seen this house in a ten-page spread already. The entire place is white with towering columns along the center, at least three stories, and more windows than I can count. The landscaping alone must cost more than my accumulated lifetime income to this point.

Rayna parks right smack in front of the place and opens her door. When she moves to get out, I snatch her arm. "Uh, what are we doing here?"

"You'll see," she replies with a wink and hops out. There's nothing to do but follow suit, so I race to catch up to her before someone comes to escort me off the premises for trespassing. We climb the wide stone stairs and don't even have a chance to ring the bell or bang the gong or whatever one does at a place like this to announce your arrival.

The humongous door swings open, and a uniformed woman with an apron and cap greets us. "Good afternoon, Ms. Thompson. Miranda is expecting you."

Rayna saunters right in like she owns the place, and I scurry to keep up. "Uh, thanks." I nod to the woman, but she's already click-clacking her way to another room.

"Now are you going to tell me?" I whisper yell to the back of Rayna's head while I try not to gawk at the surrounding opulence.

"Nope."

I have no choice but to keep up as she climbs one of two staircases, and I busy myself scanning the floor to make sure we're not leaving muddy footprints on the fancy carpet. What are we doing here?

When we reach a door the end of a hall, I'm reminded of that part in *Beauty and the Beast* where

Belle goes to the forbidden wing and almost gets her face clawed off. Rayna has clearly never seen that movie because she reaches for the knob and turns it without knocking.

"I hope you're decent, 'cuz I don't need to see your titties," she calls out, leaving me gaping like a dummy in her wake. I have no idea what I expect to see on the other side of the door, but it sure as hell isn't freaking Maria from the restaurant sprawled out on a four-poster bed with her head hanging off the edge and unfamiliar long red hair falling to the carpet. On a positive note, she is fully clothed, so there's that.

"What up, bitch?" she calls, but the second her eyes clap on me, she snaps up to a seated position. "What's *she* doing here?" Oddly enough, this finally manages to be the one thing that puts me at ease. At least it's expected.

"Shut up, Andie. Retract those claws. Jill is cool." Rayna nods toward me.

From her expression, I'd say Maria—or Andie—isn't convinced, but at least she doesn't kick me out. I'm honestly not sure if I could find my way back to the car on my own.

"We need your closet," Rayna announces before dropping onto the bed beside this pseudo-stranger.

"I'm not letting her wear any of my stuff." Andie gives me another of her disapproving once-overs. It's so odd to see her without her blond bowl cut. The red hair suits her much better. "They wouldn't fit her anyway."

I try not to be offended because, hey, I happen to think my bod is rockin', but she might be right. If I didn't think it would get me kicked out on my ass, I'd be tempted to point out that my boobs are bigger than hers. Shallow? Yes. True? Also, yes. Suck it, Maria.

"Bullshit. I'm telling you she's no threat." Rayna picks up a pair of sunglasses from the bedside table and tries them on.

"How do you know?" Andie's frown doesn't waver and she throws me another dirty glare.

I'm having trouble following this conversation, but I know better than to butt in and ask questions, so I just stand still and pretend to be one of the many statues in this mega-mansion.

"She's only staying a couple months." Rayna turns to me, showing off the sunglasses. "What do you think? Too much?"

But I'm not focused on her sunglasses. My mind is in utter panic that she somehow knows I'm not staying in town long. How does she know that? Oh, God. Is she going to tell Camille? If she doesn't, Andie/Maria surely will. She hates me.

As if reading my thoughts, Rayna pulls the glasses off. "Don't worry. We're not going to say anything."

Andie looks me over again, but this time there's a tad less hostility.

"Fine. But only the older stuff." I can practically see a tiny part of her soul die with the consent.

Rayna nods and gets up from the bed. She crosses to the other side of the room, where she pulls open a set of huge double doors. I gasp. I honestly can't help it.

Inside are row after row of what look like life-sized doll's dresses of every imaginable kind. There must be a hundred of them. Fluffy tulle-skirted ball gowns and short sequin dresses with feathers hang alongside petti-coated period frocks and ruffled sundresses. It's a little girl's fantasy closet, and I wonder for a second if I'm dreaming again.

"Don't fuck them up." Andie brings me back down to earth with a thud.

I take a tentative step forward, waiting for her to tackle me from behind, but she just stands there watching Rayna and me.

"They're beautiful," I say, attempting a smile at her.

Her eyes shift to the dresses, and after a moment she lets out a little sigh, allowing her shoulders to relax the tiniest bit. "Yeah."

I'll need about seventy hours to mull this whole Andie/Maria revelation over, but now is not the time.

"Here we go." Rayna shifts an entire section of dresses over to reveal an area full of traditional Bavarian dresses and costumes. We have officially hit the jackpot.

It's only when we're on our way back to Kure Beach with two perfect dresses that I press Rayna for the dirty details. "Okay, now are you going to tell me what the hell that was?"

She laughs, and it has an evil edge, proving that we were destined to be friends. "You should have seen your face."

"Yeah, no shit. So what is she doing working as a waitress when she's obviously richer than Diddy?"

"Okay, well, you know how Camille is a little bit..." Her finger circles her ear, and I nod. "She only got that way after her husband died a few years back. They used to live in the estate next door to Andie's—Camille's family was loaded, as you can imagine." I nod again as she turns onto Highway 421 and continues, "Anyway, Andie's parents are your typical nightmare rich pricks, and Andie ended up spending a lot of her time growing up with Camille. She and her husband don't have any kids or grandkids, so it made sense, right?"

I'm not entirely sure I want to know where this story is going, but there's not much choice.

"Well, when Camille started acting all strange, Andie stepped in to keep an eye on her. Everybody else was pressuring Camille to go to a home or facility or something, but there's nothing wrong with her apart from this weird restaurant and movie thing. Honestly, half of me wonders if it's an act. She's only seventy-two, she doesn't light her house on fire or forget which side of the road to drive on. And, as I said before, she's sharp as a tack when it comes to money and the business. So Andie told everyone to go to hell, helped Camille open the SWiN, and signed on as a silent partner so nobody could mess with the restaurant. She was at my interview and grilled the shit out of me. I was shocked as hell when I actually got hired. Andie doesn't trust anyone with Camille, which is why she tries scaring everybody away if she can."

"Well, she's good at it." I try taking in this revelation about my surly co-worker, but I can tell it's gonna take a while to unpack everything. It just goes to show that you never know what's going on in people's private lives.

"Yeah, but don't worry. We all get a feel for people after a while. Andie will ease up on you. *I* knew right away you were good people."

"How? And, by the way, how did you know about me leaving town? You must think I'm awful for not being upfront with Camille."

"Girl, you have all the signs of a runner. And you're not awful. I can just tell these things. And then when I found out you and Milo went way back, I knew I'd been right. Besides, I'm not convinced you're leaving." She throws that last part out there with a casual shrug and keeps on driving.

"Uh, girl, you're gonna have to get comfortable with being wrong for once in your life."

Her eyebrows say otherwise. "We'll see."

"Well, at this rate, I might be dragged out of town by the cops for stabbing Milo," I tell her as we pull onto his street and the old beach house comes into view.

"No biggie. I'll post bail."

This makes me laugh. "Aww, thanks, Rayna. You can always tell a good friend by their willingness to spring you from the clink."

"Damn straight."

SOMETHING IS DIFFERENT; I CAN SENSE IT THE moment I set foot in the door. I hope to God Milo didn't collapse again, because I'm not sure I can survive a repeat of last night. But, no. It's not that. There's noise coming from the kitchen, and I realize it's... singing? My feet freeze in place because nothing on this earth could tear me away from an opportunity to hear Milo Papatonis singing in what he believes is complete privacy. We've already established that I'm the tiniest bit evil, so don't even try scolding me.

I finally recognize the tune as "Simple Man" by Lynyrd Skynyrd when he reaches the chorus, and I gotta say I'm impressed. He nails it with a raspy enthusiasm I didn't know he had in him. Go, Milo. But I ruin everything when I step on one of the thousand creaky spots in this house while trying to sneak a peek around the corner.

Milo whips around mid "simple" and drops an empty metal bowl to the floor with a loud clang. "Fuck!" He bends to retrieve it. "Warn a guy next time, will you?"

"Sorry. I was just trying to catch the show. Nice pipes you got there, man."

This earns me a scowl, and I detect the slightest red tint to his cheeks. It's about damn time. "I thought I was alone."

"Yeah, I gathered that. You ever think about taking that show on the road?" I drape the dress bag over a chair, and it's only then I realize Milo hasn't just been busy playing rock star. He's cooking dinner. Chopped carrots, celery, and onion form piles on a cutting board to one side of the sink while pots and pans crowd the cooktop. "Are you... cooking?" I'm unsure if I should be impressed or gravely concerned based on the breakfast I choked down this morning. Speaking of which... "I forgot I'm not speaking to you." My hand settles on my hip.

He sets the bowl on the counter and closes the distance between us. I resist the urge to back up because I honestly haven't a clue what he's planning on with this approach. At this point, it could conceivably be anything from a well-timed wedgie to a passionate make-out session. But all he does is pick up the dress bag and push it back into my hands before dropping his voice to a quiet tone—one that has all parts south of the border begging me to forgive the man for any past transgressions and climb him like the stairway to heaven.

"Go relax, and I'll call you when dinner's ready. There's a cooler of beer and a bottle of wine on the deck."

"Uhhh." Yes, my tongue is on strike and siding with the southern coalition on this one.

Is he grinning? Shit. Time to make my exit before this gets any worse.

I take the dresses upstairs, where I can't resist admiring them one more time while pretending nothing weird is going on in the kitchen. Neither dress is really my style, but after wearing the same boring outfit currently sitting in a damp heap by the door for the last several days, I'm willing to expand my personal horizons. The first one is red and white with a built-in bustier and a low scoop neck that does amazing things for my boobs. The second is a bit more modest, but its embroidered violet flowers look great with my eyes, and it's sure to gain Camille's immediate approval.

With nothing else to do, I strip off my sweater and pad down the stairs in my t-shirt and jeans to check out this wine Milo mentioned. The deck looks brand new since I last saw it, with a rich walnut stain and a small matching table tucked between two deck chairs. It's the perfect setting to watch the ocean as well as the people strolling on the beach, so I do just that while I sip a glass of pinot grigio and try not to think too hard about how I got here.

It's less than twenty minutes until I hear the sliding glass door open and shut, and Milo takes a seat in the chair next to mine. He opts for beer, popping the top on his bottle but otherwise preserving the quiet sanctity of my beach-deck paradise. We sit in a surprisingly comfortable silence until an alarm sounds on his phone and he retreats inside again. I haven't a clue what he's thinking or why he's gone to the trouble of cooking dinner, but I'm sure all will be revealed in time. I'm honestly not sure I want to know the answers in case they present me with something I'm not ready to face—like getting kicked out of his house or Milo going soft on me and confessing some dark secret I'll never be able to unhear.

When he announces dinner is ready, it's with not a small amount of trepidation that my wine glass and I make our way to the kitchen.

"I should put a better table and chairs on the deck for eating." Milo hands me a bowl and throws his chin to a large pot on the stove. "Chicken and dumplings. I hope I didn't screw it up."

I can't help but smile at that and spoon a healthy portion into my bowl before settling at the table. There's a green salad already there, and from the delicious scents wafting up from my bowl, it's clear Milo went all out.

"Thanks. This looks great. I didn't know you could cook."

"Me neither." He shrugs and sits across from me with his own bowl. We eat in silence, and partway through the meal, he rises from his chair to retrieve the wine bottle from the deck and refill my glass. What has gotten into him? It isn't until I'm scraping the bottom of my bowl that he leans forward and clears his throat.

"So, uh, can we just go back to normal?"

I pause with my spoon stuck in my mouth and level my gaze at him. His eyes drop to my mouth as I remove the spoon, and I'm pretty sure I lick my bottom lip before common sense takes hold again. It's like he's had a personality transplant and I got here late for the briefing but just in time for the reboot.

"Normal as in bickering and tormenting one another? Or normal as in doing our best to ignore each other's existence?" I set the spoon back in the bowl.

He has the good grace to chuckle at that before responding, "I was thinking more along the lines of being friends."

"Friends." I try the word out on my tongue, and I don't hate it. I've now gathered this whole scene is his attempt at an apology, and it's a pretty darn good one.

His eyes stay on my face. "There was a time when we called each other friends."

He's not wrong. But I don't think either one of us was ever fooled that it was that simple—then or now.

"Okay," I respond after a long pause. "Let's take this out to the deck, friend. And don't forget the wine."

CHAPTER TWENTY-ONE

Twelve Years Ago

"I still can't believe it." I drop the flipper for the third time, and Milo frowns at me.

"You've said that at least a dozen times already. Now get your fins on before we both die of heatstroke." Once again, he sounds like maybe he regrets agreeing to teach me how to SCUBA dive.

But I can't help it. The casting director pulled me aside this morning and told me they might have a recurring spot for me when they restart shooting for the upcoming season. I have absolutely no details, but I've already pinched myself a dozen or more times, and I'm still waiting to wake up from what must be a dream. And, as if that isn't amazing enough on its own, the PA who asked me out was moved to another show, so I don't even have to figure out how to bail on our date! I might have been a little smug when I told Milo that part, but the guy deserved it for going all apeshit on me when he found out about it in the first place.

"I mean, I know it would be complicated, but opportunities like this don't happen all the time."

"And I'm happy for you. Now give me your foot." His impatience casts some doubt on his sincerity.

I sit on a rock and extend my leg out toward Milo. He's in a t-shirt and long board shorts again, with about an inch worth of sunscreen slathered on his closed cuts, as usual. I haven't seen the awful wound on his thigh since the other day when he rushed out of my parents' bathroom, and I hope to never see it again.

When he ran out, I wanted to call out after him and tell him to stop, but I couldn't. First it was the shock at seeing for myself how badly he'd been hurt, but then he was so agitated when he saw me gawking at it that I felt guilty and ashamed that I'd even allowed my eyes to go there—like I violated his privacy in the worst of ways.

I figured he was angry, but after two days of not hearing from him, I decided he'd had enough time to stew and called him to test the waters. He sounded surprised to hear from me for some reason, but I pushed on through, and by the end of the call, it felt like things were back to normal. So, I vowed to myself to never bring it up again, and so far I've kept that promise. It doesn't mean I don't think about it though.

Milo is the only young person I know who's come so close to dying, and I have to imagine it changes a person. It makes me wonder what he was like before the accident.

With the flippers—sorry, *fins*—secure, I push to standing.

"I feel like a penguin in these things."

Milo shoots me a grin and picks up a black vest he calls a BC. "You *look* like a penguin in those things."

"Hey!"

He holds the vest out for me to slip on. "A very stylish penguin. Is that better?"

"I suppose so. Okay, now what?"

Milo helps me put on the rest of the equipment and guides me to the edge of the rocks where he hops in the water and peers back up at me. We're not on the beach, but in a small rock-lined cove of sorts where the water is only a few feet deep. Milo said it would be a good place for me to practice with the diving equipment since the water here is shallow and still.

"I wish we could do this together," I tell him as I scooch my bikini-clad butt closer to the edge.

"We *are* doing this together. Always dive with a buddy." He points a bossy finger at me, making my eyes roll behind my mask.

I slide off the rock and land in the water next to Milo without incident. "You know what I mean."

"I know, and I promise by the time you leave, I'll find someone to lend me another set of gear so we can go on a real dive."

His fingers adjust the straps on my vest thing while my eyes dart to his face. "I just told you I'm not leaving."

"We'll see." He doesn't meet my eyes, so I pull off my mask.

"Milo, I can't pass up this chance to get my foot in the door." I'll do whatever it takes.

He sighs and takes a step back in the water. "So

you're gonna convince your parents to what? Emancipate you? You're gonna drop out of high school to become an actress? How are you going to support yourself?"

"I don't know!" I throw my arms out in frustration. "Why can't you just be happy for me for one minute?"

"I am happy for you. I'm also being practical. It's possible to do two things at once, you know."

"I know there are things to work out, but this is the best thing that's ever happened to me, and you're the only person I can tell. Don't burst my balloon."

Milo squints up at the sun for a few seconds and then brings his eyes back to me. "Fine. I just don't want you to get your hopes up only to have them crushed later."

I turn and face the area where the cove opens up to the ocean, spreading my arms wide. "But I *want* to get my hopes up. Don't you see?" I glance back over my shoulder with a smile. "That's the only way to make things happen."

"If you say so."

"I do." I pivot back to him. "You'll see. It's like I said, if you want something badly enough, you can make it happen."

He doesn't look convinced. "Maybe for some people." I know he's thinking about the line between the haves and the have-nots, but he needs to forget about that or he'll always resign himself to one future.

My toes grip the sand beneath the water as I step closer until I can see beads of seawater suspended on Milo's eyelashes. He has the most amazing eyes, and I nearly forget what I was going to say. "For anybody."

He blinks a couple times and then he gives me the

most romantic moment of my life to this point when he lifts a hand from the water and traces his fingertip down my cheek, from the apple to the spot where my jaw slopes to my neck. Water drips off my jaw, and I shiver and close my eyes, hoping to God and Buddha and Oprah that he's going to kiss me. The butterflies in my belly work themselves into a frenzy, and I'm sure he can see my pulse racing at my neck.

His voice comes from mere inches away. "Sunshine, I'll promise to be happy for you and do what I can to help."

My heart soars, and I lean in another inch to close the distance, sure he'll meet me halfway and give me the best kiss of my life. But his lips have other plans. "But you've got to know, at some point in your life, you'll have to learn to live with disappointment."

I believe an actual whine comes from my body at that point, and the next thing I know, Milo is shoving the mask back on my face and all the romance in the vicinity has sunk to the bottom of the ocean. I'm too mad to be embarrassed. I use the anger to swim away from him, letting my flippers increase the distance between us.

He thinks he's so clever. If I thought he'd listen, I'd tell him he's wrong. That there's always something more you can do—one more avenue to try—to get what you want. But he'll see. And now there are two things I'm determined to get: this acting gig and a kiss from Milo.

My legs pump through the water until something brilliant occurs to me. Milo will never be convinced by *me* getting what *I* want any more than he is by my words. He has to get something *he* wants. So not only am I going to figure out a way to get this acting job and that kiss, I'll hatch a plan to get him started on his diving business too. Then he'll see that dreams do come true—and not just for the few.

Milo calls out, and I realize I've gone farther than I thought, so I turn around and head back his way while I work out a strategy for his dream my head.

Step one will be to get him to tell me everything there is to know about the diving scene around this place. This won't be hard since he loves talking about diving, especially now that he's back in the water.

I'm not sure what step two is yet, but I'll figure it out. And in the meantime, I've got SCUBA to learn, a family to keep in the dark, a job to secure, and the best kiss of my life to steal. I've totally got this.

"So, TELL ME MORE ABOUT WHAT A DIVING CHARTER does." It's a couple days later, and I'm joining Milo for his daily walk, only this time we're headed from my condo to Wake N Bake for doughnuts. He has yet to invite me to his house, but I get the feeling it has more to do with his dad than anything. It's pretty clear they don't have the best relationship and, I don't know, maybe he's not allowed to have people over. I asked the other day why he doesn't live with his Mom since I know she's somewhere nearby, but he dodged the question, and I haven't circled back since.

I don't have to ask twice for Milo to launch into a monologue on the kind of business he wants and what the competition is like. It sounds simple enough to me. The company provides gear for tourists to rent if they don't have their own, and then a couple guides take them out on a boat to one of the established local diving sites. As far as I can gather, the most expensive parts would be the boat, the equipment, and renting out a space to operate out of. I'm sure there are more costs I don't know about to run a business—I'm not stupid—but even I know raising the money is the hardest part.

"And what if people don't know how to dive —like me?"

"People without certification would need to go to a local dive school. There are a few around here to choose from." We stop at an intersection and wait for the light to switch.

"Like the one you worked at?" I ask without thinking. But Milo doesn't act fazed by it, so I wait for him to resume talking.

"Yeah. Coastal Adventures Dive School. They do lessons and arrange charter dives. They also sell gear in addition to renting."

"But you don't want to do that?"

The road clears, and we resume walking. "Naw. I mean, teaching is okay, but I'd rather take people on open-water dives all day. Wait 'til you try it—you'll be hooked." The excitement in his voice is clear, and it makes me grin over at him.

"Can't wait." Someone in a passing car whistles, and Milo flips him off. "What was that for?"

"It's rude to whistle at women." His face twists into a scowl.

I laugh at his expression. "How do you know they weren't whistling at you?"

His scowl deepens, which makes me laugh even harder and continue teasing him for the next block. When I decide he's had enough, I return to the topic at hand. "So, what's your favorite dive you've ever guided?"

A quiet joy settles over his features, telling me I asked the right question. "There was this one group we took out to the Dredge Wreck—it's one of the man-made reefs just off the coast. You see, they purposely sink retired vessels and turn them into a home for sea life. You can find all sorts of things down there. They've got a bunch in the area, and you take different groups to different ones depending on their skill level and the time of year." He's talking with his hands, which he only does when he's really excited.

"Anyway, we had this one group scheduled for the Dredge, but it was crowded as hell that day, so my partner Devon and I decided to take them out to this other reef he knew about. The guy's been around forever, so he knows everything about these waters. We weren't really supposed to be there, but I'll never forget it. It was creepy as hell and the best local dive I've been on."

"Did you get in trouble?" I keep watching him because I haven't seen this animated side of Milo much.

"No. Devon filed the log before anyone saw it, and the divers were newbies, so they didn't know the difference."

We cross the next intersection and cut out farther from the beach, both of us close to panting at this point. Part of me wishes we were on the beach so we could cool off in the ocean, but I know it's hard for Milo to walk on the sand. And I'd rather be with him. I retie my ponytail as we walk, securing sweaty tendrils that were sticking to my face. It'll have to do until we reach the air conditioning of the doughnut shop and the most amazing doughnuts ever, as I was promised.

I glance back at Milo and see the sweat dripping from his temple down to the healing scars on his jaw. "You and rules don't exactly have the best relationship, do you?"

He shrugs, still grinning from his diving memories. "I guess not."

And then my mouth goes somewhere I hadn't intended, making me kind of want to kick myself in the face when it causes his carefree expression to drop. "So that girl you liked. She worked there too?"

He nods and stares straight ahead. "Uh, yeah. Leah. Her parents actually own the place. She works for them."

I take that in. I'm guessing maybe Leah and her family are what Milo considers "privileged" in his carefully constructed flowchart of society, but what do I know? His dad owns part of the fishing charter where he works, but Milo still regards him as one of the have-nots. Either way, though, Leah's place in society didn't stop Milo from his massive crush. I can't figure him out.

"So you had a crush on the boss' daughter, huh? Sounds messy to me. You probably dodged a bullet there." I have no idea what I'm saying, but I feel a need to say *something*. I'm equal parts mad, sorry, and jealous, so it comes out crazy.

"Yeah, probably. I mean, it was a long shot to begin with." He shoves his hands in his pockets.

"Why do you say that?" What am I doing? Trying to convince him he and this Leah chick belong together? *Shut up, Jill!*

Milo shrugs again and casually throws out a bomb. "She was too good for me."

My jaw drops, and I feel like laughing and crying at the same time. "You don't seriously believe that, do you?"

"It's a fact of life, Sunshine."

For the first time, I hate hearing that name on his lips. His tone is brittle, and the endearment sounds condescending, not special in the least.

My steps turn to clomps beside him. "When are you going to stop splitting the world into two categories of people?"

"Sorry." His response is immediate, but I don't think he's sorry at all. I think he just knows I'll get mad if he keeps insisting on this warped way of thinking. But this reaction only makes me madder.

We walk in silence for a few minutes while I try not to yell at him and he stays quiet. Then he comes to an abrupt halt, and I have to backtrack a few steps to his side.

"You see that?" He points between two buildings to where the ocean is visible.

"What am I looking for?"

He repositions himself behind me and extends his hand out in front of us. "You see those two buoys?"

His hand rests on my shoulder, and I forget why I was mad. All I can think about is that spot where his hand sits, but I manage to say, "Yeah."

"Right in between those, if you go out about ten miles, there's the Pocahontas Tug."

"Okay," I croak.

"That's where I caused the accident."

My body stills, but I can feel his breath on my hair and his hand still holding my shoulder. I want to beg him to shut up and continue talking at the same time. I stay silent instead, and he chooses to keep talking.

"There were four of us. Me, my buddy Bran, and two girls from Duke on a weekend dive getaway. Everly and Shayla. We met them on the beach earlier that day and hit it off because of the shared interest in diving. One thing led to another until I asked them if they wanted to go on a private night dive.

"Leah had been talking about some date she had that weekend and pretending she didn't know it burned me to hear it. I got mad and felt like she'd been jerking my chain, so I jumped at the chance to impress someone new and, I don't know, I guess prove something to either myself or Leah."

I try not so squirm at the mention of that name, but his story has me rapt.

"It wasn't the first time I'd borrowed a boat and equipment—and I knew I wasn't the only one who did it. But I was the first one to do it drunk and high." He huffs out a humorless laugh. "Bran scored some less-than-kosher weed from some guy who owed him a favor, and all four of us got fucked up on it. It was an idiot move and one I'll regret for the rest of my life."

"What happened?" I ask through a tight throat, hardly seeing the view in front of me.

He pauses, and I'm not sure if he'll answer at first. But he must figure he came this far already because he continues. "There was no moon. Once we got out there, I popped the engine into neutral to check if we were in the right spot since my head was messed up. Shayla got up on the gunwale for some reason and started doing some stupid dance, but she was too wasted so she fell in. She was there one minute, and then, *poof*, she was gone. None of us had our gear on—not so much as a PFD. Sorry, a life vest," he corrects for my non-seafaring brain while giving my shoulder a light squeeze.

"Bran didn't hesitate. He jumped in after Shayla, and the next thing I knew, Everly went in too. Everybody was screaming and panicking, and I didn't think. I left the engine in neutral and jumped in the fucking water. If I'd been thinking I would have cut the engine, turned on all the lights, and thrown the PFDs out. But I didn't. By the time I found Everly—which wasn't hard since she was screaming so loud—Bran yelled that he was sending Shayla my way so he could get the boat which was drifting away. Everly was crying, and Shayla was yelling at her to shut up, and they were splashing water every-where. Bran somehow reached the boat and got on board before turning it around and idling his way closer. But he didn't see Everly take off toward the boat. The girl was in full-on panic mode, and there was nothing I could do but swim after her. I think Shayla was yelling at Bran to warn him, but I'm not sure. Next thing I knew, I got hit by the prop. I heard later that Everly got a nasty gash on her arm too, but I got the brunt of it. If Bran hadn't been idling and cut the engine when he did, we'd both be dead for sure."

I cover my mouth at the mental picture he's painted, remembering the sight of his thigh wound in vivid detail. I want to turn around and hug him, but I don't think he'd let me.

"I don't remember much after that, but I know Bran and Shayla pulled us out of the water and called the Coast Guard. Turned out Shayla is a senator's daughter, and Everly belongs to some family with deep roots in the tobacco industry. They had their lawyers crawling all over this town looking for anybody and everybody to sue. Of course, I didn't know about any of this until a couple weeks later. I'm still not sure how it all worked out so well, but I only ended up with a fine to pay and community service that'll start as soon as the doc gives his okay. And, along with getting fired, I got my boating license suspended, which I'm sure comes as no surprise to anyone."

I'm not sure what to say, so I go with, "Sounds like things turned out as well as they possibly could, given the circumstances."

"Yeah, but that's thanks to Bran. I know that much."

He's still standing behind me, and I don't want to disturb this connection. He's sharing more than I ever thought he would. "It's kind of a miracle he shut the boat down when he did." I can't let myself think of the alternative outcome.

"It's more than that, though." Milo exhales, and it tickles my head. "Everly and Shayla denied that they had anything to do with the whole thing. Said we tricked them into going out there and even lied that they didn't know they were smoking weed. Bran got good and pissed, telling anyone who'd listen that it was a crock of shit—down to Everly bragging about how she guessed it was PCP lacing the weed because the feeling was so familiar. Shayla finally fessed up when she couldn't explain how her diving gear got on board, and Everly wasn't far behind. Bran took the wrap for the weed, and he's probably working on his community service as we speak."

My lip curls at this new information. "I can't believe they did that, especially with how you saved Everly."

"Some people feel entitled to special treatment."

My stomach turns at the notion that he might place me in the same category. I admit, hearing the story gives me more insight into his state of mind, but I hope he's not letting his horrible experience paint the way he views *everyone*. It never hurts to hope.

With that in mind, I choose my words carefully. "The world is filled with good people and bad people, rich people and poor people, but I'd hate to think you'd forget all the layers in between."

"I haven't." He drops his hand from my shoulder, and I can feel his absence when he steps back. "You don't have to worry about me."

But I do! I want to say.

Instead, I turn, deciding the only thing now is to lighten the mood before either one of us says something that will stick forever. "Oh yeah? I gotta say I'm kind of worried we're never going to finish this walk and get our doughnuts, SCUBA boy."

His mouth curves in a grin, letting me know he's

happy to drop the topic. I'm not sure if he shared his whole story to explain why he gets judgy and angry, or if he just felt like he could trust me. And it doesn't really matter in the end. I'm just happy he let me see inside.

We keep walking until we reach Wake N Bake and Milo gets his much-touted bacon doughnut. But the story plays over in my head until I fall asleep in the wee hours of the next morning, only to have a nightmare that Milo died and Leah sat in the front row at his funeral, telling everybody that she always secretly loved him.

CHAPTER TWENTY-TWO

MILO

The combination of wine and comfort food appears to be Jill's Achilles heel because she hasn't sent me so much as a dirty look since we sat down to dinner. Turns out I'm batting a thousand in this whole apology thing.

Now the only problem will be getting my mom to back off with all the questions. Well, that's not the only problem, but it is a big one. I suppose it's no surprise that when your son who's never cooked a damn thing other than a sandwich in his life asks for an easy but impressive recipe, the maternal wheels start turning in a nosy-ass direction. I was able to put her off for now, but we both know she won't give up that easily. Which brings me to my other problem.

Jill Holloway is lounging in one of my deck chairs with her eyes closed, humming Lynyrd Skynyrd and looking like any man's fantasy with her bare feet, tight jeans, and a cotton tee that shows off her breasts to perfection. She's two glasses into the bottle of wine, and it appears to be her mellow place, something I'm careful to make a note of in case this information could prove useful in the future.

The sun set while we were eating, so now it's just the house lights and the moon casting a dim glow on the deck while the surf plays out its dependable rhythm. I'll need to check the perimeter of the house in the morning for storm damage, but it can wait.

Jill stops humming for a minute and tilts her head toward me, her lips spreading in a lazy smile. "Why didn't you ever bring me here that summer?"

It isn't what I expected her to ask, but I can't say I haven't been thinking about the past lately too. "I don't know. I guess maybe I thought you'd think it was trashy or something."

"Seriously?" She's not truly irritated, something I can probably thank the wine for. "It's a beach house." Her arms spread wide for emphasis like this is my first time here.

"It's a shack that just happens to be on the beach, and you know it." I take a sip of my beer and shake my head at her.

"Who cares? Look at your back yard. And, besides, all it needs is a coat of paint and maybe some throw pillows."

"Throw pillows? You think that's gonna do it?" The fridge, range, and deck were just the tip of this home-improvement iceberg. Wait until her bed comes crashing down into the kitchen one of these days.

She shrugs and takes another sip of wine before

glancing back at the house. "Don't you have any pictures or anything you can hang on the wall? You've got to admit the lack of personality lends a bit of an *American Psycho* vibe."

I smile because, when she's not mad at me, she's witty as hell. "Sure. I've got a bunch from South America and a few other places."

Her mouth turns down. "No, I mean personal pictures. Family, friends, beloved childhood pets with lame names like Fluffy and Kitty."

I shake my head. "I'm sure my mom has pictures. My dad never put any stock in sentimentality." She can't be surprised by that.

"And what about Fluffy and Kitty?"

"I hate cats," I say around the mouth of my beer bottle.

"Can't really argue with you there. But what about Fluffy? He's a dog. Everyone loves dogs."

I decide to trust her on that one. "Dogs require attention, and everybody was always working—me included. Believe me, it's no tragedy."

"Well, that's just sad." Her gaze shifts to the ocean. Jill is the kind of person who probably had an entire menagerie of animals as a kid.

"I'll get over it." She's so pliable right now, I decide to test my luck. "My turn to ask a question."

When I get no response, I take it as an okay and lay it out there. "What are you doing here?"

She doesn't act surprised by my question, but she can't help being a smartass. "Like, existentially?"

I roll my eyes for maybe the first time in my adult life. "No, wiseass. Like in this town. After all this time."

She sets her wine glass down on the table between us and sits up, tucking her legs under and angling toward me. Her hair falls loose around her shoulders and I notice for the first time that her t-shirt says, *"Surely not everybody was Kung Fu fighting"* right over her tits.

"You know, I knew you'd ask me this question at some point, yet I still don't have a good answer."

"Somebody once told me a good place to start is the beginning." I wink at her, and she chuffs out a half-laugh.

"Okay, well, if you want the short version, my transmission died, I was broke, Camille needed a Louisa, and a guy named Zeb towed my car and told me how to rent a room like a common criminal. You've pretty much been around for the rest."

If I didn't know any better, I'd say she's trying to be difficult.

"Nice try, Sunshine, but give me the long version."

She takes a sip of wine and watches me for a few silent seconds before setting the glass down again. "Why do you call me that?"

Oh, no she doesn't. "Later. You still haven't answered my question."

Her lip curls. "Ugh. It's so boring." When she sees my attention hasn't been diverted, her shoulders slump. "Fine. But when you fall asleep halfway through, don't blame it on me."

I put up two fingers as a promise, and she sighs.

"Okay, here it is. I was minding my own business at

dinner one night with my sister, and the realization hit me that I'm Mike."

It's impossible to make heads or tails of this supposed explanation, so I just repeat it, hoping that helps clear things up. "You're Mike." It doesn't.

"I know. I can't believe it either. Such a disappointment." She shakes her head, and I narrow my eyes at her. "I'm getting there. Give me a minute." One more sip of wine, and she starts in again. "Mike is Jenna's ex-husband, and he's a complete dickhead, not to mention the most boring, uptight, party-pooper in the universe."

"You're really doing a bang-up job of selling yourself right now, just FYI." I'm rewarded with a grin.

"Yeah, well, I'm no prize, as you're about to find out." Her nose wrinkles. "So, I was out to dinner with Jenna, her boyfriend, Sam, and her kids—my adorable nieces, Kate and Eileen, a.k.a. the only good things Mike has ever done in his miserable life. Anyway, I couldn't help noticing that Sam never moved his arm from the back of Jenna's chair through the whole meal, even when he was eating. He watched her face when she laughed at something one of the girls said, and when she got up to use the restroom, his eyes followed her until she disappeared. Even while he held up conversation with the rest of us. And then there was this steely stare-down Sam had with the guy at the table behind us when Sam caught him checking Jenna's ass out." She raises a brow at me. "Jenna's got a really nice ass."

"Not sure what this has to do with anything, but I'll take your word for it." I'm beginning to think maybe the wine was a mistake after all.

"The point is Jenna makes Sam happy—she and the girls. And he makes her happy. I've never had that mutual fulfillment thing—never even looked for it." She brings her hands down flat on her knees with a smack, as if she's reached the conclusion of the story. Yeah, not so fast.

I happen to know from personal experience that Jill makes a lot of people happy, but I'm guessing she already knows that deep down. So the thing that must be troubling her has to do with her own happiness. But Jill and happiness go hand-in-hand in my mind and always have —well, along with crazy and temperamental. But she's the sun. The thought of her being unhappy is a jab to the solar plexus, and I hope I'm dead wrong.

"Why?" I shake my head "Why didn't you look for it?"

She doesn't meet my eye, instead picking some point beyond my left shoulder. "I guess because if someone makes you happy, they can take that away, and then you're left with... this giant, empty hole."

My skin starts to itch because this is hitting a little too close to home for me. And this is supposed to be about her anyway. So I take it from another angle.

"Okay, but since I met you, you've been making *yourself* happy, right? And there's nothing wrong with that. In fact, it's probably the healthiest way to live. You're enough. Other people are in your life to enhance that. So if they disappear, you've still got what makes you *you*." I know it's a crude simplification, but I hope some of it hits home.

She nods and shifts her gaze to me again. "I know.

That's pretty much been my mantra all along. If I'm in charge of my happiness, I'm the one with the power."

I turn my chair to face her and lean forward on it. "I've been out there on my own for years with just myself and sometimes Hobbs—but if you met him, you'd see he's not exactly friend material—and I've met tons of people here and there. But the one constant is me doing what makes me happy."

Her nod is accompanied by a sad smile this time.

"I don't see the problem," I continue, but I'm lying. Because ever since she showed up in town—and even a long time before that, if I'm being honest—I've suspected the possibility that I've been kidding myself for all these years.

"The problem is Hank," she announces.

A lead weight lands in the pit of my stomach at her words, and my chest starts to heat with something vaguely familiar that I can't put a label on.

Jill saves me the trouble of asking who the fuck Hank is, which is a good thing because I doubt I could do it without snarling.

"Hank was my boyfriend."

Was. Let's focus on this and get that blood pressure back down. That label is becoming clearer by the second. And I believe it's written in permanent green ink.

"I came home from dinner that night, and I looked at him."

She lived with this guy? Right. *Deep breaths.* I need to listen to what she's saying.

"Really looked. And I asked myself, 'Could I let this man make me happy? Could I make him happy?' Like

Jenna and Sam? That's when I came to the horrifying conclusion that I wasn't Jenna or Sam. I was Mike. I was the guy who thinks anniversaries are for investing in a new stock portfolio, and Valentine's Day is a scam for suckers, and flowers just die so why bother, and giving out raisins on Halloween is a valuable teaching moment. In other words, I was a monster!"

My inner Bruce Banner finally chills out at that, and I can't help being a little amused, especially since she's practically pulling her hair out at this point.

"Hold on now. I happen to know you'd never give out raisins unless they were covered in chocolate, and you love flowers too much to never bring them inside. Also, I hate to point out the obvious, but if you were that focused on investing, you probably wouldn't be broke and slumming it at my house right now. Just saying."

She sticks her tongue out at me and blows a raspberry.

"See, I can guarantee this Mike loser never spits at people."

"That's because he's boring like I already told you."

She flops back in her chair while I take a sip of my beer and wait for her to continue.

"Anyway, it's the *idea* of Mike. He and Jenna were married for ten years. Jenna was all in from day one, and the whole time, Mike held her at arm's length. And I don't even think it's because he's incapable of investing himself; I think he chose not to. And that's what I always do." She shakes her head, and her voice cracks on her next words. "He left Jenna after ten years, saying he just wasn't feeling it, and then he got remarried a nanosecond later, and their relationship is reportedly swell. Jenna was devastated—no, she was *decimated*."

"You're not Mike," I insist because I need her to believe me.

"All my relationships say otherwise. I never get attached enough that I can't get over a guy in days, if not hours." She curls her lip again like she's disgusted with herself. "When I went home to Sunview to help out after the divorce, I met Hank and did the same thing to him as I did with the others. I introduced him to fun, carefree Jill who likes to party and flirt and push boundaries. But don't you worry because she'll always come home at the end of the night and she'll never cheat. She won't get jealous of your friends or your Xbox either, and she'll never ever pick a fight. Being with her means good times and smooth sailing." Her eyes drop to her lap. "The problem was they never actually had the real me. A few of them realized that and ended it with me when they got smart. Hank didn't."

A nauseous feeling spreads through my gut as her story unfolds because the Jill I know is so much more than that. She wears her heart on her sleeve and gives life all she's got. When she's mad, she yells at you 'til her face hurts; when she's hurt, she cries buckets and uses your shirt as a tissue; when she worries for you, she holds you so tight like she has the power to fix anything; and when she dreams, she doesn't let anything stop her. I feel sorry for the guys who never got to see all of her, but possessive at the same time. I want to be the only one who gets all of her.

But I'm an idiot. Because she's talking about

boyfriends, partners, lovers. It was too risky to give herself over to them. I, on the other hand, have only ever been her summer-vacation friend. I'll never be a threat to her happiness because losing me is a breeze. She did it before, and she can do it again.

She doesn't notice my frown—or maybe she thinks it's one of empathy—so she continues.

"I broke up with Hank that night. He was hurt. Surprised. Angry. But it had to be done. Jenna thought Hank had been the one to break up with me because of how upset I was, but I didn't tell her it was me. She'd ask too many questions, and then I'd have to tell her that I've spent years doing to other people what Mike did to her. And I'm a giant asshole." She's pulling on her hair again, and I'm starting to worry she's giving herself a bald spot.

"Okay, calm down." I shift forward and grab her wrists to stop her, doing my best to reprise my role as her friend. Shit. "Just because you were protecting yourself doesn't make you an asshole."

"Fine, but I'm still a jerk."

"Yeah, sometimes you are. We all are. But looking out for yourself isn't a crime. People want different things. Even way back, you told me how different you and your sister were. You were the dreamer, and she was the steadfast one. Nothing wrong with either one. And, frankly, anyone who tries keeping you from being yourself is the asshole, not you. You never lied to anyone. Mike made vows in front of family and friends and God."

"But don't you see? Me making the rules kept Hank from what he wanted. I stole a chance at real happiness from him and wasted two years of his life."

"And that was his choice. If he wanted more of you or he was jealous or unhappy, nothing was keeping him from pouring his heart out except fear. And if a guy isn't going to take a chance going after what he wants, then it's his own fault when he doesn't get it in the end. Hell, you were the one who told me that yourself." I hope I'm saying the right thing.

"You know, you're pretty good at this. Have you ever thought about being a therapist?"

"I don't look good in sweater vests."

She cracks a small smile. "Yeah, I could see that."

I give her a second to make sure she's not going to yank her hair out and then deem it safe. "So you had this revelation, broke up with Hank, and then what? Came here? Why?" The idea that she'd be in a personal crisis and choose to come to my town sparks an intense feeling of satisfaction, but it's wiped out with her next words.

"No. I spent some time in Greenville, then Raleigh, and then I was on my way to Charleston when my car broke down here."

"Oh." I feel more than a little stupid, although I do remember her saying she'd been on the road a lot lately. Still, I don't like the idea of being a mistake on the way to something better.

"I just needed to get away, you know?"

I nod because my experience mirrors hers in so many ways.

"Find the life I'm meant to lead before I'm too old to do it."

"I was going to say something about your decrepit state but didn't want to be rude." I return my chair to its original position and settle back with my beer as we both focus on the night sky and the empty beach. "So, what do you think you were meant to do?"

She snorts and it's cute. "I haven't the first clue, but I'll never stop dreaming."

"Well, that's a relief." I scratch my beard. "Beaches are good places to dream, or so I've been told."

"I have to admit, I've been in worse spots." She grins and then snaps her head my way. "Speaking of which, I get my paycheck in a few days and I can finally pay you for the room."

"You're not paying me for the room."

"Of course I am. I made a deal with Felicity, and I intend on sticking to it. I even signed a lease."

"We're not going to argue about this." I dismiss her again, and she tilts her head at me.

"But we're so good at it."

We both grin at that and watch each other for probably too long.

"Yeah, that we are, Sunshine."

She throws up a finger, cutting whatever intimacy we'd built. "Now you have to tell me."

"Tell you what?" I stall for time because I already know.

"Why you call me Sunshine."

My hand goes to the back of my neck and I blurt out the first thing I can think of. "'Cuz when I met you, you had sunburn."

"No I didn't." She's grinning.

"How can you possibly remember that?"

"Because I was vigilant about skincare and obsessed

with getting wrinkles after reading an article on how even famous Hollywood actresses stop getting booked for jobs when they get their first wrinkle. A ridiculous double standard. I should have known right then that acting wasn't for me."

I don't ask about her acting career since, of all topics, it's the one most likely to cause her to murder me in my sleep after what I did. So I fess up, especially in light of all the sharing she's done with me tonight and how good it felt when we were smiling at each other just now and sharing that connection. It doesn't mean I have to look her in the eye when I do it, though.

"Okay." Here goes nothing. "The real reason I call you Sunshine is because you light up every room you're in, and no matter if you're pissed the hell off or laughing 'til you cry at some stupid joke, you make everyone around you feel alive. And it's not just what you put out there on purpose for people to see, because even when you're sleeping or sitting quietly looking at the ocean, you make me feel like I won't ever be cold another day in my life."

I chance a glance at her to see her lips parted and her eyes wet.

"You're not gonna start crying on me now, are you?" There's more frustration in my voice than I intended because I said way more than I should have and I'm pissed at myself. Not to mention, I never could handle it when she cried, and apparently not a goddamn thing has changed there.

"I'll cry if I want to, you big jerk." She reaches over and shoves my arm. "That is, hands down, the nicest thing anyone has ever said to me in my entire life." She shoves me again for good measure.

"You wouldn't know it from the way you're beating on me." I stand up and start for the door, empty beer bottle in hand. But the door sticks when I try pulling it open.

"You have to be gentle, or it'll stick." I can tell she's smiling without looking at her.

"Goodnight." I calmly close the door and reopen it with less force. And then I take my ass to bed before I say something else I might come to regret.

CHAPTER TWENTY-THREE

MILO

Twelve Years Earlier

"You are going to poo your pants when you hear this." Jill doesn't bother saying hello like a normal person.

I anchor the phone between my chin and shoulder and finish drying my hands. "God, I hope not. I'd like to think I outgrew that when I was two."

"Shut up and listen, dummy. I think I've got a gig lined up for you."

"A gig?"

"Yeah, like a private dive kind of gig."

The towel drops to the kitchen floor and I don't even bother picking it up. "What do you mean?"

"Come down to the set this afternoon at four. I'll tell the guard we're expecting you, so you shouldn't run into any trouble. He likes me."

Of course he likes her. Who wouldn't?

"Do you have a pen?"

I pull open the junk drawer and scatter the contents until I unearth a pen and an old receipt. "Yeah."

Jill recites the address, and I figure it's about ten miles from here. I'll either have to hitch a ride or see if I can borrow my dad's truck. I'll find a way there somehow.

"This is so exciting! I'll see you at four, okay?"

We hang up, and I toss the phone on the counter before bracing my body with both hands against it. There's absolutely no use getting excited about this. For all I know, Jill struck up a conversation with a cashier at Wal-Mart and is recommending me for a job selling fish tanks. Not that I don't appreciate the effort, but she operates under the assumption that things will always work out the way you want them to. I've been lectured enough times on it, I have it memorized.

The fact remains I have to my name one set of dive gear that cost four summers' worth of mowing lawns, no boat, no boating license, and no money. How can I possibly be of use to anyone with that as my resumé?

Nevertheless, at 3:45 I find myself pulling Morris' truck up to a fence near the nondescript studio and following Jill's instructions to the gray door at the north corner of the building. The door swings open at my knock, and a huge guy in a security uniform leans his body out and speaks in the lowest voice I've probably ever heard. "What do you want?"

"Uh, I'm Milo Papatonis. I was told—"

"Follow me." He cuts me off, and I don't hesitate to follow the man down the narrow hall. "You're Tinkerbell's boy."

It's not a question, and let's be honest, I don't think

I'd ever risk disagreeing with this guy anyway. He's a dead ringer for The Rock and could likely kill me with a flick of his finger.

"That's me," I say and immediately regret it when my voice cracks. This is starting out perfectly.

We go through a door at the end of the hall, and he points to a crowd of people gathered by a row of bright lights and scaffolding. Jill is impossible to miss.

The Rock disappears, and I forget to thank him because I'm too busy watching Jill. She got her head thrown back, laughing at something another girl just said, and the sound carries across the room where it settles in my chest. I glance around then, and it's no surprise that I'm not the only one watching her. The dude holding a boom microphone is smiling her way, and a couple of guys who look vaguely familiar keep glancing over while leaning in to chat with each other.

My feet move her way on their own, all of us apparently needing to be closer and not really understanding why. Her makeup is heavier than I've ever seen it, and she's wearing a blouse that dips down in the front way too far for anywhere but the beach. And then there's the skirt that barely hides her underwear with the way she's perched on that desk with her long legs crossed in front of her. My jaw ticks and I have an irrational urge to pull out my phone, call Jenna, and tell her to get down here as soon as fucking possible.

But just then, Jill's head turns, and when she catches sight of me, her expression goes from amused to—I don't even know what to call it. But I know in that second that if she would look at me like every day for the rest of my life, I could handle anything life throws my way. I don't have time to bask in it for long, though, because she launches herself off the desk and runs over to hug me.

"Milo! You're here!"

I hug her back, ignoring the pull in my right shoulder. Her body fits mine perfectly, and she's just the right height to tuck her cheek in by my collarbone and wrap her arms around my waist. We've never hugged like this before, and I'm kicking myself for it.

"Hey there, Sunshine."

She steps back and grabs my hand, and before I know it, I'm being pulled over to the crowd. Several different huddles have formed with some sharing what look like scripts while others chat or watch portable screens. Jill leads me to the two guys I noticed earlier, and when we get closer, I know I've definitely seen them both before. One is blond with a sharp jaw and the bluest eyes I've ever seen while the other is darker with an olive complexion and long hair pulled back with a tie.

"Milo, meet Noah and Tyler. Guys, this is Milo Papatonis, the guy I was telling you about."

"The diver," Tyler points to me while Noah extends a hand.

I shake both their hands and try keeping my cool. "That's me, I guess."

Jill bats my arm playfully. "I already bragged about you and your mad skills, so don't try being modest."

I glance over to see her shooting flirty eyes at these dudes while she sways side to side. What the hell is going on here? But I'll have to worry about that later because

Tyler starts talking, and I'm thinking I should pay attention to what he has to say.

"So, listen, man. I don't know if J.J. has laid it out for you, but..."

I shoot my eyes to Jill again and she giggles, but it's not her carefree, goofy giggle. I know that one, and this is not it. "They won't stop calling me that."

"Because only you could start with the name Jenna and get Jill as a nickname, baby girl. It makes no sense."

I want to say, "No shit. Because her name is Jill and she's been using her sister's I.D., you twatwaffles," but I don't. Instead, I pretend to laugh along with them. "Only you." I flash her a little glare that she pretends not to see.

"Anyway," Noah takes over. "Tyler and I are looking for, let's call it a 'diving concierge.' We've both been diving any number of times, and we're hooked. But our schedules are super unpredictable with filming and last-minute flights to L.A. and shit. We've used local charters in the past, but it's a pain in the ass and their boats are shitty."

"So, you need a local dive guide with a wide-open schedule, it sounds like."

Tyler points to me. "My man gets it. We want to be able to do our thing wherever, whenever, without all that bullshit of calling ahead days before. I like to go with the flow, you feel me?"

Oh, I feel something.

"Oh! And night dives," Noah chimes in. "We want night dives at the cool places, not just the usual spots offered by the one local company that'll even take you."

I know exactly what they're talking about. In fact, the

issues they mentioned are some of the ones I want to provide solutions to with my own business. But it's not that easy.

"All this sounds, great, guys, but I've got to be honest. I don't have a boat yet." Not to mention equipment, gear, a license, insurance—you know, minor stuff.

Jill grabs my arm and gives me a big smile. "That's the best part. Noah has a boat and a captain or driver or whatever already. He just needs a guide for diving."

"Forty-two-footer. Only sleeps four, but it works for me. She's in a slip at the St. James Marina when I'm working out here."

I flick my eyes to Jill and then the guys. I have no idea if they're solid or a couple of fucknuts, but they need a dive guide and I need a job, no matter how small.

"Tell him the best part," Jill says, still holding onto my arm.

"Oh, right," Noah says. "J.J. said you're looking to start your own full-time sitch. We know a ton of people around here who could use the same kind of set-up we're talking about. You know Dallas Bradley from *Park, Ride, Repeat*?"

I nod because I'm thinking they already assume I'm a fan of their show, in addition to all their friends' shows.

"He and his girlfriend have a boat a few slips down from mine, and they're looking for somebody local too."

"Sounds amazing." I feel a bit like I'm having an out-of-body experience because this kind of thing never happens. If you want something, you need to scrape and crawl and toil to get even a foothold, and even then it's a crapshoot. Things don't just appear out of nowhere on a platter for the taking. At least not in my world.

I turn to Jill and can't keep the grin from my face. She's smiling her sunshine smile, and another glance at Noah and Tyler says all three of us are drinking her Kool-Aid.

"So, got any plans tomorrow night?" Noah holds his hand out to me again, and I shake it.

"Nothing much. Just a night dive with my two new clients." It's smiles all around as we all shake on it—well, Tyler fist bumps me and slaps my bad shoulder, but I take it like a man. We exchange information and iron out a couple more details before the guys have to go to "makeup."

As soon as they're out of sight, Jill pulls me to the other side of some scaffolding and bounces up and down before hugging me again. "Can you believe it?"

My grin is no doubt goofy as hell. "Actually, no. How did you manage to pull that off?"

She twirls a strand of hair with her finger, and it doesn't escape my attention that, with that outfit, that hair twirl, and that smile, she is the definition of temptation. "I have my ways."

I'm not sure how to feel about that, but she continues before my thoughts go off the rails.

"I heard them talking about missing a dive they were supposed to go on, and we got to chatting. I immediately thought of you, of course, and it all just came together."

"I don't know how to thank you. This is unbelievable." I grab her upper arms, and she smiles up at me, her eyes going wider.

"And I didn't even tell you the other news yet."

"How can there possibly be more?"

"I know, right. But the casting director told me this morning that Noah wants me flown out to L.A. to audition for an even better role than the one she told me about in the first place. Eek!"

"Wow." I blink a couple times. "Congratulations." I'm careful not to voice any of my doubts or warnings and try to just be happy for her like she asked me to. It's not as hard as I thought it would be.

"I mean, it's not a huge role or anything, but I think I'd get to be at the end of the opening credits on some of the episodes. Can you imagine?" She's an open book, giving me all her thoughts and wishes and dreams with just that smile. This girl is evidence that the world can be good and right and beautiful. That *my* world can be that way if I just open myself to the possibility. I want to tell her that she's changing my life, making me a better person, giving me something I never thought I deserved with just her friendship alone. And I need her sunshine.

But a voice from the other side of the room calls a group number, and Jill's lips part. "Oh! That's me. I gotta go." She goes up on tiptoe and plants a kiss on my cheek. "Things are all working out, Milo. For both of us."

She rushes off in her short skirt, and I make my way to the hallway again and back to The Rock where, for some reason I don't understand yet, I ask him to keep an eye on Tinkerbell for me.

"Perfect night for a dive." Bran sets an air tank into its slot on the cart and closes his tailgate.

"I called ahead," I joke as I take the far handle and start pulling the cart across the marina parking lot. Bran mans the rear, and we head toward the slip where Noah said his boat would be waiting.

Since I'm not familiar with Noah and Tyler's level of experience, I told them I'd be bringing a fourth so everyone had a buddy, at least for this first dive. I prefer even numbers, but if everyone is experienced, responsible, and on the same page, three can work in the future. The guys have their own dive gear, which is either a good sign that they have some experience, or just a sign that they have cash to burn. I guess I'll find out which it is later. Bran insisted on renting his own gear, but I sprang for the air tank rentals for all of us. With what these guys are paying, it won't be an issue.

The first sign I get that I'll be earning my money is the half-empty bottle of vodka sitting on a table next to two shot glasses when we board the boat. I'm aware that my most recent dive involved both liquor and drugs, but we all saw how that worked out, didn't we? I decide to play it by ear and make introductions all around. But Bran already knows who both Noah and Tyler are without the introduction. Thankfully, he manages not to go all fangirl on them. I, however, plan on giving him all sorts of shit later about his secret man-crush on a certain pair of crime-solving vampires. I can't believe he watches that shit.

It's when I'm checking everyone's gear that the second sign rears its ugly head.

"Hey, Milo," Noah calls out from his seat across the aft lounge. "What's the deal with you and J.J.?"

I don't miss the look Bran shoots me. He and Jill haven't met, but he's heard me talk about her, and I'm guessing he's read a little too much into it.

"No deal," I respond, but the last word tries to catch in my throat.

"See, I told you." Noah throws a regulator at Tyler, and I have to stop myself from shouting at them not to fuck with the equipment. If one of those regulators breaks, there's no dive and I'm out the tank money and likely a job. I need to play this carefully.

Noah's eyes come back to me. "But you've hit that, right?"

My grip on the dive weights tightens, and I'm probably lucky they're made of lead or they'd likely be cracked in half. I want to chuck one of them at Noah's head and yell that Jill is sixteen years old and he shouldn't even be looking at her. He's got to be in his mid-twenties, for Christ's sake. And since I can't yell that, I don't say anything at all in response, instead letting my molars grind together.

"Ouch," Tyler joins in. "Better luck next time, dog." Then he goes for the vodka bottle and extends it to me. "A shot always dulls the pain, right?"

Bran, being a much better friend than I deserve, pipes up at that. "Yo! I've been known to get my drink on a time or twelve, but it ain't a good idea to dive when you're drunk."

"We're not drunk. Just getting a nice little buzz on,

right, Ty?" Noah nods at his buddy, but neither of them takes another shot.

I brush by Bran and lower my voice. "I'm dropping the cart off at the truck before I drown these assholes myself." He pats my back, and I hop onto the pier and grab the cart. I need to calm the hell down and get this dive going. When it's over, I'll draw up a contract that includes no drinking and no talking shit about underage girls. Well, I doubt the last part will make it in there, but the drinking part will for sure. Who knows, maybe they started the bottle another night and they've only had one or two shots.

By the time I get back, my pulse has evened out, and I'm no longer in danger of separating someone's head from their shoulders. I step onto the swim platform and start making my way toward the cabin where Noah and Tyler have moved. I'm about to announce that we're good to go when my body freezes at something Noah says.

"Come on, man. I get to hit that first. The L.A. bull-shit was my idea, so you get sloppy seconds. She's primed."

"Or I could spill that you're playin' her and work the friend card for my thank-you fuck. And, besides, dog, we've both seen the way she looks at me. Sweet little J.J.'s got a thing for big Greek cock."

"Keep telling yourself that. Meanwhile, I'll be over in the corner with those pink lips wrapped around my dick and an easy exit strategy when this shit wraps next week."

When I've heard people recount memories, saying everything happened in slow motion, I've always thought that was bullshit, that they were dramatizing for effect. But now I can honestly say it's true. I'd like to think my accident taught me my lesson about staying on the straight and narrow and not going looking for trouble. But this time, trouble came looking for me in the form of two vile fuckwads with zero respect for women or common decency.

By the time their asses hit the water, though, they've managed to develop a little bit of respect for the hard heel of my left boot as well as Bran's right fist. Suffice it to say, I'm out the tank money and I couldn't possibly care less.

CHAPTER TWENTY-FOUR

JILL

This pseudo truce with Milo is a weight off my shoulders. It's also weird as hell. But I think we've figured out the complicated recipe for household peace. I pretend I don't notice his "creaky noises," as I've come to call them, and never help him with anything unless he asks first. I also let him have the remote, be sure to park on the far side of the drive, and never eat the last Oreo. He, in turn, makes my coffee in the morning so I don't accidentally pour in salt instead of sugar and disturb his post-swim zen with my subsequent cursing. He also knows never to ask what I'm watching on my phone when I randomly laugh out loud, and to respond with an affirmative to any questions about fashion, hair, or wine. I've gotta say it's working quite well if the last three days of peace are anything to go by.

The morning after my confession about my Mike-ness and the mess my life has become, I felt more than a little self-conscious. But by the time breakfast was over, any embarrassment had lifted, and it felt good to have shared my troubles with someone. It didn't hurt that I had the memory of Milo's sweet words tucked away somewhere in the region of my heart. I wasn't lying when I said it was the nicest thing anyone's ever said to me. I'm just not a hundred percent sure I can believe he really meant it. We'd both had a few drinks and, I don't know, maybe he was just trying to make me feel better. Or not. I don't know, and it's driving me crazy!

Either way, though, my mind is way more at ease now, and I'm settling into a new routine with Milo, with work, and with life on the beach.

"Hey, Louisa! Heads up!" Andie raises her tray of bread baskets over my head as she passes, and I realize I've been standing in the middle of the kitchen like a zombie.

"Sorry!" I duck and shift to the side.

Last week, she would have plowed me over without a word, so it seems Rayna was right and Andie is indeed starting to warm to me.

"You will be!" she yells back. Okay, so we still have a little ways to go.

Camille walks into the kitchen, stopping to say something to Rayna before zeroing in on me. "Oh, Louisa. Just the person I was looking for." I smile back at her out of reflex because it's hard not to. "Do you have a minute?"

Since we just opened and nobody has been seated in my section yet, I nod and follow her to her office. When we're both seated, I glance around the room. I've been in here a couple times but never for more than a few seconds, so I haven't taken stock of the space until now. The walls are covered in framed photographs, some black and white, some color. There are wedding photos, landscapes, and lots of candids. I recognize a younger Camille in several, most of them with a round, smiling man who must be her late husband. Others are of people I've never seen before, but they all embody a sense of joy and love. It strikes me how different this all is from Milo's bare walls. But it's familiar too, in a way, because my parents' house feels like this and so does Jenna's. I'd like to think that by the time I leave, I can manage to surprise Milo with some photos to keep him company.

"So, I've come to the decision that you and Louisa are not the right fit."

My stomach drops. Is she firing me?

I must be awful at hiding my fears because she immediately covers my hand with hers. "Oh, no, dear. I think you're a wonderful server. The customers adore you, you're a quick learner, and you rarely make a single error."

My relieved exhale fills the room. "Well, that's good to hear. Thanks. I really like working here." And I do.

"What I meant was you have too much heart and spirit for Louisa. She's... how do I put this? A kill-joy."

I cough out a laugh. "A kill-joy?"

"Yes, you know what I mean. A buzz-kill. A goody-two-shoes. A mega-prude. A narc."

I put my hand up as I try not to snort with laughter. "I get it, Camille. Remind me to come to you next time I need a good insult." I gotta say I never thought of any of the von Trapp kids as such downers, but I've been proven wrong. "So, if I'm not a Louisa, who am I?"

"Liesl."

I can't help my fist pump at that. "Does this mean no more braids and I get to kiss cute guys?"

She shakes a finger at me but laughs while she's doing it. "No kissing. No fraternizing with the enemy. And also, no braids."

"Thank you, thank you, thank you!" I lean over the desk and kiss her cheek before thinking to ask, "Was that all?"

She nods. "I'll have your name tag ready tomorrow."

"Awesome." I turn to go and then stop in the doorway for a second. "Camille? Why don't you already have a Liesl?"

"Who says I didn't? But we all have to retire sometime, don't we?" She winks at me, and I laugh out loud, thinking that Rayna may have something there with her suspicions about Camille.

I STOP FOR A BOTTLE OF WINE AND A SIX-PACK OF THE stout Milo likes on the way home from work. Now that the trade show is over, the customers are much easier to deal with. I swear, it was like they were a bunch of spoiled college kids on spring break, wreaking havoc around town and throwing their cash around like monkeys throw poop. I hope my old motel-mates at the Misty Inn made some good money, at least. When I joked about it with Rayna, she said a customer told her his brother is a bodyguard for the ladies over there, and it's quite the operation. No pimps involved at all; just a bunch of women running their own small businesses. I was pleased to hear it and figured once they get rid of the druggies and the bedbugs, they might just have something there after all. That is if prostitution is ever legalized in the state. Minor detail.

When I turn the corner onto Milo's street, lights are still blazing from the windows despite the late hour, and I can't help the smile spreading on my face. The man might be an infuriating mix of a straight hottie with a bad temper, a killer smile, and an infuriatingly annoying habit of burrowing under my skin, but he's also fun to hang out with.

"You are looking at the newest sixteen-year-old, non-braid-wearing, sneaking-out-to-make-out-with-her-secret-boytoy, bad-ass server in town!" I announce as I saunter in the front door. "You wanna join me for the braid-destroying ceremony or should we get right to the celebration?" I hold up the wine and beer and walk straight to the living room where Milo is horizontal on the couch with bare feet, track pants, no shirt, and an arm thrown casually behind his head.

My powers of speech evaporate immediately. Holy mother of hotness. If it weren't for the scars, I'd swear he's been airbrushed. But he wouldn't be Milo without the scars, so no airbrushing allowed. All I know is somewhere out there is a swim coach who deserves a Starbucks gift card and a well-written thank-you note.

As if the current view isn't ovary-imploding enough, he uses his bajillion ab muscles to pull himself to sitting, and it's only then, as I'm perusing the smorgasbord of hot man before me, that my eyes happen to take a breather at his face and notice he's staring at me like I just deboarded the train from crazytown. Which, technically, I kind of did since I came from work, but whatever.

All I can think to do is walk over and shove the six-pack at him in a completely awkward and graceless manner.

He grins, and his eyes develop a definite glint of naughtiness. I have the sudden, irrational urge to ask him if he's been a bad boy and then offer to spank him. Abort! Time to find the corkscrew!

I turn on my heel and walk to the kitchen, careful not to go too fast and reveal my panic.

"I'm gonna need a little clarification on your opening statement. It sounded to me like you opened a dictionary and pressed shuffle." His voice is getting closer, but I don't dare turn around. If I do, I might lick him, and how in the hell am I going to explain that?

I hear him stop behind me where I'm tearing at the foil on the wine bottle with my fingernails, and I have to force my hands to slow.

"Jill?"

Get it together, man!

"Present."

That's not at all helpful.

I give myself an inner titty-punch and turn around, careful to keep my eyes focused upward at his face. But his brows are pulled together in that way that makes him look so exposed like he did a decade ago when he told me he had to break up with his first girlfriend when she went to juvie. I want to pull his face down to mine and say his name against his lips while his beard tickles my chin and I breathe him in.

"Should you have driven home?"

He thinks I'm drunk. I don't know whether to feel insulted or relieved. But this is Milo, and this is a night for celebration. "I'm not drunk. Not yet, at least." I hold up the mangled bottle. "I'm celebrating because Camille promoted me to Liesl!"

His face relaxes back into a smile, and he takes the bottle from me. "I have no idea what that means, but congratulations. And thanks for the beer."

"I couldn't celebrate alone, and you don't strike me as a wine guy."

"Let me pour you a glass." He finishes opening the bottle and grabs a glass from the cabinet.

I watch his naked biceps shift and tighten with the movements and manage to refrain from asking him to show me his manly armpit again. *Just trust me.* I accept the offered glass when he's done, and while he fetches a beer from the living room, I chug half of it down.

"To you." Milo extends his bottle, and I clink my glass to it. "And to getting all the great things you deserve."

He's getting all sweet on me again, and I'm not sure what I'm going to do about it. Chances are I'll find a way to fuck it up, but for now I just say, "Thanks, Milo."

CHAPTER TWENTY-FIVE

MILO

"And that's why you should never, ever, trust a guy wearing suspenders." Jill stabs the air with a finger and tips her wine glass to her lips, swallowing the last sip.

She's adorable as hell when she's tipsy. I thought so the other night, but this is next level. She's just finished her third glass, and this is probably a good stopping point, so I tuck the bottle behind my deck chair in case she decides to go back for a refill. I shove aside the thought that's been surfacing over the last hour—that I may never be able to enjoy this deck again after she leaves. It's best to focus on the present instead.

"Thanks for the warning. I'll remember that next time I run into Larry King," I tell her.

She sets her empty glass on the table and throws her hands up. "See! You just proved the rule. That guy's been married more times than I've internet-stalked David Gandy. 'She married me for my personality' my ass.

News flash: A thirty-year-old woman doesn't find your pervy stories funny. She's just waiting for a blood clot to work its way loose."

I bite my cheek to keep from laughing at her. "Don't hold back on my account," I manage to say.

"See. You get me." She leans back in her chair and sighs.

I watch her for a minute, unable to hide my smile. When she walked in the door earlier with her flushed cheeks, braids, and red dress that made me choke on my tongue the first time I saw her in it, I felt a kind of... rightness settle over me. Then something else came over me when I realized she was checking me out with eyes that didn't belong to some disinterested tenant just crashing in my spare room for a few nights. She wanted me. It was right there, plain as day, and I felt like sighing with relief and then pulling her down on top of me so I could see what was under that dress.

But she was also panicked, and that's never a good sign, so I let it lie and focused on celebrating her promotion or whatever we're celebrating. I'm still not sure.

So here we are on the deck an hour later, both of us having changed into warmer clothes to combat the cold breeze coming in across the water and chatting about Larry King and Jill's opinions on, well, everything.

I've been trying to work up the guts to invite her to Thanksgiving at my mom's house, but I'm afraid she'll read into it in a way I don't intend her too. The problem is I still haven't decided what my intentions are, so until I do, I can't invite her. My mom's been texting me ever since I got that damn recipe from her, asking if I'm bringing anyone. I keep putting her off.

If I only knew what was going on inside Jill's head, all of this would be so much easier. But she's hard to read these days, and God knows I haven't done a very good job of inspiring much confidence. We're like two blind people walking through a room full of spilled Legos and occasionally getting drunk together.

A glance at my watch tells me it's past midnight. I've got work at nine tomorrow, and it's probably time for Jill to start sleeping off her wine. I push to standing and hold out my hand. She takes it without hesitation, and I pull her up. We've come a long way since that first day when she pinched me and called the cops.

"Is this the part where we dance?" Her grin is mischievous, and she's so damn pretty, I can't help but smile right back at her.

"Sure, Sunshine."

"I love it when you call me that." Her voice turns breathy, and damn if I'm not dying to kiss her.

She must be thinking the same thing because she goes up on her tiptoes and closes the distance between us. The first touch of her lips on mine sends a jolt of electricity straight down my spine, and my hands lift to cup her jaw in case she has a mind to retreat. Her skin is even softer than I remembered, and her lips are sweet with a touch of wine and a warmth that has me slanting my head for more.

When her tongue sweeps across the bow of my upper lip, I groan and deepen the kiss so I can taste more of her. She wraps her arms around my waist and slides a hand up the center of my back, pulling me in closer. It's a rush of tongues and lips and teeth after that, both of us trying to get closer, get more, until I've got her pushed up against the clapboard siding by the door and her leg is circling my thigh, grinding her pelvis against my painful hard-on.

Nothing is stopping me from stripping her bare right here on my deck and taking her against this wall until neither of us can talk or breathe. I've never wanted anyone so badly in my life. I've never been so damn hard in my life. And she's making whimpering noises and pulling at my shirt, begging me, "please," over and over. We want this. We need this.

I break the kiss, and she gazes at me with dazed, lust-drunk eyes before leaning back in, but I pull her with me to the door instead, intent on getting us somewhere horizontal. When I jerk the door open, the damn thing sticks, and I let out some choice expletives.

Summoning a shocking level of composure, given the circumstance, Jill closes the door slowly with one hand before pulling it fully open. "You have to be gentle, or it'll stick."

I respond by bending down to kiss her hard and then pulling her inside with me, making her shriek with laughter and slap my ass. We're both smiling like idiots by the time we reach my bedroom door, and then it's a freefall into that lust-haze again, both of us practically clawing at each other's clothes to remove them as quickly as possible.

We both lose our jackets and shirts, and then she goes for the button on my jeans while I drop my eyes and take in the sight of her glorious breasts straining the confines of her pink lace bra. I need my mouth on them as soon as humanly possible. But she's struggling with my button, and when I study her face, I see her concentrating hard on the task. My first instinct is to laugh and tease her, but then I remember the wine. The fucking wine.

I grab both her hands and still her movements.

"Third time's a charm, I promise," she says on a laugh and looks up at me from her kneeling position on my floor. Her smile drops when she sees my expression. "What's wrong?"

"You've been drinking."

"So?"

"You're not thinking clearly."

"Thinking is for suckers. Let's get naked." She sends me a naughty smile and pulls her hands free, but I take a step back.

"Jill, we can't."

"Yes, we can. You see, it's a simple matter of physics. The round peg goes in the round hole. Ta-da!" She makes a crude gesture with her hands that would normally have me laughing, but both my good sense and my case of blue balls are killing my sense of humor.

"You know what I mean. The last thing I want is for this..." I gesture between us. "to happen, and you wake up regretting it.

"Milo, it's just sex." She's tipping the scales from amused to perturbed.

But I've already fallen off the cliff to dumbstruck. Because there's no way on earth that anything between Jill and me could ever qualify as "just" anything. She's always been more to me, and even when I've tried to deny it, I never believed it for long. It's the reason she's followed me around all these years, and it's the reason it feels like hot daggers in my chest when her actions and words let me know I'll never be more than a pitstop, a time-killer, a project to her. She's my sunshine, but I'm just her summer vacation.

I don't say anything. I can't.

"Fine." She picks her shirt up off the floor and stands. "God forbid you ever break the rules when it's something *I* want."

I'm not sure what she's talking about, and maybe it's the wine, but I let her finish without responding.

"Milo Papatonis, author of the most complicated moral rulebook in history, ladies and gentlemen."

I don't follow when she stalks out of my room and up the stairs, shutting her door with a quiet snick instead of the slam I was expecting.

I DON'T SEE JILL FOR TWO DAYS, WHICH ISN'T ALL that surprising since she works both lunch and dinner shifts most days and Bran said Rayna and Jill have been hanging out a lot. I admit part of me was holding out hope that Jill would come down the morning after and announce that she was not only sober but crazy about me and jump my bones. Yeah, I wasn't holding my breath. Maybe she's embarrassed because she got a little drunk and I saw her without a shirt. Or maybe she was trying to scratch an itch and doesn't even remember. Or maybe—

and this is the one I'm betting on—she regrets kissing me entirely and is pissed off I took advantage of the situation.

Either way, I'm left in the same boat with firm evidence that Jill's lips taste even better than I'd imagined and a dick that gets hard every time I think about it. Not even my morning swims in the cold ocean can make a dent.

It doesn't help that I've got the day off work today and nothing to do with it, so I resolve to pour my sexual frustration into some long-overdue repairs to the house's exterior. Since I don't own more than a few basic tools, that means I'm headed for Mom and Morris's place, where there'll be no avoiding the inquisition.

Morris answers the door, and we shake hands as usual. "You're looking good," I tell him, and it's not just out of courtesy. He had a heart scare a while back, and my mom's been keeping him on a healthier diet.

"That's kind of you to say, my boy." He ushers me inside and calls for my mom. Morris and I are of the same opinion when it comes to small talk, so unless we're planning on staring at the walls for the next ten minutes, it's best just to summon my mother sooner rather than later. "I've got the truck all loaded up with whatever you might need. You can just bring her back when you're through."

I thank him, and in comes my mom wearing a pink velour sweatsuit with a matching ball cap. "You still haven't RSVP'd for Thanksgiving," she says, apropos of nothing at all before she gives me a quick hug and stands back to survey me. She must not see anything particularly upsetting because she makes no comment and keeps on about the holiday. "You missed last year, and with

Felicity out of town, you don't have to feel bad about not going to Sherry's." She says my sister's name like it tastes bad on her tongue. Sherry's mom was wife number two, right before my mom, so there's always been a bit of bad blood there, not to mention the fact that Sherry used to steal money from my mom's purse when she was over and never once copped to it. But my mom has never let that color her affection for Felicity.

I nod, knowing my mom is right about Thanksgiving with Sherry, and if I can avoid my sister and her boyfriend under any circumstances, I tend to do just that. But I don't want to commit to dinner yet, and I definitely don't want to tell my mom why. So I try dodging the question.

"I just talked to Felicity this morning. She said she's narrowed her college choices down to about twelve places now, and she's looking into being adopted by her friend's mom." I'm only half joking.

"Well, I'm not surprised. She's so creative and smart —and I'd want to be adopted too if I were her. It would also solve your problem about the house." She says, taking a seat on the sofa next to Morris.

"There's no problem about the house. Why do you think I'd be fixing it up only to turn around and sell it to someone who's planning on tearing it down?"

She puts her hands up in surrender. "I'm just saying." As if that's an explanation for anything. I glance over at Morris, but he's no help. He's got his sudoku book on his lap and is shaking his head at me without even having the decency to look me in the eye. "Anyway, will you be RSVPing for one or two?"

You know, I saw this coming, yet I still dragged my ass over here. I give deflection one more go.

"What's with this RSVP thing? Isn't it just going to be you and Morris?"

She nods, brushing some nonexistent lint from her sweatpants. "And Brandon and Rayna. And a couple friends of theirs I haven't met yet, but I think their names are Tim and Helen."

"Ted and Haley?" I think the veins in my forehead are in danger of rupturing.

"Yes. That's what I said. Ted and Haley."

I close my eyes to give myself a moment and then start again with a more agreeable tone. "Don't they have families?" Okay, forget the agreeable part.

Her brows snap together. "Well, that's rude. Brandon said Rayna's parents are snowbirding in Florida, and I don't know about Tad and Hermione because I haven't met them yet. Would you like me to call them up and invade their privacy with a bunch of insensitive personal questions?" She leans back on the couch and crosses her legs, knowing she's pulled out a clear victory on this one.

I sigh. "No."

Her lips curve. "So. One or two?"

"Is tomorrow too late to RSVP?"

CHAPTER TWENTY-SIX

JILL

"Are you sure that cat's not sick or something?" Zeb ashes his cigarette on the newly stained deck, and I have to bite my tongue really hard not to yell at him.

I follow his gaze to the sliding glass door where Lollipop the cat is hissing at us from the other side with both paws splayed on the glass and his face pressed so close his breath is fogging up the window. "No. I'm pretty sure that's just his personality."

Zeb nods, accepting my answer at face value and taking another drag on his cigarette. I try not to cough when the breeze brings his exhaled smoke to my chair. The disturbing thought that I'm breathing in air that was just in this stranger's lungs hits me, and my stomach lurches. What am I doing?

My inner voice chimes in. *"This is what happens when you shove your feelings down in the trash compactor of your soul and let anger guide the way. You are essentially a large child with a killer rack at this point."*

I can't argue, but I also can't turn back because I just heard the front door open and close. Here goes nothing.

"Gimme a cigarette." I motion to Zeb. There's no time for manners, and he clearly doesn't mind because he immediately holds his pack of Marlboros out for me to take one. A glance through the glass door reveals nothing but the cat, so I turn back to him. "Do you mind lighting it for me?"

He pulls a cigarette out and puts it between his lips next to the one he's smoking. I fight a gag reflex and focus on bringing up the playlist I prepared on Spotify earlier today.

Just as Zeb hands me the lit cigarette, a string of curses sounds from inside the house and I see that Lollipop is not at his post anymore. I hit play on my phone and turn the volume up as the opening chords of "Welcome to the Jungle" by Guns N' Roses blares from the surprisingly decent speaker.

Less than five seconds later, Milo pulls on the door handle with a fuming expression, and—I could not have planned this any better—the door sticks with only a few inches cleared.

I suppress my laugh and gesture to the door, pretending I don't see his expression. "You've got to be gentle, or it sticks," I shout over Axl's vocals.

Milo's face gets even redder as he closes the door and opens it more slowly this time. Then his eyes bounce from me, to Zeb, to the two beers on the table, to me again, then to the cigarette dangling from my fingers, then back to me. "Do you mind telling me what the hell is in my kitchen taking a shit on my floor?"

"Oh." I nod and take a quick pull on the cigarette, forcing myself not to cough before continuing, "That's Lollipop. I got him from your friend, Haley. She said nobody would adopt him for some reason, so I told her you'd take him." I turn to Zeb and shrug. "We've all gotta do our part, right?"

"How did you even—" Milo cuts himself off. Probably smart. "And the food and dishes all over the counters?" He tries again. I almost forgot about the giant mess I left in there.

"Huh?" My hand cups my ear as I cock my head to the side.

His jaw tenses, and I can almost see right up to his brain with the way his nostrils are flaring. He turns to Zeb and speaks in a tight voice. "I'm Milo."

Zeb stands and smiles, reaching his hand out in greeting. "Zeb. Great to meet you. You've got a sweet place here." The boy is oblivious.

"Thanks." Milo shakes Zeb's hand, but his gaze shifts to me. I know he remembers the name from the other night, and I inwardly snicker. Serves him right for making me feel like a total idiot and for not wanting me like I want him. Gah! I need to stop thinking about this and focus on the sweet nectar of revenge.

So maybe I was a little drunk that night, but that doesn't mean I didn't know what I was doing. Like I said, it's just sex. I've had a lot of it, and I'm sure Milo has too. We're both adults, so what's the big deal?

Except I know what the big deal is. This is me and

Milo. This is the one dream I never got over. When the acting thing didn't work out, and the dancing petered out, and the singing—well, I never was that good of a singer—I found my peace with it all. There were always more dreams to explore, so I traveled and met people and landed in a profession that could take me anywhere—people always need a good waitress. But then Mike dumped Jenna, and I went home to take care of her and the girls. And I met Hank. And I treaded water until I couldn't anymore.

I grit my teeth and push it all back. Milo has always, *always*, been the one holding back. Not believing in me, in us, in possibilities. Nothing I can do will make him take a chance, and it's time I learned that lesson for good. He probably did me a favor the other night. But I've got years and years' worth of anger stored up, and today is the day I'm letting it loose. The only problem is now it doesn't feel so good anymore.

My thumb ticks the volume up one more notch on my phone and I take another drag of the cigarette, trying to rekindle my Milo-torture buzz. I forgot how awful these things taste.

"Come on out and hang with us." I paste on a fake smile.

Milo glances back at Zeb. "Try not to ash on the deck. I just stained it."

Zeb puts his hands up and drops his eyes to the wood slats. "Aw. Sorry man. No problem." Then he drops his cigarette into his empty beer bottle and relaxes back in his chair—in Milo's chair.

Milo doesn't look at me again. He slides the door

closed, and a few seconds later the aluminum storm door at the front of the house bangs shut.

I am officially the biggest jerk in the Wilmington metro area—if not the entire state of North Carolina—or the world. Yeah, let's go with that.

AFTER MILO LEAVES, I SEND ZEB ON HIS WAY. HE only came by in the first place to give me three hundred bucks and the rest of my stuff from my car because he found a buyer for it. It just happened to be convenient timing, so I invited him onto the deck for a beer. He really is a nice guy—just not the guy for me.

The cat, the loud music, and the dirty kitchen, however, were premeditated. I was trying to cross off everything on Felicity's original posting for the room rental. No pets, no loud people, no messes. And I did a bang-up job if I do say so myself. I even violated the no-smoking rule, although that required a shower and several rounds with a toothbrush afterward. And I knocked it out of the park with the asshole stipulation, that's for damn sure.

I swipe the last of the crumbs into the trash and go upstairs to pack my bags. I've already cleaned off the deck, mopped the floor, and done the laundry. Haley came for the cat an hour ago, thanking me profusely for taking him off her hands for the afternoon. She and Ted are cat-sitting for one of her veterinary clients for the week, and Ted was threatening to commit felinocide if Lollipop pooped in his shoes one more time. I waited on them at the restaurant last night. We got to chatting since we all know Rayna, and the whole plan just evolved from there.

Today is the first time I've seen Milo since our almost-naked kiss the other night, and I'm betting we won't cross paths again. Of all the times I wondered if each goodbye would be our last, the idea that this will be our last memory is enough to make me cry. But there's plenty of time for that. I need to get out of here before he gets back, and since I'm not on shift tonight, the only logical thing to do is grab a room at some hotel and eat my weight in Oreos. Everything else can wait until the morning.

I finally got my paycheck and all my tip money today, and combined with the cash from Zeb, it's enough to get started at an extended stay hotel or another rental. And it's past time I said goodbye to Milo—even if I don't get to say the word itself.

When I hear my Uber on the gravel outside, I drop the keys to the Tercel and the house on the kitchen table and walk quietly to the door where my bags are waiting.

But when I open the storm door, it's not the Honda my Uber guy is supposed to be driving. It's an unfamiliar gray pick-up truck with Milo in the driver's seat.

I freeze, hoping that maybe if I'm super still he won't notice me, but it's too late. He's staring right at me, and he doesn't drop his gaze once as he opens the door, climbs out, and stalks over to where I'm standing in the open doorway. He's hardly even limping, which tells me right away that he's on some mission and I'm probably not going to like the outcome one bit.

But as he gets closer, he doesn't slow down, instead walking directly into me and pushing me back inside where my back hits the entryway wall, and Milo's mouth hits mine. *Dayum.* That was hot! But that's as far as my brain gets because Milo's tongue is sweeping my lower lip, and I'm opening to him and pulling him to me while I kiss him back with everything I've got. He smells like sawdust and leather and hot man, and I'm very much into all those things right now.

I moan his name into his mouth, hoping it says all the things I want to say. *I'm sorry. I miss you. I don't know how to do this. I need you. I love you. I always have. Don't let me go.* But his name is enough for now.

That is until a car horn blares from the drive, and Milo's head snaps up. "That better fucking not be Zeb." His eyes burn with lust and probably some anger too, but I ignore that part and put up a finger between us indicating I need a second. Then I peel myself off the wall and walk with shaky legs out to the waiting Honda, where I tell the driver I won't be needing his services after all since I'm about to get laid by my childhood crush and to wish me luck. Okay, I don't say those last things, but I'm sure he could read between the lines.

When I get back to the door, Milo is staring down at my gathered bags. "You were leaving."

I bite my lip and nod because it's no use lying. Or putting off the conversation we need to have now that he's kissed my face off instead of murdering me. "Let's go inside." I know this must be what love feels like because I've never in my life been mature enough to put off hot sex for a heart-to-heart. I can practically hear Jenna clapping with pride all the way from Sunview.

Milo nods, and I follow him to the living room. Part of me hopes he'll just throw me on the couch and have his way with me, but I'm not surprised when he takes a seat in the armchair and leaves the couch for me. We both lean forward with our elbows on our knees, and I can't decide if it's to be closer to each other or to be prepared to flee at a moment's notice. It's probably best if I don't overthink it. So I take a breath and go for it.

"I'm sorry. About the cat and the mess and the stupid cigarettes. And about Zeb too. He was the guy who towed my car the day I came to town, and he was just dropping off some stuff for me. There's nothing going on there."

"I know." This is all he says.

"You know?"

"Yeah. Ted told me about the cat earlier this week, I know you hate messes because you called me a monster the other night when I left the cap off the milk, and you turned an interesting shade of green even though you didn't inhale with the cigarette."

I have to admit, this news doesn't make me happy at all. I didn't fool him for a minute, and here I was feeling all horrible and shit. Not to mention, that damn cat ate my favorite lip balm, and they don't make that flavor anymore so I can't even get a new one.

"What about Zeb?" Surely, he at least had a moment of doubt with that one.

Milo's chin dips as he eyes me. "Come on."

"What? He's good looking."

"If you say so. He's also about ten years younger than you, and he has a set of gold balls hanging from his trailer hitch."

"Eww." I probably should have seen that one coming. "Fine then, Mister Smartypants. I'm taking back my sorry." Milo is looking entirely too smug, but this just makes him grin. "Wait, if you knew all this, why did you storm out of here?"

"Because." His eyes narrow at me, and his smugness subsides.

I gesture for him to expand on that.

"It doesn't mean I wasn't pissed. You've been avoiding me for two days, and when you finally decide to talk to me, it's covered up in all that bullshit? Not cool."

I chew my lip for a second. "Okay. That makes sense. You can have your sorry back."

He exhales and shakes his head. "Just for the record, I'm sorry too."

"What are you sorry for? Wait, you didn't bring Lollipop back, did you?" My back straightens and my eyes scan the room for the cat.

"Fuck no. I hate cats."

"Phew. There's something seriously wrong with that thing."

Milo waits until he has my eyes again. "I'm sorry for the other night. For letting you walk out without talking about it."

Even though I know this is the real issue we need to discuss, I suddenly have cold feet. As in, ice blocks. I stand up before I can think and dart over to the kitchen.

"Where are you going?"

"To get..." My eyes hit the loaf of bread in the corner. "Toast."

"Toast?"

"Yes. I'm starving. Must be the cigarettes." I thunk my forehead with the heel of my hand. What the hell am I talking about?

"Does it have to be right now?"

"Yeah. I'll just be a minute." I shove two slices in the toaster and press the lever down, trying to think of what I'm going to say. Do I spill my guts or wait to see what he has to say first? What if I tell him I love him and he says "Thanks?" But if I let him talk first, he might say something I don't want to hear. Maybe he's going to tell me we should just be friends with bene-fits while I'm in town. Maybe he's planning on screwing me and then locking me in a room with Lollipop as revenge for today. Maybe he's going to ask me never to leave and to stay with him forever. My heart does this pitter-patter thing and drops some hot goo in my belly. That's the only way I can explain it. Love is so weird.

"Jill."

I jump at Milo's voice and turn around to find him standing only a few feet away. How did he get so close without me hearing him? Oh, that's right, I was busy obsessing over all the horrible possibilities before I got distracted by the love goo. God, he's handsome.

"I meant what I said about not wanting you to regret anything between us. But I remembered something." I'm too freaked to speak, so he continues, "You said your heart was different with me."

"I did?" Not that it isn't true, but when did I say that? Oh God, I must have been more drunk than I thought.

His hands are shoved in his pockets, and he looks like he did at eighteen. "You did. I was standing in the street, and you looked over at me with all these tears pouring down your face."

What is he talking about? I don't remember going out to the street the other night at all. I just went up to my room and alternately cursed his name and cried.

"You said, 'I thought you were different, Milo.' You were so mad, and you wouldn't let me explain." He shakes his head. "And then you looked at me, and I swear I actually saw your heart break, and you said, 'My heart was different with you. But now it will hate you forever.'"

My nose starts to sting with tears because I remember with perfect clarity what he's talking about.

"Milo. I didn't mean the last part. Well, I did at the time, but I was sixteen."

The corner of his mouth lifts. "I know. Well, I *didn't* at the time, but I was eighteen."

"I was a bit of a drama queen, wasn't I?" I allow myself a ghost of a smile.

He steps closer and tucks some loose hair behind my ear. My entire body shivers. "It's one of your many charms."

"Are you saying I'm still a drama queen?" My voice shakes a little, but I need to keep up the sass to preserve my sanity.

"Were we in the same house a couple hours ago?"

"Right. Good point." My eyes drop to my feet. "I can't believe you remembered what I said verbatim."

"I remember a lot of things where you're concerned."

"I always have strived to be hard to forget." I go for flippant, but my heart is threatening to crack my ribs.

Instead of playing along with my little procrastination game, Milo cuts to the chase. "Did you mean the other part?"

I swallow hard because this is the moment. I can be a coward, or I can reach for what I want, get my hopes up, jump off that cliff, and trust that fate is on my side and that everything has led to this.

So I lift my head and look Milo straight in his gorgeous multi-colored eyes and go for it. "My heart has always been different with you. It always will be."

CHAPTER TWENTY-SEVEN

MILO

Something releases in my chest and it has me feeling like I could float right up to the ceiling or go out and run a marathon. But I don't try either one. Instead, I reach out and cup Jill's face with both hands, holding it gently and feeling the warmth of her smooth skin sink into my trembling fingers. Her eyes watch me closely.

"That's good to hear, Sunshine." I drop a soft kiss on her lips, and she sighs, making me want to sweep my tongue inside and kiss her breathless. But she needs to know I'm all in. "And just so you know, my heart's yours to do whatever you want with it. Always has been."

Her lips curve up, and I move in for another kiss, this one longer and deeper. Jill's hands run across my shoulders and then up where they thread through my hair. I press her into the counter, and I know she can feel how turned on I am, but I still need to get closer, so I run my hands over to the backs of her thighs and hoist her up onto the counter. She circles my ass with her long legs and locks them behind me, pressing her center against me and making me groan out loud.

"Fuck, I need you," I murmur against her lips.

This makes her squeeze her legs and pull me in even closer. "Me too."

I don't want her legs to ever let go, but as I've said before, I try my best not to be stupid. And the stupidest thing I could do right now would be to drop her ass on the floor while trying to make my way blind to the bedroom. I barely got her in the front door that first night without my leg giving out, so I'm not taking any chances.

I give her ass a good squeeze and ignore the insults my dick throws at me as I pull back and grab her hand. "Come on."

She hops off the counter and runs her tongue across her bottom lip, making me think maybe taking her right here wouldn't be a bad idea. But I need to take my time with her. This is Jill. I'm not rushing through anything with her.

That doesn't mean I don't haul ass to my bedroom, though. She laughs at me and my less-than-smooth moves, but she shuts up real quick when I push her back on the bed and pull my shirt off. She rolls on her stomach before crawling on the bed toward me, nothing but pure, carnal want in her eyes. I can work with this.

Her hand slides up my bare skin from the waistband of my jeans, over my stomach, and on up to cover my left pec. I shiver when she leans forward and traces her tongue just above my navel and up to my sternum. My dick is hard as a rock and one impatient bastard, but

I've got a long list of things I want to do with this woman.

I reach toward her and strip her of her long-sleeved shirt, interrupting her tongue's journey across my skin. But that's okay because it's my turn.

"Let me see you."

Her eyes lift to me and hold my gaze while she sits back on her heels and reaches behind her to unclasp her bra. Her gorgeous breasts tumble forward, tipped with tight pink nipples the same color as her perfect lips. She tangles my hair in her fingers when I bend forward over the bed and take one firm tip in my mouth. My tongue swirls over the tight tip as I taste her skin and moan my satisfaction.

I move forward on the bed, pushing her down to her back while I get my proper introduction to her lush tits. She's soft and round and so sensitive, pulling at my hair and wrapping her legs around me to pull me closer. I have to concentrate to keep myself from rutting at her through our jeans like some kid.

Once I've tasted and touched every inch of her breasts, I move my mouth down her stomach, tickling her with my beard and dropping kisses and licks along the way until I come to her waistband. The button releases with a flick of my fingers, and then I'm pulling down both her jeans and her panties at the same time. I almost pass out when I see the tiny strip of dark hair and find her absolutely bare everywhere else.

"Fuck." I breathe out.

"Yes, please," she says on a half giggle as she pulls at my shoulder, trying to get me to come back up.

But I'm not going anywhere. Her jeans, panties, boots, and socks land on the floor half a second later, and I'm swiping my tongue up through her folds from bottom to top and drinking in her flavor. She moans and thrusts her hips up toward my face, and I circle her clit with my tongue before lowering again and thrusting it inside her. I can feel her muscles tightening around my tongue as it strokes her, and I can't wait to feel her around my cock. But I'm not done eating her yet. I continue to lick, nibble, and tease with my fingers and tongue until she moans a series of filthy curses and spasms around me. I'm pretty sure she takes a chunk of my hair with her, but I don't give a single shit. I'll go bald if it means I get to make her come like this another couple hundred times.

"Milo." She pulls at my shoulders again, and this time I obey, pausing only to wipe my beard with the sheet before settling myself over her gloriously naked body.

"You're so beautiful." I kiss her lips. "And you taste like heaven."

She goes in for another kiss, not shy to taste herself on me, and if that's not a fucking turn on, I don't know what is. I let her flip me over to my back and straddle me, and I'm rewarded with the sight of her naked breasts hovering over my mouth and her wild waves of hair falling all around us. I bite her nipple, and she shrieks, grinding herself down on my crotch and making me see stars.

And then she's lifting herself up and unbuckling my belt. I watch as she strips my pants and boxers off and my cock springs free, hard and ready. My brain threatens to shut down when she bends down and licks me from base to tip and then circles her tongue around the head.

"If I don't fuck you now, I might actually die." My tone is dead serious, but she just smiles at me around her tongue as it circles one last time. This is, hands down, the greatest moment of my life. No contest.

But I change my mind about three seconds later when Jill holds my stiff cock in her hand and lowers herself onto it, letting it part her folds and sink deep inside her. She moans and closes her eyes, dropping her head back as she fully seats herself on me. She's silk and honey and heat all around me, holding me so tight I can hardly catch my breath.

And then we both start to move. I thrust my hips up, and she meets my movements as I withdraw and surge back in again and again, first slowly and then faster and faster as I grit my teeth and she whimpers. Her tits bounce madly with our movements, and my fingers and palms massage and squeeze them while she writhes over me. I lift to take a nipple in my mouth and bite and lick until I'm driven half insane with the pleasure of it all.

My balls start to tighten, but I'm not ready for this to be over, so I gently draw her to the side and move us so I'm settled over her, between her soft thighs, where I slide back in.

"You feel so good," I tell her, and she shuts me up with her lips on mine, smiling against my mouth.

I continue my slow thrusts while we kiss and run our hands all over each other, and then she wraps her thighs around me again, and it's no use. I quicken my movements, surging in and out as the pressure builds and she meets my every movement with her own. Her whimpers get louder, and I can feel her begin to tighten and spasm around my cock, so I don't try to hold back any longer, speeding my movements until my own release takes over.

I'm panting into her collarbone, and her hands continue to stroke my back as I finally still on top of her, both of us spent and ready to pass out. At least I know I am.

But leave it to Jill to have the energy to speak.

"I'm happy the over-achiever in you is alive and well."

I smile into her skin. "Go big or go home, right?"

Her laughter wraps around me as her legs do the same, and I roll us over while holding her right there.

"Thanksgiving? I totally forgot that was next week." Jill sits cross-legged on my bed wearing just my shirt and playing with the ends of her hair.

I've just lost my mind and asked her to Thanksgiving at my mother's after having the best sex of my life. This is what sex does to a man's brain. It scrambles it until we can't think straight to save our lives. I doubt I could even do simple math at this point.

It's impossible to tell if Jill is horrified or just amused at the fact that my mind jumped directly from sex to holidays with my mother. I want to assure her I'm disturbed enough for the both of us, but she saves me.

"I'd love to meet your mom. She won't think it's weird if I come along, will she?"

I let out the breath I was holding and drop my hand to her bare knee. "Definitely not. She's been on my case since I called for her chicken and dumplings recipe." I can't believe I'm still talking about this while I'm naked and Jill is only wearing a shirt, but what's done is done.

She leans forward and kisses my chest, letting the neck of the shirt fall forward so I can see her tits underneath. My dick starts getting ideas again. "Oooh. You told your mom about me?" She's laughing softly and it tickles.

"Well, not exactly. If I remember right, you pretty much despised me right about then."

This makes her laugh some more, and she bites me. "Sounds legit." She moves up and drops a quick kiss on my lips. "But I don't despise you right now. In fact, I'm feeling all sorts of positive things about you."

I can't resist pulling her down for another kiss, this one longer. "I'm glad."

She straightens again and peers down at me where I'm propped up on a pillow, not bothering to cover myself. It took a long time, but I haven't been self-conscious of my scars in quite a few years. They are what they are, and besides the pain and trouble they cause, I don't give them much thought anymore. Jill's eyes run over my body, and I don't miss the glint in them. If she's even half as turned on by me as I am by her, then I figure I'm doing all right. She brings her eyes to mine again, and they go a little soft.

"Thanks for coming back for me today. I wouldn't have blamed you if you'd stayed angry."

I reach up and run a finger down her cheek. "I just had to blow off a little steam, but I knew before I left that I wasn't going to let you get away."

She rolls her eyes. "Oh, right. I forgot you were onto

me the whole time. I should have known you wouldn't buy the whole Lollipop thing."

"Well, I can't say I don't wish you'd just talked to me, but that whole scene did clear some things up for me."

I take her hand and pull her a little closer. She goes down on one elbow next to me, the shirt riding up and making it hard to concentrate.

"How's that?" she asks.

"I guess I figured if you'd go to all the trouble of setting up such an elaborate revenge strategy, you must have been really angry."

"I was. I was so mad at you. And myself, but mostly you." Her finger jabs my chest while she tries not to smile.

"Which told me that when I pushed you away the other night over the whole wine and sex thing, you were genuinely hurt. It wasn't just a flesh wound to your pride or some minor inconvenience to your raging libido."

I'm quick enough to grab her this time when she goes to punch my arm, and I push her to her back, my hands holding hers above her head. "I'm being serious." I smile at her. She just scowls up at me, which makes me smile even harder.

My head lowers and I plant one on her before letting her go and finishing what I was trying to say before she got all violent on me. "If it was 'just sex' to you, there wouldn't have been much to get upset about, now would there?"

She loses the scowl and goes back up on her elbow, kissing the scar on my jaw—the one that's still visible through my beard. "That's because it's not just sex. Not with you."

"I know." I touch her cheek again and can't believe how lucky I am to be lying here in this bed with her. But I'm also realistic. "But there are still a lot of things that could screw everything up." My head sinks back into my pillow again. "I'm a temperamental asshole."

"So am I." She grins.

"We fight all the time."

Her head tilts to the side. "Duh. Because we're good at it." I know she's trying to make me laugh.

"And you're leaving."

That one sits out there for a few seconds. She doesn't have a quick answer for it like she did for the others. But it's worth the wait when she finally speaks.

"I don't have to."

CHAPTER TWENTY-EIGHT

"I should have brought my *Uncanny X-men* #308." Ted frowns at me, and I shift my eyes to Haley for an explanation. She looks pretty and festive in her fall colors and perfectly matching auburn hair swept into an updo.

"It's probably best not to ask," she tells me from the corner of her mouth, not even attempting to drop her voice at all.

"Hey. It's a Thanksgiving classic. Where's Felicity when I need her?" Ted mutters and then wanders off to the kitchen.

Haley grabs my arm and laughs. "Don't worry. He'll get over it. I'm apparently doing an awful job standing in for Felicity with all the comic book talk. I've been told nodding my head doesn't count as being an active participant in a conversation."

"I don't know how you do it. I never understood the fascination."

"That makes two of us. But, hey, when a man is good in bed, you make certain allowances."

I almost choke on my wine, and Haley laughs. "Warn a girl, would ya? But, as your new friend, I'm happy to hear you're being properly taken care of." I pat her arm. Ted is definitely a little on the nerdy side, but damn if that smile and that ass don't make a girl look twice.

The doorbell rings, and I see Rayna and Bran walk into the living room a few seconds later. We're all at Milo's mom's house for Thanksgiving dinner, and it's turning out to be fun. His mom, Delia, and his stepdad, Morris, are a super cute couple. Morris obviously dotes on her, and Delia strikes me as a free spirit. I'm thinking Milo got some of his independence from her.

She didn't make any particular fuss over me when we were introduced, and I was happy about that. This thing between Milo and me may have been a long time coming, but it's still new. The last thing I want is to draw all sorts of attention to our relationship and have people examining it through a microscope.

But it was really no use when it came to Rayna and Bran. They came over for drinks the other night, and it took Bran approximately two minutes before he pointed at both of us and announced, "You're totally boning each other." Rayna gasped and smacked him, I laughed into my hand, and Milo threw one of the brand-new throw pillows at him.

Otherwise, we've been keeping things pretty quiet. Which isn't hard since we pretty much spend any time when we're not working in bed. Or on the couch. Or in the bathroom. And then there was that one time on the deck. That was HOT. Neither Milo and I nor the neighbors will forget that one anytime soon.

Suffice it to say, things are going swimmingly. I even bit the bullet and called Jenna to tell her I wouldn't be back for Thanksgiving. She was disappointed and a bit worried at first until I told her Milo and I had worked out our differences and I'd be spending the holiday sitting on his face. Well, I didn't actually say that part, but I'm pretty sure I can make it happen by the time we go to sleep tonight.

She was excited for me, and I could hear in her voice that she was relieved, so I must have sounded happy. I haven't told her yet about my decision to stay here, but I will eventually. And she knows me better than anyone, so she probably already guessed.

I did finally share with her what happened with Hank and me and how I realized I'd been holding myself back from men. Predictably, she reacted the same way Milo did when I confessed my regret at being the Mike in all my relationships. It's a relief to leave that chapter behind because there's no holding back anything with Milo.

I promised her I'd be there for Christmas, and I'm hoping Milo and maybe even Felicity will join me, but I've been away for a long time, and my family will always be my home. Well, one of them.

Rayna waves me over, and Haley heads to the kitchen for more wine while I go hug Rayna and tell her she looks hot.

"Hey, if you guys aren't too stuffed after this, you should stop by the restaurant later. Camille and Andie are boycotting the holiday and getting together tonight for leftover lamb and all the desserts on the menu. There was also talk of watching a movie, but don't let that scare you."

I laugh at that, and then Milo comes to say hi. He's clearly too accustomed to it just being the two of us because his hand goes directly to my butt and I have to wiggle away before everyone gets a show. And that's definitely not how I want my first time meeting his mom to go.

"Sorry." His word choice is right, but his tone and his eyes say the exact opposite. I'm one crazy-lucky girl.

"Everybody to the dining room," Delia announces, and we all start making our way there. It's a bit cramped, but we're all friends, so it doesn't matter. And, besides, it just means I get to feel Milo up under the table.

"Who's missing?" Milo gestures to a remaining empty seat and place setting, but the doorbell rings again a split second later.

"I'll be right back." Delia leaves the room, and we all busy ourselves filling water and wine glasses. The scent of roasted turkey and fresh bread fills the room and has my mouth watering.

"Here she is." Delia is back, and she's followed by a blond woman wearing a conservative burgundy dress and carrying a bottle of wine.

"Leah." The surprise in Milo's voice is clear, which is the only thing that saves his foot from my heel. Because it's a universal rule that you always inform your current girlfriend of the expected presence of an old flame at any upcoming function. There are no exceptions to this rule, and excuses such as "I forgot" or "it's no big deal" are never deemed acceptable and will immediately result in either bodily harm, a drink in the face, or a nasty case of blue balls. Sometimes all three.

But Milo is just as surprised as I am, which is good because I'm really enjoying this wine and don't want to waste it.

My eyes immediately flash back to study the woman more thoroughly. She's pretty with straight, shiny hair hanging just past her shoulders and very subtle make-up. There's not a hair out of place, and I can tell from her toned arms alone that she takes meticulous care of her body. A quick glance around shows I'm not the only one checking her out. Rayna is doing her own examination and doesn't look impressed. It makes me want to laugh and hug her at the same time. I don't dare look at Milo.

"Hey, Milo," Leah says in a casual yet confident tone, smiling politely at all of us. "Vicky and Bill are on a cruise, so your mom invited me over."

Delia puts a hand at Leah's back and guides her toward the empty seat. "We ran into each other the other day at the grocery store and got to talking. Here, dear. Have a seat." They both sit, and introductions are made around the table.

We pass the dishes around, each of us taking healthy portions of the delicious-looking turkey, stuffing, and all the usual Thanksgiving favorites. Compliments are given to the chef, and everyone engages in small talk around bites of food and sips of wine.

Leah is nice. Polite. I really don't have anything negative to say about her, apart from her decision to put only vegetables on her plate. But I can tell Milo's uncomfortable because his leg won't stop moving under the table.

"So how do you all know each other?" Haley asks, looking between Leah and Delia.

"She's my boss," Milo blurts out and then grabs his water glass like it's attempting to evade capture.

Several pairs of eyes dart to him and Leah in turn.

"Well, technically, that's true. But we've been friends for a long time," Leah says, trying to make up for his bluntness.

"Why didn't you tell me you were working for the diving school again?" Delia frowns at Milo, who simply shrugs.

"I guess I forgot."

My eyes narrow at him. How could he forget to tell his mom? Even I knew about his job from the first day he got it, and we weren't even on speaking terms.

Delia watches Milo too, and then she sends a polite smile to Haley. "We all go way back. Leah's family owns a diving business, and Milo used to work for them when he was in high school."

"That sounds like an awesome after-school job." Haley's face brightens. "I feel like a sucker for working at Taco Bell."

A few of us chime in with similar work regrets, and I relax again, the awkwardness having passed.

Until it returns with a vengeance.

"Milo has always known what he wanted to do," Delia chimes in with obvious pride in her voice. "He's never let anything get in his way."

"Even the law," Leah says into her water glass, loud enough for everyone but Morris to hear.

Milo freezes next to me.

The table falls silent and Delia's smile drops. "Yes, well, your family was very understanding." She's holding onto her hostess hat with a death grip at this point if the vein in her forehead is anything to go by. She obviously wasn't expecting Leah to go all passive-aggressive like that. After all, it's usually relatives who ruin family holidays, not random acquaintances. I mean, come on, Morris hasn't had a chance to chime in all evening, and everyone knows it's the old quiet guys who drop the biggest bombs at the holiday dinner table.

But Morris will have to wait because Milo stands, pushing his chair back. "Leah, may I have a word with you in the kitchen?"

Leah actually has the nerve to point to herself and widen her eyes like she can't believe it's her name he said. Then she smiles politely and sets her napkin on the table. "If you'll excuse me for just one moment."

Milo stalks to the kitchen, and Leah follows more slowly. None of us but Morris even bother to pretend we're still interested in the meal.

And either Milo has forgotten the size of this house or he just doesn't care, but at this point, they may as well have just stayed at the table because we can all hear every word.

"What are you doing here?" That's obviously Milo.

"Your mother invited me. Why? What's the problem?" Leah, of course.

"The problem is you're my boss."

"Oh, please, you never let that keep you from trying to blur the lines."

Bran coughs, and several of us shush him.

"And I like to think we're friends," Leah continues.

"That was a long time ago."

"Look. I did you a favor by giving you a job. You don't think I knew you were back in town, getting turned down by every other outfit for twenty miles? I'd think you'd be a little more grateful."

A couple people grimace at that one, and then there are several seconds of silence from the kitchen. My jaw starts to go tight, but finally Leah speaks, her voice much sharper than before. "Oh, come on. I thought we were on the same page."

Did she just...? Oh no, you don't, bitch. Haley reaches out and presses on my arm when I move to get up. She's probably right.

Leah keeps talking. "If you're going to be a child about it, I'll leave. No big deal."

"I think that would be best." I can practically picture Milo's face, and I kind of want to high-five him before showing Leah to the door.

But she's not done. "You know, you should be more grateful. Not just to me but to my parents and yours too."

Bitch, he just told you to go home.

Milo responds, "I already thanked you for giving me a job, and I thanked your parents a long time ago for not pressing charges. You worry about you and let me worry about me."

Bran makes a hissing sound, and I can hear him

mutter, "Dang, son, are you trying to get fired?" Rayna glares at him.

But we all shut up then because Leah barks out a laugh, and it's not a nice one. "You still don't know, do you?"

Delia suddenly shoots up to standing and shoves her chair back, throwing out an apology and trying to scramble around the gathered guests in their chairs.

But Leah keeps talking in the kitchen. "Why do you think your mom invited me over after all these years?" When there's no response, she continues, "You don't know how much time we spent together trying to keep your ass out of jail and all of us from going broke because you decided to get wasted and try killing yourself."

Morris stands too, and everyone scoots in or stands to let them by as they hustle toward the kitchen. But it's too late because the damage has been done.

"What else." Milo's voice is a demand, not a request.

"My parents' insurance went through the roof because of your stunt, and we were going to lose the business. Your dad mortgaged his house and sold his half of the fishing charter to pay us back."

"That's enough, Leah!" We're all surprised to hear Morris's voice boom through the kitchen and out to the dining room where we're gathered. "It's not yours to share."

His voice acts like a catalyst, and we all snap out of our quasi-zombie modes. Everybody starts gathering dirty dishes and doing whatever we can to tidy without going into the kitchen. We purposely talk loudly about anything that pops into our heads while we pretend World War III isn't threatening to start in the kitchen.

Leah stalks in the room and grabs her purse from the floor by her seat before hauling ass out the front door without another word.

We all look at each other, unsure of what to do. We want to give Milo, Delia, and Morris privacy, but we don't want to be rude and just leave. So we make a compromise by grabbing our drinks and heading out to the front patio.

"Not to be insensitive, but that was the most exciting Thanksgiving dinner I've ever been to," Rayna says once we're all seated on the porch.

We smile and do a silent toast because she's not wrong.

I want to go to Milo, but I think this is one situation where it should just be him and his family. For now, at least. There will be plenty of time later for us to talk about it.

"I still can't believe his dad did that and never even told him," Rayna says before glancing over at Haley and Ted. "They didn't have a great relationship."

We all sit on that for a few moments, and then Bran speaks up. "Although, it kind of makes sense when you think about it."

"Well, sure." Ted shrugs. "No matter the trouble in a relationship, parents tend to always look after their kids. Ideally, that is."

"Yeah, but that's not what I meant." Bran sets his beer glass on the patio next to him. "Milo has always gone above and beyond for other people, even though he pretends not to give a shit. And he had to have gotten that from somewhere. Looks like his dad was that way too. We just didn't know it."

"I could see that. Milo saved that girl from getting killed by that boat engine," I offer up.

Bran points at me. "Exactly. He didn't think about his own safety. He saw her in trouble and dove in headfirst."

"Wow. I didn't know that." Haley covers her mouth in surprise.

"And remember that asshole Shawn back in high school?" Rayna smiles and looks at me. "Milo got suspended for knocking this guy out after he spread a rumor that I gave him a blow job." She raises her finger. "Which I did not."

"That guy was such a dick." Bran shakes his head and frowns before putting an arm around Rayna. "You know I would have done it if I'd gotten there first, right?"

Rayna kisses his cheek. "I know."

Bran grins, and then he turns my way again. "Oh, and he gave up his dive business to keep those actor assholes from fucking with Jill."

Rayna smacks him, and he throws his arms out. "What? She says 'fuck' all the time. And you just said 'asshole.'"

The sound of them bickering fades as all the blood in my body rushes to my head. "What did you just say?"

"Fine." Bran glares at Rayna. "I'll stop throwing f-bombs at family holidays if it means that much to you."

I feel around by my side for a flat surface and set my wine glass down, never taking my eyes from Bran. "No.

What did you say about Milo's dive business and the actors?"

"Those guys from *Brothers of Moon Bay*. I stopped watching that show after we shoved those assho—I mean jerks—into the water that summer." He turns to Ted, and I feel the blood buzzing across my skull. "Oh, man, you should have seen it. These pretty-boy Hollywood pricks were talking shit about Jill, and Milo comes tearing around, pulling one of them by the shirt, and then he kicks him square in the chest over the side of the boat. Guy didn't know what hit him." Bran puffs his chest out a little, but it's like I'm watching him through a cloudy filter. "I took care of the other one. Gave him the old one-two punch."

"What did they say?" My voice is louder than I intended, and everyone turns to me. Rayna stands and walks over, clearly understanding something is very wrong. She squats down and puts her hand on my back, but I'm still focused on Bran.

"What do you mean?" Bran's brow is furrowed, and he's gone still.

My voice is quieter this time because it's caught in my throat. "What did Noah and Tyler say to make him do that?"

Bran shakes his head. "Jill, you don't want to hear that. It's not important. You know what happened."

"No, I don't." My nose stings, and my eyes fill with tears. If what Bran's saying is true, then I don't know what to do. What to think. If what he's saying is true, then Milo ruined his chance at his dream... for me.

I stand and stumble forward. Rayna grabs my arm,

but I shake her off. I need to get out of here. I need to think.

"Jill, it's okay." Rayna's voice comes from behind me, but I don't stop. I run down the porch steps and to the sidewalk and keep on going, ignoring the sound of my name being called.

CHAPTER TWENTY-NINE

Twelve Years Ago

"So when is this mysterious Milo showing up? I'm so curious to meet the reason we've hardly seen you these past weeks." Jenna sets down her book and grins at me from the bed.

"Whatever. And you already met him." I pull a brush through my hair and frown at her through the mirror. She's way too pleased about this.

"For two seconds. I'm just glad I'll get to introduce myself properly and without sitting on his lunch."

I turn around to face her, lowering the brush. "Just promise me you won't fawn all over him. He hates being the center of attention."

This makes her laugh. "Then you two are perfect for each other."

"There's nothing going on between us. We're just friends." I'm quick to shut that down. The last thing I need is Jenna trying to "help" where my crush on Milo is concerned. I go back to brushing my hair and ignoring her.

The doorbell to the condo rings a minute later, and the brush drops to the floor with a clatter as I try wrestling my way in front of Jenna to get to the door first. I'm going to kill her if she embarrasses me.

"Stop it or you're going to have a black eye at your wedding," I say through clenched teeth as she laughs her ass off and finally lets me go. I take advantage of my hard-won freedom and almost slide on the tile as I barely beat my mom to the door and swing it open.

"Hey!" I'm breathing hard, and half my hair is in my face—so much for the trouble I took getting ready. But I don't care because Milo is standing in the condo doorway with his hands in his jeans pockets and a sky-blue polo shirt that brings out the blue swirls in his eyes. He's wearing a nervous half-smile, and I want to kiss it off his face, but I manage to get ahold of myself and invite him in instead.

"Hello, you must be Milo." My mom steps forward, extending her hand, and Milo shakes it.

"Nice to meet you, Mrs. Holloway." His voice is a little hesitant, and when my mom turns to lead us into the living room, I can't help but nudge him with my elbow.

"They're not going to stab you and eat you for dinner. Relax."

Jenna chooses that moment to saunter into the room. "Milo, it's nice to officially meet you. I'm Jenna. But I'm sure you knew that after all the times we've been on the phone." Luckily, she's smiling and being normal instead of offering to show him my naked baby pictures.

"Nice to meet you too. Milo Papatonis." They shake hands, and he refrains from telling her he's a badass. Then it's on to the open living room where Milo meets my dad. Everyone is behaving and not asking a bunch of prying questions, so I begin to breathe a little easier.

When I called this morning to invite Milo to dinner, he sounded weird, and I regretted it immediately. But I told myself he'd probably been out really late with Noah and Tyler on their dive and was just tired. Which also explains why he put me off when I asked how the dive went.

But my parents insisted they meet the guy I've been hanging out with, and what was I going to say? Making excuses would only get them on my case, and it's not like it's that big of a deal anyway. Sure, he's been helping me lie to them, but he's a rule-breaker by nature. He said so himself.

Dinner with people I love shouldn't be a chore. But since we met, it's mostly just been me and Milo in our own little bubble. And I know him. I know he gets quiet when he watches the ocean. I know people littering on the beach makes him mad. I know when he hears Aerosmith, he can't help himself from nodding along. I know the furrow in his brow means he's taking his time choosing his words. I know he can't pass by a homeless person without saying hello. I know when he forgets to favor his leg it's because his emotions have taken over. And I know when he's backed into a corner, the only thing he knows to do is lash out.

And I don't want to put him in a situation where any one of his actions or words, or lack thereof, might be misconstrued by the people who love me. But I also know my family are good, loving people who want what's best for me. And my friendship with Milo is just that.

By the time we sit down to dinner, he seems to have relaxed a bit and even managed to laugh at one of my dad's lame jokes. My mom went all out and got lobsters for dinner, saying we may as well take advantage of the coast, so we all dig in and laugh at each other moaning over the rich, tasty meal. Jenna asks about local gems that tourists might not know about, and that gets Milo talking about some of his favorite spots, including the cove where we practiced with his diving equipment.

"Milo's teaching me how to SCUBA dive," I tell them, picking up my water glass.

"Well, not officially," he's quick to insert. "And only in shallow water until she passes all the usual tests."

"Wow, that sounds like fun," my mom says. "It's nice to have a pro like you as a friend." She sends him a warm smile, and I reach over and squeeze Milo's knee under the table.

"He's even opening his own private diving business. He has his master diving certification and everything." I know I sound too proud, but I can't help it.

Milo spills a little water down his shirt, and I eye him curiously. He sets down his glass and rubs at the spot with his napkin. "One day." The quick glance he throws my way tells me he wants me to drop it, and I realize he's afraid I'm going to forget myself and start talking about Noah and Tyler—which would surely have everyone suspicious as to how in the world I know two Hollywood stars.

I smile back at him and nod, trying to tell him without words that I got it.

"You seem to have accomplished quite a bit already for someone so young." My dad looks up from where he's pulling the meat from his lobster tail.

Milo shrugs, never one to brag about himself, and I lean forward to do it for him when his phone rings. All eyes turn to him, and his face reddens immediately. "I'm so sorry. I forgot to turn it off." He reaches for his back pocket and pulls out the phone.

"That's okay, I never turn mine off," Jenna says before popping a bite of asparagus in her mouth.

"That's because you can't stand the thought of missing a call from Mike," my mom teases her, while Milo fumbles for the volume button with nervous fingers.

I pull the phone from his hand to help him silence it while also taking advantage of the opportunity to give Jenna a hard time of my own. "She sleeps with it under her pillow." I roll my eyes and then drop them to the phone where I see a very familiar number. It's Dana, the new P.A. for *Brothers of Moon Bay*. I gape at Milo, and he drops his eyes down to the phone too.

Then his mouth turns down, and he tries pulling the phone back from me. I yank it closer and narrow my eyes at him while my family talks on about Mike and Jenna, oblivious to the battle raging on our side of the table. I need to answer this call. It could be about the L.A. audition, and I'm not missing out on that. Sure, I can understand Milo not wanting to be rude at the dinner table, especially with this being my parents' first time meeting him, but I'm taking this call.

I push to standing, my chair scraping loudly against the tile floor. "Be right back." I'm in the bedroom with the door shut in two seconds.

"Hello." I'm afraid I've just missed Dana, and my finger hovers over the disconnect button when I hear her voice and sink to the edge of the bed in relief.

"J.J.?"

"Yeah. It's me. Sorry I took so long to get to the phone."

"That's okay." Dana clears her throat, and I cross my fingers.

"What's up? Do you need me down at the set?"

"No, that's not it. Listen." She sighs, and a little thread of doubt starts weaving its way through my stomach. "We're going to have to let you go."

"What? Why?" My head is hot, and my vision goes fuzzy.

"You lied about your age. You gave us a fake ID, J.J."

I open my mouth to deny it, but I can't. Because I did exactly what she said.

"Look, didn't you know that all you needed was a letter of consent from your parents?" She's being nice to me. Nicer than I deserve. But what good will it do to tell her my parents wouldn't have signed it?

"Yeah."

"Well, I'm sorry, but I can't do anything about it at this point. We really like you, and I wish you the best, okay?"

"Thanks," I manage, but it's weak, and the tears are

already spilling down my cheeks. I close the phone and drop it to my lap.

There's a knock at the bedroom door. "Jill?" Jenna cracks the door open and peeks her head in. When she sees my face, she rushes over to me. "What's wrong? What happened?" She glances down at the phone with a furrowed brow. "Who were you talking to?"

"Nobody," I answer on a sob, and she pulls me into her arms and starts stroking my back.

"It'll be okay. Just tell me what's wrong."

"Jill?" Milo's voice comes from a few feet away, and I can hear the worry in his tone. Without thinking, I pull from Jenna's arms and stumble over to him where I throw my arms around his waist and bury my face in his neck. He doesn't hesitate to wrap his arms around me and pull me in tight, making shushing noises and running his hand over my hair in a soothing rhythm.

I hardly even notice the sound of the door closing and Milo walking me over to the bed. He sits us down and draws me away by my upper arms so he can see my face. I know I'm a mess, but I don't care.

"What happened?"

"Th-the-they fired me." A new round of tears starts, and I swipe at my eyes with my knuckles.

"Shit." He reaches up and strokes my hair again, and I want to sink into him and pretend this day never happened.

"They found out my real age."

Milo's nostrils flare, and it's just like him to get pissed off on my behalf.

I try a shrug and a sad laugh. "It's my own fault. I'm

the one who lied in the first place." My fingers attempt to smooth down his collar where my tears—and probably a good amount of snot—have soaked it.

"It's my fault," Milo says.

My eyes shoot up to his face, and my mouth opens to refute it, but his neck is stiff and his jaw is clenched tight, and there's something in his eyes I know I've seen before. It's regret. It's the same look he had on the pier when he called me a kid and said he was only hanging out with me because he was bored.

"Wh-what?" I don't want to believe him.

He drops his hand from my hair to the bed. "It's my fault. I told Noah and Tyler you were sixteen."

I stand so fast black spots float in my vision and have to grip the duvet so I don't fall over. "What? Why would you do that?"

He stands too, and my head tilts up so I can watch his eyes as my vision clears. I expect the regret to still be there, for him to tell me that he and the guys were just shooting the shit and it slipped out by mistake. That he's sorry. But the regret is gone, and sharp anger is in its place.

I've seen this expression before too. But only once. It was outside the corner store when he glared at me like I was scum and called me an entitled rich girl. I can see right through him and into his darkness as I watch his eyes get harder and his lips curl around his next words. "I had to."

I let go of the bed and back up a step. He had to? That doesn't make any sense. Those words and this expression can't be coming from the Milo I know. But maybe I never knew him after all.

"Get out." I try to make my words ice, but a tremor gives me away.

"No," he says and takes a step forward. "I need to—"

"Get out!" This time it's a scream, and I can see him freeze through a new haze of tears. I turn and race from the bedroom to the front hall, needing to increase the distance between me and this stranger before I go completely insane.

I hear Jenna and my mom call my name, and I glance over my shoulder to see Milo coming down the hall. He loses his balance and glances off the entry table, sending a figure of a pelican crashing to the tile. My mom shouts in surprise, and Jenna dashes forward, but I'm out the door, intent on getting as far as possible from the boy who just broke my heart.

Gripping the railing tight, I make my way down the stairs without falling and sprint out to the sidewalk. I have no idea where I'm going, and I don't care.

"Jill!" Milo's voice echoes behind me.

"Go away!" I yell, running even faster, my sandals slapping the sidewalk. I'm hoping his leg slows him down enough for me to duck down a side street and lose him, but he's been getting stronger and stronger, and I can hear him still chasing me. I cross the street, not bothering to check for traffic, but my side is cramping and my lungs are burning by the time I reach the opposite sidewalk. The tears keep coming, and I'm so tired. I stop at a lamp post and lean my forehead against it, gasping for air.

"Jill. Wait." Milo's words come out on deep gasps of his own.

I lift my head and look over to see him standing in the middle of the street, a good twenty feet away with his hands raised in surrender. My arms go limp at my sides.

"Why? Why would tell them, Milo?"

I watch as his hands curl into fists. "Because they were assholes!" His voice bellows into the air, and a few random people on the sidewalks turn our way. We're making a scene, but it doesn't matter. I've had enough.

I laugh, but it's more maniacal and devastated than funny. "Seriously? This again?" My teeth grip the inside of my lip and I pin him with a glare. "How many times are you going to beat this dead horse, Milo? Just because they're not Bran, and they didn't grow up here, and, okay, they have money and boats, doesn't make them assholes!"

His head is shaking hard before I'm even done. "You're just going to have to trust me on this one. You're better off without them."

I can't believe him! "Trust you?" Another crazy laugh slips out. "You ruined my big break just because you decided they were assholes, and you want me to trust you? Are you listening to yourself?"

"I know what I'm talking about Jill. I've dealt with these kinds of pricks before."

"They were nice to me!" I cut him off. "They were trying to help me, Milo. They're not the assholes; you are!" Why did I think I could ever change his stubborn mind about anything? "You can't stand for anyone else to be happy because you need to surround yourself with people as miserable as you. Well, congratulations, because you just broke my heart."

He steps forward, and I immediately back up farther on the sidewalk. "Just listen." He raises his hands again. "I can explain it if you just shut up and listen!"

My mouth falls open at his nerve. "You're never going to change."

He runs a frustrated hand through his hair and locks his jaw in silence. He looks defeated, and I hope it means he's done talking and he'll go away. But I have one more thing to say to him.

"I thought you were different." I blink back tears and stab my finger into my chest so hard it hurts. "*My heart was different with you.* And now it will hate you forever." I can't bear to look at him ever again, so I turn to run down the sidewalk, my vision once more blurred by my tears.

"Jill!" I hear Milo shout my name even louder than before, but there's no way I'm turning around. I stumble forward and catch movement flashing in my vision, but there's no time to even begin to react. I'm lifted off my feet, and pain rips through my arm and shoulder where it crashes into something hard. I hear a cracking sound, and I can't tell if it's my arm or my head before blackness closes in and there's no more pain to feel.

CHAPTER THIRTY

MILO

"Well, where the hell did she go?" I can't believe this. Any of it. First Leah, then the bombshell about my dad, and now Jill has disappeared.

"I don't know, man. We tried going after her, but that chick is fast."

Rayna steps in front of her boyfriend before I have a chance to shove him. "Look, Milo, she was clearly upset and wanted space. She has her phone and wallet, so I'm sure she'll call when she's ready. She might even be at your house now."

I hit Jill's contact and bring my phone to my ear again. It goes to voicemail, just like it did the first two times I called it. I hang up and scrub at my hair in weariness.

My talk with Mom and Morris lasted longer than I intended, but I needed to understand exactly what everyone had kept from me and why. I still can't fully grasp the sacrifices my dad made for me and that I never even knew about it. It's going to take a long time to come to terms with that and everything it means. Mom and Morris both said he made them promise not to tell me, so I don't know that I can be too upset with them for keeping their word. He had to have had his reasons, and God knows I never understood the guy. But I guess this explains why my mom always had a soft spot for him.

I can think about all this later, though. First I need to find Jill.

I know she was as surprised as I was to see Leah waltz into my mom's dining room, and I'm guessing she probably wanted to be in the kitchen with me while I talked to her. But I was pissed Leah had shown up in the first place. Sure, I'm grateful she gave me a job—she didn't owe me anything—but things at work have gotten even more uncomfortable since that day she offered me a massage. I've been keeping my distance as much as possible, but she's been finding ways to brush up against me, drop innuendos, and make reference to the old days like we used to be a thing. Her memories must be different from mine because I just recall her always rebuffing my advances and then parading other guys in front of my face.

Turns out she was a game player then and she's still one now, something she proved when she tried to maul me with her mouth in the kitchen tonight.

Does Jill know about that? Does she think I wanted Leah coming onto me? I've got to fix this now because there is nobody in this world I want besides Jill Holloway —and she needs to know that.

"Tell me what happened, and don't leave anything out."

Bran speaks up again but still apparently thinks he's funny. "Look, she was fine. She didn't seem pissed about Leah at all. I mean, it was pretty clear Leah tried to get herself a little Milo action in the kitchen, but we all heard you shut that shit down."

"Wait. Why would Jill care about Milo and Le—oooohhh." Haley gets herself up to speed from her spot across the porch. "Right on." She throws me a thumbs up, but I don't have time for this right now.

"No, I don't think it was that either, Milo." Rayna looks up at me. "I think it had to do with some guys you took diving one time?" She shakes her head, and I don't know what she means. "We were talking about your dad, and Bran was saying you always do things for people without needing thanks or credit, just like your dad apparently did for you. We mentioned the incredibly moronic girl from the night of your boat accident, and then the time you punched Shawn Mendenhall for me in high school. And then some story I didn't know about, but I think that's what upset her."

"Right," Bran steps forward and scratches his cheek before propping both hands on his hips. "Uh, it was those two guys from the show Jill was on that summer."

My head starts buzzing, and I close my eyes because I know I'm not going to like what Bran says next.

"I might have said something about you blowing your shot at starting your dive business because you had to set those assholes straight about Jill."

My teeth clench because everything makes sense now.

"You told me she knew about that." Bran's tone turns a little panicked.

He's not wrong. I did tell him she knew about it. Just not the whole thing. I open my eyes and start for the steps, patting Bran's shoulder on my way. "Not your fault, man. Thanks."

It takes me less than ten minutes to get home on my bike, but Jill's nowhere to be found. I consider that maybe she's trying to walk home, so I retrace the path, hoping to see her along a sidewalk somewhere. But it's no use.

I spend the next thirty minutes checking the beach and even the old pier before calling my mom, Bran, Ted, and anyone else I can think of in case she showed up somewhere while I was out searching. But nobody has seen her. She's nowhere.

Then something from earlier in the night hits me, and I'm back on my bike, heading for the SWiN.

"WE'RE CLOSED," CAMILLE SAYS FROM BEHIND THE glass door, sending me a disinterested look. Her silver hair is in its usual curls, but she's dressed in what appear to be pajamas.

"Mrs. Blume, can you please open up? I know Jill is in there."

She tilts her head and puts a hand on her hip. "There's no one by that name here."

Shit. I forgot who I was talking to. "Louisa then. Can

I talk to her, please?" I can't believe I have to play this game with her.

Camille puts a finger to her chin like she's wracking her brain for some recollection of anyone by that name. I want to bust through the door, but I'm ninety-nine percent sure she'd call the cops on me.

"Nope. No Louisa either." Crazy or not, now I know she's lying.

"I know she's here because I've tried everywhere else. Just let me in."

"I'm telling you there's no Louisa here." Her brows are raised in a challenge, and it's only then I remember Jill going on about her promotion meaning she gets to be a new character. Some girl who hates braids and kisses the mailman or something. I promise myself to pay better attention to detail from now on because I can't for the life of me remember the girl's damn name.

"Mrs. Blume, please. I can't remember her new name, but I know she doesn't have to wear her hair in braids anymore. Isn't that enough?"

She pretends to think about it and then responds with a firm, "No."

But I must have done something right in my life because a woman I don't know with long red hair and a gorilla onesie comes up behind Camille. "You're Milo, right?"

"Yes!" My shoulders slump with relief, and I grab for the door.

"Not so fast," the new girl says. "Are you the one who made Jill cry?"

She's crying. Shit. I close my eyes again and drop my

forehead to the glass of the door. "Yes. No. I honestly don't know. I just need to see that she's all right."

I hear the lock turn a second before I stumble forward into the restaurant, the annoying but familiar tune playing over my head until the door shuts behind me.

When I straighten, I find myself face-to-face with Camille and the redheaded gorilla, who's now got a finger in my chest yet a completely bored expression on her face. Who is this?

"You break Liesl, I break you. Got it?"

Liesl. That's it!

I nod because there's nothing else to do.

"Wait here." She turns toward the kitchen doors. "Come on, Camille, we're only halfway through the dessert cart. That strudel's not going to eat itself."

Not wanting to poke the bear—er, gorilla—I wait where I am as they both disappear into the kitchen. Less than a minute later, Jill pushes through the doors.

Her eyes are red, and her makeup is gone, but she's the most beautiful woman on earth.

"Hey, Sunshine."

And that's all it takes for her to cross the floor, throw herself in my arms, and start blathering. "You gave it all up for me. This whole time I thought you..." She trails off and hugs me harder. I hug her back just as hard, running my palm over her hair and breathing her in, feeling the softness and warmth of her body against mine.

"I didn't give anything up. Not really."

"You did." She pulls on my shirt and sniffles.

"No. It was just a job in the grand scheme of things."

"It was your dream," she protests again.

"*You're* my dream." I squeeze her tighter for emphasis. "I'd give up anything in this entire damn universe for you. No question."

My words must be the right ones because they have her kissing my throat and crying on me at the same time. We keep holding each other for another few minutes, and then I settle us on the same side of one of the booths, keeping my arm around her. Her nose is pink, and smudges of black surround her eyes from her mascara. I can't help but lean forward and drop a quick kiss on her lips before pulling back again.

"I didn't know." She wipes under her eyes, finished crying for the moment. "If I'd known..."

"It was for the best that way."

"No! If I'd known, if I'd listened to you, trusted you, we wouldn't have lost all those years without each other."

"You don't know that. We both had a lot of growing up to do, a lot of living to do. It's better this way."

"It would have been better with you," she insists with one last swipe of her finger.

I take her hand, needing her to hear me. "No, Jill. It wouldn't have. I had such a chip on my shoulder, and try as you did to knock it off, it was still there for a long time after we parted ways."

"But—"

"No buts. Didn't you wonder why I never tried to come see you after that damn woman ran you over with her bike that last day?"

"Oh God. That lady." Jill's brows draw together, tears forgotten. "Who rides their bike on the sidewalk when there's a bike lane? Jenna just about punched that woman after they got me all sorted and my arm in a cast."

I try not to grin at her, but it's hard when she goes from crying to ranting on a dime like that.

"Scared the living shit out of me, I can tell you that. I thought you cracked your head open." I can't help but run my free hand over her hair again.

Jill drops her eyes to our clasped hands where they rest on my knee. "I did wonder why you didn't come see me. I told myself I didn't want to see you ever again, but deep down I think I knew I was lying."

I shake my head, remembering that day so clearly. "When you got hit and your sister came running a few seconds later, I kind of lost it. I spent quite some time after that in an embarrassingly pathetic place, beating myself up, telling myself I was no good for anyone, feeling sorry for myself, you name it."

Jill's head snaps up, and I can tell she's going to refute what my eighteen-year-old brain was telling me, but she doesn't need to.

"It seems you weren't the only drama queen in town back then." I raise a brow at her, and she gives me a small grin. "I wallowed for a couple days, not letting myself come see you. Telling myself you'd never let me in the room anyway. You know, the usual drama queen stuff." I smile over at her, and she manages a little laugh this time.

"And then my dad called me into the kitchen one night and sat me down at the table with a beer."

I want her to hear this because I need her to understand that I had my own journey to go on, just like she had hers. And I can't have her blaming herself for anything.

"I know it's no surprise he and I never talked. I mean never. It was always just single-word answers and occasionally working on things side-by-side in silence. Even that first night I was released from the hospital and he had to help me into the house, he just dropped a bottle of water and a bag of chips on the bedside table and that was about it."

I play with Jill's fingers for a second while I try to figure out how to say the next part.

"But that night, he talked to me. Not *at* me like he did when he was drinking, but *to* me. He said he'd seen me getting into trouble, doing stupid shit, and basically living my life with no direction. I, of course, talked back and told him I knew what I wanted to do but the world was pretty much against me." I dip my head at Jill. "Feel free to refer back to that drama queen comment from a minute ago if you feel the need."

She smiles again and squeezes my hand. "He pretty much told me to stop being a baby. Said the world doesn't owe me anything and to stop expecting life to be fair. He said the best advice he could give me was to pick one thing and put all my energy there. Then once I had that sorted in a way that pleased me, pick something else. I don't know that I took his advice precisely how he meant —and let's be honest, I didn't exactly want to emulate the guy. But three months later, I wrapped up my community service, and I was on a bus to Florida. I hooked up with some other divers and eventually found my groove traveling the world and focusing on one thing: diving."

"And that whole time, I thought you were back here running your own diving business with clients like those two dillholes—I can't believe they talked such shit about me! They acted all nice to my face, but I gathered from what Bran said, I should have nut-punched both of them the first day!"

"Simmer down there, Rocky." I grab both her hands, which have gradually balled themselves into fists over the last ten seconds.

Her eyes meet mine again. "But you did it for me, and it cost you. It's so infuriating. If it weren't for them—"

I cut her off with a quick kiss. "No. I like how things turned out just fine."

She watches me for a minute as if she needs to see for herself that I'm being sincere. And then she sighs, and I know I've convinced her.

"I like how things turned out too. I wasn't meant to be an actress. But I love being a waitress. I get to talk to people, joke around, earn decent money. And, hey, here at Schnitzel with Noodles, it's not just dinner, it's drama too." She winks at me.

"God help us all." I pull her in for another kiss, glad to have this behind us.

"What about your dad?" she asks a couple minutes later.

"You mean what Leah said?"

She nods and shifts in the seat so she's leaning back into me. I wrap my arms around her and rest my chin on top of her head.

"I don't know. My mom said he made her promise not

to tell me so that's why I never found out. He must have had his reasons, but damn."

Jill squeezes my arm and finishes my thought for me. "You would have liked to thank him."

"Yeah." I sigh. "The guy never let on that he really cared. It would have been nice to try again knowing that he did, but there's no going back since he's gone."

"He obviously didn't want that. Maybe he didn't know how to give in to emotions and preferred to keep them separated."

"I guess so. It sure explains why all his wives left him."

She tilts her head up to consider me. "Yeah, why in the world did he keep getting married if he wasn't an emotional guy?"

"Honestly? I think he just didn't know how to cook."

Jill gasps, and I laugh into her hair.

"No. I'll probably never know most things about him, but he did practice what he preached. He focused on one thing, and it pleased the hell out of him."

"What was that?"

"The ocean," I say, thinking about how my dad and I actually were similar in some ways. In that way especially. The ocean is my touchstone like it was his. I thought the itchy feeling I've had since being home was about missing my nomadic life in the sea, but the truth is I was feeling unsettled long before I came back here. I spent a long time following the ocean, and we understood each other well; it was time to turn my focus elsewhere. Who knew that I would find exactly what I needed right back here—in this town with this woman.

"Speaking of the ocean, I think it's about time we went home. It's been one long-ass day, and I need to go to bed." She turns in my arms and winds her arms around my neck. "Thanks for coming to get me. I just couldn't get past the idea that I ruined everything for us."

"You didn't." I kiss her again. I'll never get tired of kissing this woman.

Her lips slowly release mine and she opens her eyes. "But I need to make you a promise right now."

I pull my head back so I can see her better. "What's that?" Her expression is serious, so I want to give her my full attention.

"I, Jill Holloway, will never ever *ever* again call you an asshole, a dickhead, or a jerk."

"Wow."

"I know. It's big."

"And very romantic."

"What can I say? I do my best."

This time, she kisses me and it's anything but quick. When she starts working on my shirt, I have to remind her Camille is only one room away and won't hesitate to remove my balls with whatever kitchen tool she has handy. This, of course, gets her grinning again.

"I still can't believe she hates you so much."

"The woman can hold a grudge, I'll give her that. Maybe one of these days, she'll fall further into her crazy and forget."

"Oh, I wouldn't count on that." Her grin turns sly, and it scares me a little.

"I'm obviously missing something here."

"When I came in all upset earlier, she called me *Jill*

and told Andie to move the—and I quote—'movie shit' over so I could have room to sit. She must have felt really sorry for me—either that or she's drunk from the empty schnapps bottle those two have back there—because she confessed that her whole von Trapp spiel is complete bullshit." She throws her hands out. "Turns out she just likes the attention. Well, that, and she said an oddity always draws customers so it's a sound business strategy."

"I'm pretty sure you just blew my mind."

"I know, right?" Jill sits up straight and grabs my hand. "Now take me home and do dirty things to me."

She never has to ask me twice, so I let her pull me to the door. Then I take her home on the back of my bike and give her whatever she needs to make her happy. And because my luck has finally taken a turn for the better, she gives it right back.

EPILOGUE

"Who's winning?" I plop down next to Milo on the couch and throw my knees over his lap.

"The Irish," Sam answers for him.

"Ooh." I poke Milo. "That reminds me, we should plan a trip there. I've always wanted to go."

We've been talking for weeks about new places we'd like to explore together, and it would be fun to visit Ireland. I'll have to add it to our list.

"Not Ireland." Sam's eyes flash to me from his spot in the armchair. "Are you even—"

"Don't bother. She doesn't care about football," Jenna cuts him off, finding her own seat on Sam's lap. "She just likes the tight pants." My sister grins at me and pops a pretzel in her mouth.

"What's not to like?" I glance around for anyone to offer a valid argument, but nobody is paying attention to me. Camille and Andie are talking to Rayna in the kitchen, Kate and Eileen are upstairs with Felicity doing who knows what, and Bran's outside in the driveway checking out a motorcycle with some guy he invited over. Even Milo just pats my knee and keeps his eyes on the TV.

It's New Year's Day, and Milo and I are hosting a little get-together so we can pig out on junk food to feed our hangovers from last night. Although I think I'm the only one who had a hangover—I blame Jenna for that. She told me over Christmas that she's preggers but doesn't want to share the news until she's a little further along. Sam knows, of course, but my nieces are still in the dark, along with everyone else. Which meant that every time anyone handed Jenna a drink last night, she pretended to drink it, but really just switched glasses with me. By the time I caught on, I was already halfway in the bag and decided to just commit. I can't wait to have a new niece or nephew to snuggle and spoil and give me excuses to buy cute stuff.

"We're going to head back to the hotel soon so the girls can swim," Jenna tells me. They're staying nearby at one of the local hotels that does not host any small businesses of the illegal variety but does have an indoor pool.

"You don't want to swim in the ocean like Milo?"

"Milo is insane," Rayna joins in, circling the couch to take a seat on Milo's other side. "Even if he does wear that whole insulated get-up when he swims, the man needs to understand it's winter."

"Winter is for the weak." Milo leans forward to grab his beer from the table.

"I think we'll just stick with the nice heated indoor pool, thanks." Jenna gives Rayna a thumbs up.

Camille calls to me from the kitchen, and I get up again to see what she needs. Turns out she just wants to offer me some decorating advice, which I politely turn down since all evidence indicates her suggestions might be a little too Salzburg-in-wartime for a beach house. Call me crazy.

And Milo likes the place the way it is. Besides the throw pillows—which do wonders for the mood of the room, by the way—the walls are now painted a crisp white, and the main living space is accented with blue and orange touches everywhere. I spearheaded the project, but I wanted Milo to make all the final decisions. This house is his legacy, and even though we're sharing it, I think it's important for it to feel like he truly belongs here. It's also a way for him to honor his dad, something he's still been struggling with a little, but he's getting there.

That said, I did cover the walls in pictures as a Christmas surprise for him. Delia helped, and I even threw in shots of my family and all our friends. Milo didn't cry when he saw it, but I think he secretly wanted to, or at least that's what I'm telling myself.

Andie pulls on my sleeve. "Did Milo tell you I got my official SCUBA certification?" She rolls her eyes at me, and I grin back.

"Yes. And congrats by the way."

"Ugh. Whatever. If I'd known how strict he'd be about his rules, I never would have invested."

"Liar." I stick my tongue out at her because she's full of shit.

Since Milo's been hanging out at the restaurant more, he and Andie have gotten to know each other pretty well. I suspect it's their innate tendency toward distrusting strangers that bonded them, even though he denies it. He claims they bonded over his business plan for his new diving outfit. Which is probably sort of true too, because Andie ended up investing in it so Milo could finally get the thing up and running. Everything is going perfectly so far, and it should be all systems go in time for spring diving season which, apparently, is a thing.

In the meantime, he's been doing some flooring work with Morris, trying to save up money since giving his notice at Coastal Adventures the day after Thanksgiving. And he's promised that we'll finally go on that open-water dive together as soon as I agree to put my toe in the freezing Atlantic Ocean. I'm thinking I should be good to go by July.

The front door opens, and Bran comes in, scanning the room with an expression I know well.

"What did you do now?" My hands land on my hips as I face off with him. Another guy, who I'm assuming is his friend, comes striding in after him looking decidedly more relaxed. I choose to leave the friend alone since I don't know him—and because he's a total hottie and I don't want to scare him away. He makes excellent eye candy with his dark hair, pretty brown eyes, and a swagger you just can't teach.

Bran scratches the back of his neck. "Well, uh, I kind of backed his bike up into the white Mercedes out front."

"What the hell?" Andie comes storming out of the kitchen, red hair flying. Uh Oh.

The new guy steps in front of Bran, intercepting her as smooth as can be. "Is it yours?"

Andie stops in her tracks, and I have to bite my cheek not to laugh. I've never seen her struck dumb like this, not that I blame her.

"Maybe." She tries oh-so-hard for her usual bored expression, but it just misses the mark.

I'm pretty sure everyone in the room is watching this little exchange now.

"Sweet ride." The guy puts his hand out. "Name's Nick Amante, but you can call me Ponch."

Andie eyes his hand and then his face again, and just as I'm trying to decide which way this is going to go, her lip curls. "As in the sleazy man-whore from that eighties show?"

Aaaaand, she's back.

"Well that was fun, but I'm glad they're all gone now so I can have you to myself." I reach my soda can across the deck table to clink with Milo's beer bottle.

We're seated in our usual spots, bundled in sweatshirts and enjoying our view. Felicity went over to Haley and Ted's to hang out since they just returned from traveling for the holidays. She heads back to Virginia tomorrow. It's been fun having her around and getting to know her, not to mention seeing Milo interact with his niece gives me a whole new insight into my guy. I'd never have guessed it, but it's actually super hot seeing him go all parental.

"Ditto. How about you come over here and let me have a look at what's hiding under your sweatshirt?"

I grin at him since it's impossible not to, but a loud knock at the front door steals our attention. It comes again, and when Milo moves to get up, I motion him to stay where he is. "I got it." Someone probably forgot something and is just coming to pick it up.

I go through the sliding glass door and make my way to the front where I swing the door open with a smile. But it's no one I recognize. A pleasant-looking older man in dress slacks and a thick sweater stands outside.

"Oh, hi. Can I help you?"

"I hope so. Is Milo Papatonis here?"

"Um, yeah. Come on in." I open the door a little wider for him to grab. "Can I tell him what it's about?"

"Sure." He takes a half step into the foyer. "I'm Trent Laherty from Blue Bay Realty."

And that's all I need to hear.

"Oops. Sorry." I block his path. "Care to back it on up there?"

His smile drops, and when I lower my eyes to his shiny black shoe on the linoleum, he pulls it back and shrinks from the doorway.

"Let me make this real simple for you, Trent. Milo is not now, nor will he ever be, selling this house. It's his home. Can't you understand that? Now go back to your home and spend the holiday with your family."

I don't wait for a response. Instead, I close the door in his face and stalk back through the house, where I jerk the sliding glass door open, ready to tell Milo all about the asshole at the door who's taking tenacious to a whole new level and may require a restraining order.

But I come to a dead stop and close my mouth right back up. My eyes drop down and then up again to the back of Milo's head.

"Uh, Milo?"

"Yeah."

"The door is fixed."

He turns in his chair, a sly grin on his lips. "You noticed that, did you?"

I slide the door closed and walk over to his chair, smiling like an idiot the whole way. "Tell the truth. You got tired of trying to make a dramatic exit only to have the door stick in your face."

"I plead the fifth."

I straddle his lap and wrap my arms around his neck, no longer interested in the realtor or anything except being with Milo. "I have my ways of getting you to talk, you know."

His hands skim over my hips and cup my ass through my jeans. Then he kisses my neck and slides his tongue up toward my ear where he bites the lobe. "I'd rather use my mouth for other things if that's okay with you."

And, really, who am I to argue?

Jenna asked me over Christmas if I found what I was looking for when I left Sunview without a word. I think she was trying to make sure I wasn't going to run again, but she has nothing to worry about. I thought I was going out to find my "purpose" or I was taking a journey to "find myself." But it turns out I just needed to recover something I once had and misplaced for a while. And now that he's right here by my side, I'll never let either of us get lost again.

I HOPE YOU ENJOYED *NEW JERK IN TOWN*. UP NEXT is Ponch and Andie in *The Last Good Liar*, coming February 2021.

You can catch Haley and Ted's story in *The Nerd Next Door* and Jenna and Sam's story in *Then Again*, both available in ebook, paperback, and audiobook. Stay tuned for excerpts.

ABOUT THE AUTHOR

Sylvie Stewart is a *USA Today* bestselling author of romantic comedy and contemporary romance. She's married to a hilarious dude and has crazy twin boys who keep her busy and make her world go 'round. Her love of all things North Carolina is no secret, nor is her ultimate wish of snuggling her very own pet baby goat. If you love smart Southern gals, hot blue-collar guys, and snort-laughing with characters who feel like your best friends, Sylvie's your gal.

Keep up with new releases, promotions and giveaways:
Subscribe to my newsletter... http://bit.ly/NewsSylvie

Hang out with me and other fans:
Join my reader group on Facebook... **Sylvie's Spot - for the Sexy, Sassy, and Smartassy!**
http://facebook.com/groups/SylviesSpot

Thanks! XOXO,
Sylvie

ACKNOWLEDGMENTS

This book was written in the midst of not only my worst case of writer's block ever, but the Covid-19 pandemic. With that in mind, I'd like to send out a huge thank you to all the healthcare workers, teachers, first responders, and essential workers who continue to work tirelessly and put their health at risk for the rest of us. I hope when the dust settles, you'll continue to receive the recognition you deserve, as well as more appropriate compensation for everything you do!

Big thank yous to my family for supporting me through my grouchy months and my amazing author friends for encouraging me when I wasn't sure I'd ever get back to my weird writer self (Junkies - you know who you are!).

I must also send a shout out to Amy Duli of Duli Noted for saving my ass when I was so behind! Not only did you save my book, you saved my sanity.

Lastly, huge hugs to all you readers out there who make everything possible! When the world around us is falling apart, there are always books.

Chapter One

HALEY

...Pulling up to our building in a dark blue late-model Mazda is the object of my... fascination? Obsession? Slightly stalkerish tendencies? *Jesus.* Who's the creeper now? The car settles in a spot by the curb, the driver's side door opening shortly after. And out steps Ted Jones. *My* Ted Jones. Well, he would be if I had my way about it.

I tilt my head to the side and admire him for a moment or two. Now, here's a man who knows how to rock an elbow patch. *Oooh, yeah.* I don't know what it is about Ted Jones' particular brand of nerdiness, but it is friggin' hot. I've done a little, let's call it... investigating and discovered he teaches in the liberal arts school at NCUW, so I know he's whip smart. He also wears the sexiest black-framed glasses over brilliant blue eyes, has little to no affection for his razor, and exercises a habit of smoothing his hair down to fight a stubborn cowlick. It never obeys, much to my delight, making him sport a constant just-rolled-out-of-bed look.

In contrast to that, he is always dressed neatly, often in a traditional tweed jacket with elbow patches which he pairs with jeans that do amazing things for his ass. Something about that combination of tweed, leather, and denim sets off an odd Pavlovian response in my uterus. I can't explain it. To top that all off, he's a runner, and I've seen the muscles of his thighs and calves bunching as he powers through his evening runs, leaving him coated in sweat and me with plenty to think about when my head hits the pillow.

It's safe to say I'm gone over Ted Jones.

The only problem is we've never actually had a single conversation.

To be fair, we *have* spoken to one another—on several occasions, in fact. But you couldn't exactly call these interactions conversations. As I recall, my first word to him was, "Hi." To which I got zero reply.

It was the afternoon I moved into my apartment, the unseasonably cool temperatures making my fingers sore from cold. I'd just returned a borrowed cart to maintenance and was trying to remember which walkway would take me to my building when I got my first glimpse of my future boyfriend (positive thinking is always recommended). Although, to be honest, it was the teenage girl speaking to him who first caught my attention and caused me to do a double take.

The two stood on the sidewalk while the brisk early-spring temperatures caused us all to tighten our coats around us. When I first saw the girl, I could have sworn a bag of cotton candy rested on her head—the classic dual pack with sugary clouds of half pink and half blue. But, no, it was just her hair, so my attention quickly shifted to take in the man beside her.

He wore a dark wool coat and I could see the puffs of his breath on the air as he laughed at something the girl showed him. It was a magazine of some sort, called *The Weatherman*, although I'd never heard of it. Both the girl and man were seemingly enthralled and neither one noticed me as my insides turned to mush. His laughter skipped toward me on the breeze and made my stomach flip—and this was before I'd ever even seen him in his tweed, denim, and leather trifecta of hotness.

The two spoke animatedly, the girl gesturing with wide sweeps of her arms as her cotton-candy hair swished around her ears. He flipped some pages until he found what he was looking for and they both buried their noses —and every other sense, it seemed—into the magazine. I felt oddly left out, even though I'd never laid eyes on either of these people before in my life. After a few moments, I stole one last look and retreated down the cement walkway to what I was almost certain was my building.

So it was no surprise that I all but gasped when I found myself on the elevator of my apartment building not two hours later with the very same man—sans teenage girl this time. I mean, what were the chances of him living in the same building as me in such a huge complex? It was clearly a sign, as was the uptick in my heart rate as I got my first close-up view of him. I drew in a breath and uttered my very first word.

"Hi." Yes, I am available to teach flirting lessons should anyone need my brilliant advice.

He didn't even glance my way. Here I was in an enclosed space with this delicious guy who immediately pushed all my buttons—making me want to push the emergency button on the elevator and make out with him in a really dirty way—and he wouldn't even acknowledge me.

I've never been great with guys, but I do okay. Certainly well enough to spark up a casual conversation in an elevator. When he left me hanging, I felt a sharp pang that this guy who was friendly to *Weatherman* girls and was my type in every way was actually kind of a rude jerk. That was, until I noticed he was wearing some of those weird wireless earbuds. This discovery brought some relief, but I still stood awkwardly until we reached the third floor where I got off.

Refusing to concede defeat, I waited until the elevator was about to close behind me and turned to give him my best smile and a friendly wave. Unfortunately, I missed the small fact that he had stepped out after me. Which meant when I whipped myself around, my forehead made audible contact with his very defined cheekbone, causing us both to stagger back.

"I'm so sorry!" I put one hand to my head and one out toward him, as if my hand held a magical power that dulled the pain from blunt-force trauma.

He held his cheek and blinked a few times, his jaw working as if to test the level of injury. Then he pulled out an earbud and shook his head, his gaze dropping to the floor.

His voice was a deep, quiet rumble when he spoke. "No problem."

Then he snatched a set of keys from his pocket like he thought I might attack again and made quick work of the lock to apartment 3-C. The apartment right next to my 3-B. Ack!

"Happens all the time," he mumbled before disappearing behind his door. I continued to stand in the hallway, unsure of what had just happened and wondering if I should run to the store for some frozen peas or something. But I got the distinct feeling that would just make things more awkward.

Little did I know, awkward would be our go-to vibe for all subsequent encounters.

Like the time my grocery bag split and a bottle of wine, a huge roll of chocolate-chip cookie dough, and a box of panty liners came tumbling out at his feet. Instead of just picking them up like a normal person, I, for some unknown reason, felt compelled to share that I was PMSing.

Because that's exactly the topic that's gonna make your crush confess his undying love for you. *Oh, Haley, there's nothing I find sexier than the mental image of you stuffing your panties with cotton personal products before binge drinking and shoving raw cookie dough in your face. Come to daddy!*

Yeah. That's pretty much how things have gone since.

But not today! Today, I'm going to have a real live conversation with Ted Jones.

I straighten my back and then glance down at my clothes. The old t-shirt and capri leggings can't be helped. I take a quick sniff in the general direction of my armpits and resolve to just keep my arms glued to my sides during the course of our scintillating discussion. Hell, he's a runner. Maybe he's into girls who work up a sweat.

I stride forward, pulling Tank along as I watch Ted stop at the communal mailboxes on a grassy patch of lawn. He stands with his back to me, his legs shoulder width apart and covered in the familiar denim.

I can do this. I'll be confident and charming and not even a little bit weird—I'm sure of it. That is, until I actually reach the mailboxes and catch Ted's scent. Lordy, he smells like pencil shavings and leather. I want to bite my fist and then lick his neck. Instead, I pretend to search for my mailbox key which I know to be sitting in a dish on my entry table at this very moment.

Ted doesn't turn his head or acknowledge me in any way. He closes his mailbox and removes his key before sifting through the stack of white envelopes and coupon fliers.

It's now or never. I take a deep breath and turn to him, one hand on my hip and the other gripping the plastic handle of Tank's leash. "Beautiful evening, huh?"

Dammit! *The weather? Seriously?* I'm a walking cliché, but it's too late, so I widen my smile. Ted turns to me and, upon taking in my overly enthusiastic smile, takes a step back.

Right into the pile of shit my dog just dropped behind him.

Get your copy of **The Nerd Next Door** to continue reading Haley and Ted's story!

Also available in audiobook

CHAPTER ONE

Holy mother of ... abs.

I bit my lip hard and let the blinds fall back in place.

"Stop being such a pussy and get your ass out there!" Jill hip-checked me, almost sending me to the floor.

"Just give me a minute. Jeez." I took a cleansing breath and let it out slowly.

She rolled her eyes. "They're just men." She parted the blinds again to have another look while I attempted to gather myself. "*Dayum*. One of them took his shirt off— did you see that? If you can't close the deal I might have to break up with Hank and get me a bite of that one."

"Wow, you're so classy, Jill. Please, teach me your ways." I let my flat tone communicate my insincerity.

She dropped the blind again and gave me a scowl. "Enough stalling. If Mom's lemonade doesn't work on the hottie neighbor or his friend, then nothing will." She looked me up and down. "Unless you're willing to reconsider the bikini top."

I gave a half-laugh. If one of us was going to wear a bikini it would have to be Jill. Although we share the same dark, wavy hair, that's where the resemblance ends. She's willowy while I lean a bit more toward curvy. But she somehow lucked out and got the same size boobs as me. "Yeah, that would be more likely to trigger a rapid retreat. Nobody wants to see my stretch marks." I flattened a hand over my stomach where a few stubborn extra pounds liked to rest.

"Badges of honor, sis. You carried two watermelons in there for nine months! Fuck anybody who cares about a few scars." She had her hands on her hips at this point, posturing in mama-bear mode—regardless of the fact she's six years younger than I am.

My lips twitched and I pulled her into a hug. "You know I'm only giving you a pass on the cussing jar because the girls are gone, right?"

"Yeah, yeah." She pretended to be aloof, but hugged me back anyway. Then I felt the sharp sting of her hand on my ass. "Now grab that tray and get on out there! Hot men are waiting to be seduced."

I pulled back and looked down at my outfit. I'd gone with a snug pink tank that showed off my assets, and a denim skirt that was probably a bit too short for a thirty-four-year-old, but I tried not to think about that. I smoothed my shirt down and went to the counter to retrieve the tray of sweet lemonade our mother was known for. Condensation already beaded on the pitcher, and I wasn't even out in the heat yet.

Jill opened the door for me, and I swear, if I hadn't been balancing a laden tray, she would have physically pushed me outside—probably with a foot to my ass. "Tits out," she commanded before closing the door and leaving me on my own. I sighed.

You see, a new neighbor moved in this week. A very hot and apparently very single new neighbor. I'd spotted him coming and going as contractors worked on his house over the last week. He was tall and muscular, with dark hair that was a touch too long to be conservative and an ass that was a touch too nice to be ignored. I had yet to introduce myself, feeling a bit stalkery if I ambushed him on one of the days he met with contractors. But today was clearly move-in day. He'd arrived this morning with a full truck and a friend to help him unload it. The same friend whose abs I'd just seen through the window and was about to get a closer look at—whether I was ready or not.

Unfortunately, I'd made the colossal mistake of telling my sister about the new neighbor, and it had taken her less than thirty minutes to shove her tiny little ass into my day and my business. Thus, my current errand to deliver lemonade—and myself—on a platter for the taking.

I could say I didn't know how I'd gotten myself into this situation, but I knew exactly how it had happened. And I chose to blame it all on Mike, my asshole ex-husband. Of course, Mike hadn't always been an asshole. In fact, he'd been the love of my life. It just so happened that I, apparently, had not been the love of his. That realization was a blow I wouldn't wish on my worst enemy.

But back to the tasty lemonade and the even tastier

new neighbor and his friend. *Come on, Jenna, you can do this.* I took another deep breath, straightened my shoulders, and pushed the girls out as far as they would go. God, I hoped I didn't look like some puffed up tropical bird. The ice clinked against the sides of the pitcher with each step down my driveway. I kept my eyes firmly planted on the tray until I worked up the nerve to raise them.

There he was—tall, dark, and sweaty. And living right next door to me. It couldn't be mere coincidence that had landed this man in my path the very same week I'd vowed to get back my love life—sex life—love life? Hell, I didn't know. But I knew it involved a hot man who shared absolutely nothing in common with my ex. I swallowed thickly and plastered what I hoped was a casual yet flirty smile on my face.

"Well, welcome, neighbor!" I called out as I approached.

Both men turned simultaneously to face me and it was a wonder I didn't drop the tray. I was caught in a laser beam of hotness as two sets of eyes took me in. Holy crap! Jill and I had been watching them play basketball through the blinds like two total creepers, but this close up it became a bit overwhelming. White smiles, bright eyes, glistening sweat. Why didn't women carry those little fans around with them anymore? I could feel the heat rise to my cheeks.

I forced more words from my throat. "Pretty hot out here. I brought you some lemonade. Didn't know if you'd had a chance to unpack dishes and whatnot yet." They both looked at the pitcher appreciatively.

"Haven't unpacked a single box," hottie neighbor responded in a friendly tone. "Thank you. Very kind of you." His blue eyes practically sparkled as he continued, "I'm Erik."

He extended a hand, but soon realized I didn't have one to spare so he gave me a little wave instead before gesturing to his shirtless friend. "And this is my friend who helped me unload everything—Kyle."

I took in all that was Kyle and considered changing my mission to focus on him instead. I'd never seen an eight-pack in real life before. I kind of assumed they were a myth along the lines of unicorns and abdominal—ahem, I mean abominable—snowmen. *Oh, shut up, Jenna! And stop staring at his stomach, for God's sake!*

I forced my gaze up to a more respectable level. "So nice to meet the both of you." I smiled again, but was pretty sure my nervousness was announcing itself loud and clear. These guys were out of my league. If I didn't know for a fact that Jill was staring daggers into my back at that very moment, I would have turned tail and run. Grrr.

"Jenna Watson," I said. I needed to switch the focus back to them. "I'm just next door to you. Are you new to the area? Or just the street?"

"Just the street," Erik's sweaty hair fell over his forehead as he answered. "I used to live in a condo downtown. Time for more space." Ah, but space for what?

Kyle took a step forward. "Can I help you with that?" He gestured to the tray with a curve of his lips.

Damn—hot *and* a gentleman. Who was I to refuse?

"Thanks. That's so kind. It's heavier than I imagined." Jesus, I was practically cooing.

Kyle took the tray and I immediately set to the task of pouring lemonade into the two glasses resting alongside the pitcher. I cursed my hands as they shook. "So, it's homemade. The lemonade," I clarified and handed the first glass over to Erik. And then I freaking giggled like some pandering idiot and practically batted my eyelashes at him. I wanted to punch myself the face. I was supposed to be putting out the strong and sexy vibe, not some ditzy teenager act. But, damn if he didn't smile right back at me. Huh, maybe I was better at this than I'd thought. I went ahead and offered Kyle his glass, trading him for the tray. "I hope it's not too sweet."

They both took a deep swallow and I had the urge to look around to see if anybody else was benefitting from this particular view. I was thinking about grabbing Jill and pulling up a couple lawn chairs so we could have a long afternoon of ogling.

"It's perfect," Kyle finally said. Jill had been right— Mom's lemonade worked wonders.

"So, is it only you? Or did your girlfriend take the day off? Or wife," I added hastily. *Real smooth, Jenna.*

He smiled. "Nope. No wife or girlfriend." Then he downed the rest of the lemonade as Kyle followed suit. "This really hit the spot, Jenna." They both returned their glasses to my tray, and I felt a shift in the air. I got the sense that I was being given my dismissal—a kind one, but a dismissal nonetheless. Maybe I'd been too forward? Or too much of a spaz? Either way, it was time to retreat.

"Well, I should get back." Thank God I had the tray

to occupy my hands or I probably would have embarrassed myself further by giving them the double guns or something. I turned to go.

"Terrific meeting you," Erik called after me.

I gave him a backward glance and maintained the painful smile. "The pleasure was all mine. Welcome to Juniper Court." *Where psycho single moms throw themselves at you because they haven't had sex in over two years!*

"Thanks." I heard one of them say, but I was too intent on getting back inside my own damn house to look back again. My front door opened just as I approached it, and I didn't even stop to see the look on Jill's face. I marched straight to the kitchen, slammed the tray down on the counter, and stuck my head under the kitchen faucet.

To continue reading Jenna and Sam's story, get **Then Again**, now available in ebook, paperback, and audiobook.